Scars

The Recovery Series
Book 1

By J.A. McCoy

Scars is the first book in The Recovery Series.

Cover design by J.A. McCoy

Dagger art by Bethany Lackey

ISBN: 979-8-9951571-0-6

Printed in the United States of America.

First Edition: 2026

HUMAN AUTHORED

Reg #: 1685708

https://authorsguild.org/human

Content Warnings

This novel explores the gritty details of varying levels of trauma through a grimdark lens, with the following Trigger Warnings:

Grief & Loss, Violence & Gore, Body Horror, Child Loss, Graphic Childbirth, Animal Death, PTSD & Panic Attacks, Abuse & Harrassment

Dedication

At the risk of sounding ridiculously cheesy, this book is dedicated to my wife. For the many hours over the course of four years I spent at the desk, or the dinner table, writing this story. Thank you for believing in me. Thank you for pushing me to do it. Most of all, thank you for listening to me whine when the days felt hard. It wouldn't have gotten done without your support.

-Jake

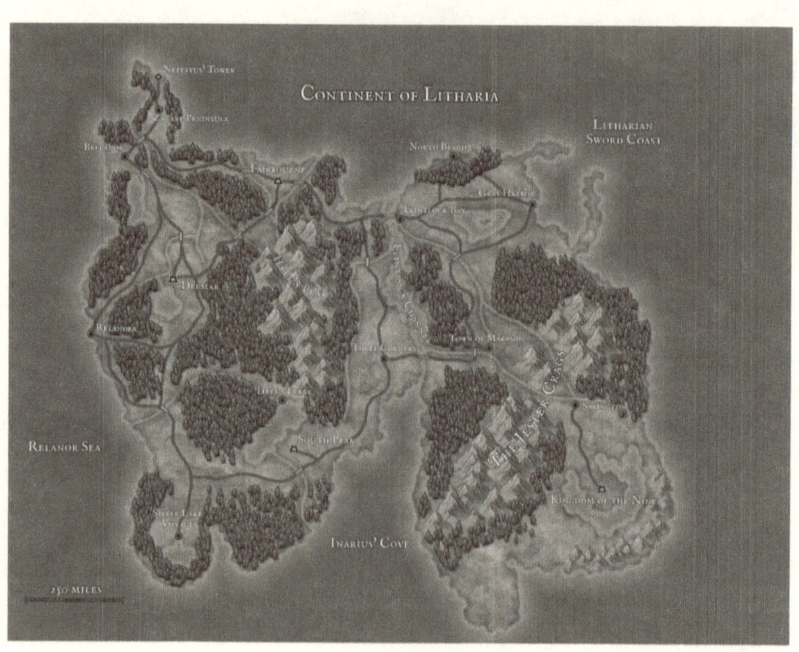
Nefestus' Tower
Zavisi Peninsula
Bellanor
Fairboline
Continent of Litharia
North Beach
Litharian Sword Coast
Gray Harbor
Laidlock Bay
Delmar
Finestra's County
Relanora
Town of Marason
Three Corners
Hill Town
The Jester Crags
South Peak
Norhelton
Relanor Sea
Kingdom of the Nine
Silver Lake Village
Inarius' Cove
250 Miles

Prologue

Nefestus burst through the door to his tower, shuttering the bar behind him to impede the mob of angry townsfolk chasing him. Eyes darting back and forth frantically, his mind raced with potential scenarios. He was the last known sorcerer of the time, and not of the formerly known "good" kind – not that such a distinction mattered anymore.

Nearly a decade prior, an angry lord had begun a crusade against the gods, and thus all magic, to which the rest of the population quickly latched on. The lord's crusade became known as the Reckoning, and countless users of the mystic arts were hunted down, burned at the stake, stoned to death, keel-hauled, or even hacked apart limb by limb by those they used to defend from monsters of the various magical planes of existence.

As one who wields the shadow arts, Nefestus was a natural selection for torture and he knew it, so he had begun to run from town to town hiding his magic as best as he could. But it seemed his time had run out. After feeling the first villager ram their shoulder into the door he was barricading, he knew he had no choice but to stand his ground.

Drawing a dagger from the folds of his robe, the old man sliced his own forearm and drew forth a small amount of blood, willing the shadow magic within the weapon to fuse with his very essence. With the clench of a single fist and a jerk of the same arm, he magically ripped the very foundation from the center of his tower and formed from it a well – into which he cast the dagger before turning to face his imminent death.

Even as the bangs grew louder and more intense, Nefestus couldn't help but wonder what the world would be like without magic. He reflected back upon his own childhood, to the memory of the time when he first discovered his affinity to the shadow realm, when the schoolyard bullies were beating him senseless.

Their screams filled the air as tendrils of shadow exploded from Nefestus' small frame, gripping their torsos tight and flailing the bullies violently side to side before throwing them half a stone's throw away. Those bullies never bothered him again, and Nefestus knew from that point on that he would blindly follow whatever benevolent god had given him this power.

But as the Reckoning began to take root, and magic users were destroyed one by one, the creatures of the magical planes of existence began to retreat to their home planes. The gods themselves began to pull away from their chosen. Nefestus had but a few spells left from the Baron of Shadows, but he wasn't about to abandon his god, even if the Baron had left him. He would stand his ground, just as he had with the bullies, to show the world that magic would never be bested by brute strength.

The door splintered under the weight of a makeshift battering ram, and Nefestus began to chant in a low drone. The words he spoke hummed with dark power, and the very air around him started to vibrate.

Scars

Another crash blasted a hole in the door and the villagers let loose a primal scream of glee. Unfazed by the wooden shrapnel that peppered his frail body, the old man continued his incantation, feeling the power collect within him. His eyes drained fully of color to a pale white, just as the tower door was vacated of its' position and the first bloodthirsty villager charged in.

As the would-be assailant thrust forward his crude spear to make a shish kabob of the necromancer, Nefestus spoke forth the final word of power and exploded in arcs of shadow lightning. The lightning burst through the chest of the first assailant, and again through the second, third, fourth, fifth, and sixth intruders of his domain.

The very bedrock upon which his tower stood shook violently with the booming retort, and the tower itself began to crumble, burying Nefestus, the villagers, and the well of shadow with it.

Nefestus felt his consciousness fading at the same time his body started to crumple. He knew he was dying, but he smiled as he saw the devastation around him. His spirit retreated from his body to the Realm of Shadow, and took with it the souls of those he'd liberated from their bodies.

He would feed upon them slowly, sustaining himself while the world celebrated the death of the last known magic user. He would wait patiently, while the world forgot about magic.

Stone by stone, the tower collapsed, entombing the well of shadow so that none who survived knew of its existence. It sat for a hundred years, hiding the last vestige of magic on the planet. The world moved on, raging with war after war, before civilization began to calm itself. Nefestus' spirit lay in wait, slowly feasting on the souls of those he had damned.

***

The Lord's decree came swift and harsh: a divine judgment upon a wicked sorcerer. The very earth had rejected him, they preached. And the people, desperate for an explanation that didn't shatter their fragile understanding of the world, latched onto it. The site was declared cursed, a place to be avoided, its true nature slowly buried beneath layers of fear and manufactured truth.

They wouldn't say "magic." They'd say "divine wrath," "a demon's curse," "the earth swallowed him whole," or "a catastrophic accident."

But never magic.

Zaulyl's Log
The Darkness

It's funny, really. One might think that being alone was the ultimate path to freedom. But since her death, all I feel is chained. Imprisoned. I find myself not knowing what to do. What path to take. Where to go. What meal to make.

The silence in the mornings is the loudest thing. No longer the soft rustle of her dress as she moved about, no scent of the tea she'd always brew before the sun was fully up. Just... nothing. A vast, echoing chasm where warmth used to be.

Every sunrise feels like a betrayal. Why should the world continue spinning when mine has stopped? I used to wake with a purpose – to earn enough, to protect, to return to her. Now, the rising sun merely illuminates a list of tasks that feel utterly meaningless.

Even choosing what wood to lay on the fire feels like a monumental task. Every decision, no matter how small, used to be filtered through her. What would she like? What would make her happy? Now, the path ahead is a tangled, dark forest, and I've lost my compass.

What do you do when the person you thought would be with you until the end is taken from you? What do you do when the very bedrock of every action you've taken or plan you've made is no longer in the picture? What do you do?

Am I supposed to act like nothing is different, as if my very reason for staying alive isn't gone? Am I supposed to act like she was disposable? The Sergeant seems to think so. The General seems to think so. Hell, my mother seems to think so... the old viper, already eyeing the eligible daughters of merchants and farmers like fresh produce.

'A good wife ensures a man's future, Kel'rak,' she'd cooed, patting my arm with a hand that felt like a spider's touch. As if one woman could simply be replaced by another, a cog in the family machine. As if her ghost didn't still sit across from me at every meal.

Sergeant Wynon clapped me on the back with a forced cheer. 'Right then, Zaulyl, chin up. Plenty of good women in the garrison town, eh? Time to find another to warm your bed.' His words were well-meaning, I suppose, but they tasted like ash. He saw a body, not a soul ripped to shreds.

"People die son, you know that better than most," the General had told me, as if it was another day on the job. "You cannot stop living your life when another life ends."

Screw him. I will do whatever I damn well please.

I live in a world where I worry every single day that I won't come home to her. I have lived every single day of our decade of marriage with the fear in the back of my mind that if I screw up - if I fumble a blade, or trip on a rock, or lose a handhold - I will leave her without a way to care for herself. Without money to pay for our home, or for the food she so lovingly prepares every night assuming that I will make it back.

I never thought I would be the one sitting at the empty table.

The answer then, seems simple. Embrace the empty.

Sure, they will call me a deserter. I will be hunted down for treason if I return. I do not know that I care. Treason? What is treason to a man whose world has already been decimated? They ask me to serve a flag, a king, a purpose. My purpose died with her. Let them hunt. Let them judge. Their laws mean nothing to a man who has already lost everything worth living for.

If I sell our holdings, it might be that I can afford a few things that will allow me to take on this new life. But how does one sell memories? I thought them to be needless wastes of time in the moment, but now, I find myself unable to let them go.

The portrait she commissioned Nerecio to paint of our wedding day hangs above the mantel. I remember accompanying him to the field where the willow grows tall to this day, how he commented on the way the sun was setting perfectly behind it. He captured that silhouette so well. He had a sly grin that day, teasing us about our impatience.

He'd spoken of the 'golden hour,' and how her hair, spun like threads of sunlight, would catch the last light of the day. I remember her laughter, soft like chimes in the breeze, as I held her hand, my heart swelling fit to burst. He captured not just our image, but the very essence of our joy, a joy I now struggle to recall with anything but pain.

When she asked her grandmother to make the blanket, I looked at her like she was crazy. We don't even live close enough to the mountains to warrant something that thick. Nor did my pay from the laird's army afford us a large enough bed for it to fit upon. I didn't know until later that it would give us some of the best nights of my life, laying next to her under the stars as we found pictures in the sky.

I remember her spreading it out, a riot of greens and browns and deep blues, smelling of lanolin and forest floor. Our first night under it, the stars felt close enough to touch, each one a tiny lamp illuminating our whispered secrets, our shared dreams for a future that now feels as vast and empty as that night sky.

Then there's the collar of the dog we always talked about getting, but never could find the right one. She kept it by her bed side, and I have yet to move it. She dried and crushed the cornflowers herself to dye the cord that vibrant blue - was so proud of it. She'd spent a week on those cornflowers, crushing them between smooth river stones, her hands stained indigo.

'Our faithful companion deserves a collar as vibrant as his spirit will be,' she'd declared, her eyes bright with the promise of a future that would never arrive. I can still see her, kneeling by the hearth, meticulously weaving the cord, her tongue caught between her teeth in concentration. Now, it rests there, a silent accusation of all the tomorrows we will never share, all the wagging tails that will never greet us.

I wish I could bring myself to burn it. I crave the oblivion of fire, the cleansing heat that would erase not just the collar, but the memories it clings to. But my hand trembles. My will falters. I am a coward even in my despair, unable to sever the last, agonizing threads.

I will find someone to give the memories to. Her grandmother will love the portrait. Her grandmother, old Elara, with eyes like deep wells of wisdom. She deserves this piece of her own blood, a legacy of light in the twilight of her years.

But placing that wooden frame into her trembling hands... it would be like handing over a piece of my own living heart, still beating, still breaking.

The young couple next door will find a use for the blanket. They speak of starting a family, of quiet evenings by the fire. The blanket, so vast and comforting, will swallow them whole in its warmth, just as it swallowed us. It's a painful irony, that something so steeped in our intimacy will now be shared by others, oblivious to the countless stars we traced beneath its folds.

Perhaps a kid will take the collar and beg their mother to get the dog. Some grubby-faced child, eyes wide with longing, clutching it tight, begging their mother for a companion. A small, desperate hope that this last piece of her, untainted by my current despair, might finally find its purpose. It feels like the smallest possible penance for my own failure to provide her with that joy.

At least finding people who need the memories will feel like honoring the woman she was. This isn't an act of generosity, not truly. It's an exorcism. A desperate attempt to sever the cords that bind me to this agonizing past. But perhaps, in severing them, I can release a small fragment of her light back into the world. A tiny, flickering hope that her memory won't die with me, forgotten in the dust of this forsaken home.

Without those tying me to this place, it will be easier. I can sell the rest. Every stone of this cottage, every blade of grass in our small yard, is a tether pulling me back to a life that no longer exists. They are anchors, heavy with the weight of happiness lost, dreams shattered. To cut them free, to burn the bridges behind me, is the only way to breathe, even if that breath tastes like ash and desperation.

I can gather supplies, and go somewhere far away. Away from the pitying glances, the well-meaning platitudes, the suffocating presence of what was. Away from the ghost that haunts every corner of this house, every moment of my waking nightmare.

J.A. McCoy

Embrace the empty. Embrace the void. The empty calls to me. Not the emptiness of a broken home, but the vast, boundless emptiness of oblivion. A place where pain cannot reach, where memories cannot torment. A void where nothing is asked of me, and nothing can be lost. It's a terrifying thought, but less terrifying than staying here.

Perhaps I'll die on the road. Perhaps I won't. I just cannot stay in this house any longer. This house... it has become a tomb. Not hers, but mine. Every breath I take within these walls is a gasp for air that isn't there. Every silence screams her name. I must leave, or I fear I will become a part of the dust and shadows myself, a ghost haunting my own living grave.

Chapter 1
The Fall

This seemed as good a place as any. Wide open views of the plains for as far as the eye could see, with salty ocean air cascading up from the crashing waves on the nearby cliffs. Nowhere for wild, vicious animals to hide that would otherwise attack his livestock. There was an unsightly pile of overgrown rubble on the ocean side of the land, but that could be cleared in due time.

Surrounded on both sides by a thin line of forest and rolling hills, the land was effectively a wide alley leading to the ocean. The large patch he had chosen was flat, but raised up from the rest of the land, a slight decline all around that would keep any rainwater from running under the foundation.

Kel'rak Zaulyl was a simple man. Entering his mid-thirties, he now lived a simple life, with simple linen clothes, and a simple mindset of living out his days without conflict away from the prying eyes of a kingdom or any sort of government therein.

An unnamed section of land at the northwestern-most tip of the continent of Litharia, about five days' ride from the nearest town, he had chosen it for its proximity to...well... nothing. Though it would never make it onto anyone's map, he decided to call the place Zaulyl Peninsula. It wasn't much, but no one else was here, so now it was his.

Kel'rak's skin was tanned from his time on the road, having ridden either on the wagon or by horseback without any cover, quite a ways and quite a few days from his old home. Having elected to make this move during the late spring, it was a hot journey. He kept his head clean-shaven – both a habit from his past life, and due to the ease of maintenance for a life on the road with naught but a knife and an axe.

His green eyes went beyond the typical shade of emerald, leaning further into the dark depths of a forest. Keen, and honed from a life of hardship, they searched constantly for threats - even when there appeared to be none. Especially when there appeared to be none.

His frame was muscular, but wiry rather than bulky. He moved with the grace of practiced motion, his steps making barely a rustle. He had sired no children, and rarely spoke to anyone short of making trips to town for supplies.

He preferred it that way – people tended to be fake and conniving, while simple cows made for better company. They never interrupt, offer up the occasional moo in response to conversation, and most importantly never judge.

"Yes," he said aloud to no one in particular. "This can be home for now."

As the wind rolled over the open plain, rustling the tall grasses in rhythmic waves, Kel'rak took a deep breath and tasted the brine on the air. It reminded him faintly of the coast near Gray Harbor, though there, the sea had always smelled of rotting fish and desperation. This air was cleaner. Wilder. It made his muscles relax in a way they hadn't in years.

Still, there was a part of him that remained coiled, waiting for something unseen. Peace was an unfamiliar rhythm, and his body didn't trust it yet.

He ran a hand over the stubble on his jaw and glanced back at the wagon. The bulls had begun to nuzzle each other in lazy camaraderie, while the cows grazed without care. It occurred to him how strange it was to envy a cow.

Kel'rak set to work unhitching his two bulls from the wagon, allowing them and the four cows to roam and feed, clearing the land of the grass that he would need out of the way to begin building.

With no one around to help for miles, he started the lonely job of unloading some of the larger logs from the wagon and shaping them with his crude carpenter's tools to make a rough frame for what would become his house. At times he would whistle a sailor's shanty to himself, chopping with his axe in rhythm to a tune he picked up in a seaside tavern.

On his breaks, he would go lay out in the warmest spots of the nearly empty wagon and let the hot wood soothe his aching back as he munched on a honey-loaf he'd bought at the market on the way out. It was turning stale, but after laboring in the sun it was like a sweet gift from the gods. Simplicity.

That was his new mantra. With simplicity, came appreciation for the small things. He smiled to himself during one such break, just scanning the sky for shapes in the clouds, seeing if perhaps he could find any cows among them.

Before the end of the day, he managed to erect the frame for his home, with rafters placed that would allow the eventual roof to be built. Unfortunately, there just wasn't enough time in the day to get that part up, so he would have to spend another night beneath the starts.

All-in-all, it wasn't so bad. Just another simple pleasure to enjoy as he embraced this new life. He did, however, manage to finish the floor using boards he had paid a small ransom for in town. The money was ultimately of little use to him, but having the flooring down on the first night allowed him to place his belongings somewhere dry and off the dirty ground, which was a win he was willing to pay for.

As the sun began its descent on the horizon, the simple man mounted his horse and rounded up his cattle, bringing them back to the wagon and tying up the lot of them so no one wandered off.

Deciding it best to go ahead and start a fire – even if there were no ambush predators to be seen or heard – he rounded up some overgrown dry grass for kindling and grabbed a few reserved logs from the wagon before setting it all to burning in a nice clearing of dirt. As Kel'rak sat gazing at the coastal horizon, watching the sun drop fully under the water line, he couldn't help but notice that overgrown pile of rubble again.

Even from this distance, something about it felt off—not just the unnatural shape, but the way the moonlight seemed to bend subtly around it, as though the pile resisted illumination. When the breeze passed over it, the tall grasses nearby leaned toward the ruin rather than away.

Kel'rak rubbed his arms without thinking. The fire crackled comfortingly at his back, but the sight of the ruins sent a slow chill along his spine. He told himself it was just a trick of the moon and the sea mist that crept in with nightfall—but the farmer in him had learned long ago not to dismiss his gut. The ruins felt... hungry.

They looked distinctly darker than the rest of its surroundings. Pinned against a backdrop of sky and moonlight, the shape was more distinct now, if only minimally so. While still very much a mount of rubble, there was a distinct cylindrical shape to it.

Scars

Based on the location, Kel'rak figured it was plausible it was once a lighthouse of some sort intended to keep ships from colliding with the cliffs in the fog. That was the only thing that made sense. What still did not make sense though, was why the darkness seemed so much more intense than everything else around it.

He decided he would ride over and investigate once the sun had risen – for now, it was time to turn in and trust that the cattle and/or the horse would sound the alarm if any threats approached. The exhausted, simple man rolled his back towards the fire so his night vision wouldn't be ruined, before drifting off into troubled dreams.

***

Kel'rak awoke from a night terror with a bloodcurdling scream, hatchet cocked and ready to throw, before realizing that the only thing he was threatening were his poor terrified cows; meanwhile, the bulls were starting to snort and stomp. Throwing the hatchet to the ground like it had burned him, he rose in one fluid motion to settle them, making hushing noises all the while.

These night terrors were becoming more frequent, and more vivid, and he wondered how soon it would be before he actually attacked something. Wondering whether he should start sleeping further away from the animals for their protection, Kel'rak grabbed the deerskin pouch of remaining water and splashed some of it on his face to wash away his internal demons.

The water had gotten a bit colder overnight than he'd anticipated, but it was just the refreshing wakeup he'd needed to get over the anxiety attack. Having been anchored back to reality, the simple farmer took note once again of the lack of water in his pouch and set to the morning routine of sending the cattle to pasture before mounting up in search of a watering hole he had seen yesterday before arriving, on the way to investigate the coastal ruins.

The mare, whom he affectionately called "Sugar", kept herself to a slow trot as he twisted all around in the saddle taking in the surroundings. Sugar had been with Kel'rak since he had bought her as a two-year-old filly, some ten years ago. Their bond was such that he could do as he was now, or even bend forward and fall asleep with his arms around her neck, and she would just keep going to the next water source; which she was doing now.

The water they found was within a ten minute's easy trot from the home-site; the farmer made a mental note to clear a small path leading to it so he could travel by foot for baths if needed.

With a lazy creek of fresh water running into and out of it, the waist-deep divot in the earth was surrounded by shady trees and some large rocks that baked in the sun. Those rocks would serve as a great spot to dry his clothes after washing the sweat and grime off. The water was cold and crystal clear, a source he felt he could reliably drink from.

Upon arrival, Kel'rak first brought Sugar to the water's edge and let her get her fill, before unloading his four waterskins and filling them to the brim then tying them off and tossing them over the saddle. Shielding his eyes from the sun still low on the horizon, he scanned the landscape and figured he and Sugar would probably reach the ruins within thirty minutes.

Scars

Once he spotted it, he found he couldn't look away. The pile of stones had a definitive shape to it in some places, but he couldn't quite make out what. All Kel'rak knew was that it stuck out like a sore thumb. Whatever the structure used to be did not fit with the rest of the surroundings, so it deserved investigating.

When it was clear Sugar had had enough rest, he saddled up and they set off for their destination. The closer the pair got to the salty sea air, the happier the mare seemed to get. She went from her slow trot to an all-out gallop as her excitement grew, and jumped around in circles once they reached the cliff edge.

Unable to contain his own mirth at her rare outburst of youthfulness, Kel'rak couldn't help letting out his own rare chuckle. He needed this short trip with her, unburdened from the haul of their prior travel.

As they turned back towards the final destination, however, he began to feel an intense sense of sadness. As though something horrible had happened there.

The closer the pair got to the site, the more Sugar's mirth was replaced by agitation. She began resisting his insistence that they continue forward, so much so that he would have mistaken her misbehavior for a wild stallion. Once within a few hundred feet of the ruins, she outright refused to move another step.

The farmer knew his girl, and knew when she was set in a way she wouldn't budge, so he dismounted and gave her an apple from his pack as a reward in getting him so far. He didn't bother with tethering her, because he knew she was a good girl and would wait for him where she was.

He lingered a moment beside her, running his hand down the slope of her nose and resting his forehead gently against hers. She snorted and huffed, her breath warm against his neck, but didn't nuzzle him the way she usually did. Her weight shifted nervously from hoof to hoof.

Her fear was raw, untainted by human reason. She didn't have stories of the Reckoning, or sermons about divine judgment. She simply felt the wrongness of the place, the subtle pull of something ancient and hungry, and her instincts screamed for flight. It was a purer understanding than any man possessed.

"You don't like this either, huh?" he whispered, even though he knew she couldn't answer.

She stamped once in the dirt and looked to the sea, ears twitching. Something in the way she wouldn't look back at him made his stomach tighten.

Still, he turned toward the ruin, one last glance thrown over his shoulder. "I'll be quick," he promised.

Kel'rak proceeded on foot, the inexorable pull of this ruin drawing him forward. There was no real explanation for it - he just felt like he should be here. It felt like if he didn't, there was a piece of himself he would never discover; however, the rational part of his mind screamed at him to stop.

It yelled, smashed, and clawed at his psyche, telling him that this was a point of no return. That he was doing something incredibly stupid.

The closer he got to the dilapidated pile of stone and overgrowth, the more he became depressed and apprehensive. Now within touching distance of the pile, he could see distinct lines in the ground where no grass grew. No flowers surrounded this place. No bees buzzed around and no birds chirped nearby.

Aside from the sound of waves crashing against the cliffside far below, there was utter silence. The air grew thick and hard to breathe, but no matter how much dread replaced happiness, Kel'rak found himself going deeper and deeper into the area.

He climbed onto a few of the stones in the pile, looking for an explanation as to what might lay underneath. Taking out his belt knife, he cut away some of the thorny overgrowth and dislodged a few large stones that had cracked apart when the structure had collapsed.

Eventually, after some continued work, the farmer and would-be adventurer managed to form a hole in the rubble big enough to climb into. He gave Sugar, still in the same spot about three hundred feet away, one final look to assure her everything was okay and slipped inside the pile.

He winced when he heard her let out a panicked whinny but knew she would be okay. Squinting his eyes to try and see better in the lack of daylight, Kel'rak made out a singular spot within the collapsed area that was darker than the rest. In fact, the darkness there was so absolute, he doubted any light could penetrate it.

He found himself doubting so much suddenly. Self-doubt as to whether he would come out of this alive, doubt at his incredulous idea to even come here in the first place, and doubt in the silly concept of building a farm far away from anywhere anyone would notice him needing help. But even through all of the doubt, he kept pushing forward, without even realizing it.

Before he could even get all the way there, a large piece of rubble fell - still attached to a vine - and swung to hit him directly in the temple.

The blow sent him stumbling forward, reaching for the retaining wall of what he could vaguely make out as a well in the back of his mind. Instead of connecting his hand with the wall, his blurred vision and his momentum took him straight over the edge, into blackness.

The last thing Kel'rak remembered as he plummeted down the shaft was cutting his arm on something intensely cold, feeling something icy and slimy crawling on him, and smashing the side of his head on the way down into unconsciousness.

Chapter 2
The Dagger

"Ah, he wakes," a raspy voice said from somewhere very nearby.

Kel'rak winced at several broken ribs and an intense migraine, and he turned to figure out who was talking to him. But then he realized he didn't hear anything – not even his own breathing.

He couldn't hear! The fall had taken away his hearing. So how had he just heard someone's voice?

"I'm in your head, farmer." The voice was much louder this time, boomingly so, and thoroughly unimpressed.

Making a visible effort to tamp down his feelings of sheer terror, Kel'rak sat himself up at the bottom of the pit – which was absolute blackness – and reached out with what he could best describe as his mental voice.

What is going on?, he asked with timid quiet.

"I should think it's quite obvious. You fell into a dark pit, experienced a traumatic brain injury, and thus lost your hearing. What is there to not know?" the voice asks, then continues. "Of all the rotten fortune in the world, I have to end up with a simpleton that asks obvious questions."

A strong-willed person, Kel'rak stiffened at the insult, and winced at a sharp pain in his lower left three ribs.

Obviously, I know I fell down a hole, he snapped back. *I mean who are you, and how am I hearing you in my head?*

"In due time, lad" the voice interjected. "For now, I believe you need to focus on getting out of here before the structure over your head collapses – I'm sensing vibrations in the ground around you."

Exactly how am I supposed to do that? Kel'rak snaps back. *I am stuck at the bottom of a pitch-black hole with at least three broken ribs and I'm fairly positive I'm still bleeding from whatever cut me on the way down!*

The voice groaned with dramatic effort in annoyance. "Feel slowly to your right, you will find a blade. It is mine. Grasp it firmly and concentrate on the sources of your ailment, I will do the rest."

Kel'rak decided to follow the order after squinting his eyes in disbelief, and found the dagger a handbreadth from his right hip. He grabbed it first by the blade, to a sharp hiss of irritation from the voice, then found the hide-wrapped hilt and gripped it tight.

Upon doing so, he immediately felt a cold sensation originating at his wrist and slithering up his arm, across his chest, and down towards his broken ribs. After first jumping in surprise at the cold, the farmer breathed a sigh of relief and sucked in a deep breath of air his lungs had been craving but that the pain had prevented.

He then swiped his left hand over the cut that had been on his right forearm, and felt no wound – though the blood was rapidly drying and flaking off.

What did you do? Kel'rak asked in amazement.

"Again, later!" the voice replies, as the ground began to tremble. "Now, can you climb?"

I think so, but these walls are slick with moss and I can't see a thing.

"Hold that thought."

Once more, the cold feeling washed over Kel'rak, and he could swear his vision temporarily darkened as the coldness swept over his face. Once the strange experience stopped, he felt invigorated with a grip that could halt a bull mid-charge and a weightlessness that would allow him to do hundreds of pushups on end without tiring.

Deciding to test this theory, he cut the sleeve from his shirt and wraps the blade of the dagger with it before stuffing it in his boot, then reached for the nearest wall. Though it is definitely still slimy, Kel'rak found that he had no trouble keeping his grip.

In fact, if he so chose, he could probably rip this brick from the wall. The ground rumbled once more and he decided to table that thought for later. Going by pure feel, the farmer scaled the wall with relative ease. His muscles did not burn for even one second as he climbed at a speed that should not be physically possible for anything other than a lizard or spider.

In short order, he brought himself over the lip of what he now realized and remembered to be a well; however, there was no time to rest as the ground began to quake with a fury and small pieces of rubble started falling at an increasing rate.

"Run!" the voice implored.

Kel'rak exploded into movement, still energized by whatever gave him the strength to climb, and dashed towards the beam of light that was his man-made entrance. Large chunks of what used to be the supporting structure were falling all around him, but he had no time to panic.

His heightened reflexes were the only thing that kept him alive as a stone the size of his chest dropped directly above his head, requiring him to dive into a roll just before reaching the opening. Acting on instinct, he exited the roll in a front handspring, effectively leaping to safety as the remaining structure collapsed in a heap of dust.

Sweet Sugar whinnied in fear from her chosen guard post, where she had not moved since Kel'rak had disappeared. Hunched over and huffing from the sudden exertion, the farmer glanced back one last time at his near-death experience and stood up tall, not fully believing what he'd just done.

Chuckling at the incredulity of it, he turned back towards Sugar and approached her cautiously with hands raised in an attempt to calm her.

"Shhhhh, good girl. It's okay," he said aloud for the first time since the fall. Remembering he can't hear himself speak, he brought his thoughts inward once more while climbing into the saddle.

Alright voice, explain.

"You're not going to believe me," the voice replies.

I just: fell unconscious into a well, lost my hearing, miraculously healed myself, scaled said well more easily than I've ever climbed anything in my life, and am talking to YOU inside my own mind. Try me, Kel'rak said as a matter-of-fact.

"Well, technically, I did all of those things for you" it clapped back with a terse clip.

You know what I mean, you royal ass.

"Is that any way to thank the entity that lifted you from certain death? Fine, I take it back."

Kel'rak suddenly felt all his prior pains return with no warning, making him double over in pain and lose his grip on the reins, thus falling five feet from the saddle to the road.

Screaming with rage and pain, he forced himself to his feet as Sugar started circling him with worry in her eyes.

What the hell? He starts, gritting his teeth through the pain of each shallow breath.

"You made it clear you did not appreciate the help of a 'royal ass', so I took my help back. Would you like to apologize for your rudeness?" the voice asked, with a smug grin that Kel'rak could feel inside his conscience.

I apologize, he started. *You must forgive my objectively frustrated behavior; this is all a bit weird. Please, help take this pain away. It is unbearable.*

"My pleasure, lad!" the voice returned, as the cold feeling washed throughout the farmer's body once more. "Now, as to your explanation…you will get one. But I am famished – expending that much power at once for the first time in a long time nearly drained me."

It was all Kel'rak could do to hold back his fire-like fury at this point. *You already promised me the explanation! …and what do you mean "power"?*

"Again, I feel as though this should be obvious. Magical power. My very life force, you twit. Are you going to continue complaining or am I going to get to feed soon?" the voice complained in an uncharacteristically whiny way.

Hold on – back up a few steps there mister voice –

"Voidtooth" it interjected.

V-Voidtooth? What?

"That is my name," Voidtooth replied, "now you may continue."

Okay then… Voidtooth. I'm going to need you to slow down a little bit. Did you say 'magical power'? And what the hell kind of name is Voidtooth?

"T'was the name given me by my creator when I was forged. Surely you didn't think I was some kind of person in your head did you? I *am* the dagger you brought with you – by the way, thank you for wrapping my blade so gently. I do so hate being cold and dirty; say, might you find me a nice cozy sheath?" Voidtooth finished, its tone rather excited.

As Sugar continued down the road at a casual pace, Kel'rak needed to trust her direction blindly as he rubbed the bridge of his nose and his temples vigorously in an attempt to fend off the ensuing migraine.

His mind was reeling from the sheer amount of information he has had to accept since waking up not even ten minutes ago, and now he's not just talking to some kind of spirit, he's talking to a magical weapon?

This is ridiculous, he thought to himself.

"I assure you it's not," Voidtooth replied in a curt tone.

UGH! My own personal thoughts aren't even an escape from you now?

"To your misfortune, no – though to my needs it is already proving to be a turn of luck! I see from your most recent memories you have a herd of bovine; one of them will do nicely."

Excuse me? Kel'rak replied, taken aback.

"For lunch. I told you, expending that much energy drained me. I am starving!"

As Voidtooth finished the final word it imparted its' own feelings of hunger upon Kel'rak, who suddenly felt as if he has not eaten anything in recent memory. The pain and thirst was enough to nearly drive him insane in an instant, but he persevered through sheer willpower and pushed back against Voidtooth's presence.

You can't have my cows! They are my livelihood and my only companions, aside from Sugar, Kel'rak implored.

"Well I can have a 'cow' as you call them or I can just start slowly eating your soul, which would you prefer?" Voidtooth replied with what can only be described as a cat-like purr.

Terrified, Kel'rak fumbled inside his boot for the dagger and threw it far into the fields of tall grass, hoping that to be the end of it. As he shook off a chill from the rising anxiety inside himself, he felt a puff of cold air on the side of his calf and glanced down to his boot, where the last vestiges of a cloud of black smoke was now blowing away with the wind.

"I told you already farmer, I am inside your head." Voidtooth claims. "You cannot just toss me into the wind. Once my blade tasted your flesh and soul, I knew I finally had a way out of that prison – so, rather than consume you, I decided it was in my best interest to bind myself to you. Given that most recent interaction and the further expenditure of power, I apologize for what I must now do."

An intense sadness came over Kel'rak, accompanied by a sharp pain in his chest, as a childhood memory came to the forefront of his mind. His oldest cousin and best friend, Tre'rak, was sprinting as fast as he could down the lane towards his childhood home.

Kel'rak looked up from the dirt drawing of a wolf that he had been working on for some time, as his face lit up with glee at the sight of Tre. That glee soon faded though when his cousin's face came into focus under the glare of the late day sun, and the puffy eyes and tear-streaked dirty cheeks became clearer.

This was the day the family split ways, he remembered. His aunt and uncle had come to the agreement that their family business would profit more from a multi-front and multi-city approach. Since that day, he had never seen Tre again... and never would, he realized, as the memory started to fade and Voidtooth breathed a mental sigh of relief.

"You have no idea how long it's been since I've tasted a fresh piece of a pained soul," it began.

D-did you just eat my memory? Kel'rak interrupted.

"Always the obvious questions with this one. Yes, how observant of you. Would you like a cookie, wee lamb?" Voidtooth responded, its' voice dripping with sarcasm.

How dare you! That was the last memory I could remember of my cousin!

"Calm yourself, Lambie. How can you rightly long for someone whose face you don't even remember? I told you I was hungry, and you didn't listen. You made me waste even more of my power and put me on the brink of hibernation. Actions have consequences farmer; I know you know that; I've been through your memories. I only took one that didn't matter."

Forcing himself to bury his panic, Kel'rak shut his "mouth" and glared at the horizon. How could this... this...weapon, possibly understand what consequences are? How could it possibly know his pain? Remembering that it can read his thoughts, he shut down that track and moved towards another.

Fine. I will take you to my herd and you may have just one cow – no more. I had intended on surviving only on crops and trapped game until the winter, but it is very clear that I have no choice in this matter.

"Delightful, we're finally seeing eye to eye!" Voidtooth replied. "Now for your explanation, should you decide to open your mind to it."

I am all ears, considering you're the only voice I can hear now.

"The lamb has a sharp bite! How exquisitely fascinating!" the weapon began. "As we've already discussed, the only reason you're still alive is because of magic; alas, having been through your memories, I've discovered that you don't believe in magic."

There's a difference between believing and being told that it doesn't exist anymore, for your entire life. Laird Privvel's Reckoning extinguished it from the face of the planet. The gods themselves pulled away their favor and left humanity to its' own devices, once they realized they no longer had anything they could entice us with. We were victorious!

"Just because that's how that bawbag wrote the history books, doesn't mean it's the truth Lambie."

Would you stop with the ridiculous nickname?

"No, I'm quite fond of it actually. Now, as I've stated, my existence is due to the existence of magic here on the earthen plane. More specifically, my power feeds on the emotions of fear and hate, otherwise known as dark energy. These energies are all around you humans – you writhe within it! Your emotions, your feelings. Your anger, your sadness, your loneliness, your joy; even your...love," it made a fake gagging sound at the last word.

Sugar just continued to plod along, oblivious to the conversation going on in Kel's head. She raised her snout in the direction of a nearby tree, smelling fresh fruit, and turned that direction after feeling no resistance from the farmer.

"The gods were never the source of the magic, they just harnessed it in ways that humans can't imagine and taught their followers to do the same. Can you explain in any other way how I managed to free you from your deep dark prison?" Voidtooth finished.

Kel'rak took a deep breath, knowing already that it was a rhetorical question.

No, I cannot, he replied.

"Grand, we've moved beyond that paradigm shift!" the dagger exclaimed. "I worried with your simple mind that would take all day."

I get it, I'm a dumb farmer. You can drop the schtick. This still doesn't explain how you managed to affect my body in the way you did. Isn't magic supposed to be accompanied by finger wiggling and words only wizards can understand? Kel'rak responded in his most sardonic tone. *One second, I was dying of hypoxia, the next it was like I not only never got hurt, but I was stronger than ever!*

"Ooh, the lamb's a medicine man too? Impressive," Voidtooth answered equally as sardonic. "Has magic really been missing from the world so long that that's how the stories have evolved? Finger Wiggles? What I wouldn't GIVE to feast on the idiot historian who wrote that!"

As Sugar finished her fruit feast, she turned her head back towards Kel'rak, who realized he hasn't acknowledged her presence in ages and gave her a quick neck rub for good measure before signaling for her to carry on with the journey home.

Voidtooth decided to continue, "In the same way that an emotion is a feeling, so too is magic. There is no need for words for the most basic of uses. No ridiculous finger wiggling. For the truly powerful magics, yes, there are incantations that must be recited but those are the more advanced variety that used to be provided by the gods to their chosen. Given that I am a magical being and not an entity of the earthen plane, I am less bound by these rules."

So you're telling me that I only need to harness the energy from my emotions to do magic? Kel'rak asked, still with a hint of skepticism.

"If it were that easy, do you not think that every royal old prune in their castle would have figured it out by now, given that they have nothing better to do with their time?" Voidtooth responded, with more than a bit of irritation.

"There are additional factors to consider: one's own ability to tune into their emotions, the lengths of their imagination, and their natural affinity to one of the various types of energy and their related emotions. There are of course those with the ability to control their emotions like a beast on a leash, whom are a terrifying sight to behold, and then there are people like you whose life experiences reek with fear and hate. That's why I chose you."

Back up again, what do you mean you chose me? I thought you said the second your blade ripped my skin, you knew you had a way out?

"Eh – not entirely truth. I could feel the life force radiating from your body as you got closer to the ruins. I could also feel your hesitation as you got closer, and the fear that accompanied it, so I fed on that fear and pulled you closer, because I knew immediately that I couldn't let you go. Instead of just feeding on your soul like I had with every other unfortunate passerby for the last hundred years, I decided you might actually be of some use to me given our same affinities."

"Now, you don't need to walk around in fear anymore, Lambie. Now, you have me. And together, we will humiliate, destroy, and consume any bastard unfortunate enough to cross us!" As Voidtooth finished its' last thought, Kel'rak felt this time a surge of pleasure as the dagger imparted its' own emotions and eagerness into his mind. That rush of pleasure was accompanied by murderous thoughts that Kel'rak hadn't had in a long time – a very, very long time. And even though he knew Voidtooth was just fishing for reasons to feed, he knew in his mind that Voidtooth's proposal was one that he would be stupid to turn down.

Finally, Sugar rounded the last bend in the road and the beginnings of the cottage he'd started earlier that morning came into view. The herd had stayed close by, given the sheer amount of vegetation available to eat, so he didn't have to travel much farther.

Upon arrival, Kel'rak dismounted Sugar and pulled the weapon from his boot, removing the makeshift outer wrapping and trying to decide which cow he was willing to sacrifice. However, as soon as the outer wrapping was removed, he felt the blade tugging his hand towards the herd. Voidtooth started promising him all of the desires of his heart, so long as it could feast.

Though it pained him to allow it, he went against his own words and promised the dagger a feast worthy of a king – so long as one of the bulls were left for them to bring to a market for sale. Voidtooth agreed immediately and flexed its' power for Kel'rak to behold. Unleashing a shadowy wave of fear, it rendered the entire herd completely immobile, frozen with terror.

Suddenly, the weapon pulled on his arm so hard it felt like it might fly out of his hand. His feet started moving of their own accord, eager to sate the hunger of the dagger. As he closed in on the first cow, it looked him directly in the eye with all of its' fear on display, and Kel'rak wavered with his own internal horror; but Voidtooth won out in the end as it willed Kel to plunge the blade deep in the heifer's neck.

As it drank from the cow's life force, Voidtooth began to cackle, like the laugh of a madman. "AHA! – Ahahahaha!" Using its' newfound energy, the weapon infused Kel's body with more strength and agility, encouraging him to leap from cow to cow, slaughtering each in turn with more and more efficiency.

With just the last two bulls left, Voidtooth picked the weaker of the two – true to its' word that it would leave the more sellable alive – and savored the approach to this final death.

As Kel'rak severed the bull's spinal cord with one swift motion, Voidtooth halted the forward progress of Kel's arm to keep its' blade firmly planted in the bull's body, and began to release a corrosive shadow which started melting the bull from the inside out. "AHA! – Ahahahaha!" This time, Kel'rak found himself to be the one cackling maniacally, as Voidtooth consumed the bull's essence leaving nothing but a melted pile of blood and bones where fifteen hundred pounds of bull once stood.

The would-be farmer leashed the remaining bull and walked it over to Sugar, tying the leather strap to a loop on her saddle. He turned back towards the beginnings of a house frame that he had started on in what seemed like a lifetime ago and just stood there, wondering at the pathetic turn his life had nearly taken.

Raising his arm and thus Voidtooth to face-level, Kel'rak simply grinned and gave the mental affirmation, *Deal. Let's get to work.*

Chapter 3
The Reaping

Amelia Atwater was a kind woman. Her nondescript linen clothing was plain, brown, and otherwise unremarkable; however, her cherubic face lit up any room she walked into. She was known as the healer of the town of Marasol, using various herbs and tinctures to remedy common ailments.

The healer's home sat on the edge of town, so every restock trip carried her past the homes of those she'd helped over the last few years. She loved this part the most, because she got to watch as the children she had saved from deadly fevers would grow up, and the littlest ones would run from their front door to give her hugs as she passed by on the main road.

One appreciative mother always had a fresh, warm bread roll ready for her as she walked by, to give thanks for the work Amelia had done to bring her husband back from the brink of death after a particularly brutal round of pneumonia contracted from working in the fields during a rainstorm.

Today was no different – the sun shone down on the town of Marasol as it shyly peeked over the wintery caps of the distant Jester Crags. They were so named because of their late Fall, early Winter habit of getting blanketed with snow one day and immediately thawing out the next, as if they were playing a trick on all who watched and eagerly awaited the first indicator of Winter.

As Amelia strolled down the lane, appreciating the warm buttery goodness of that bread roll, she reflected on the lives she'd saved since moving to this town and the new life growing in her belly. The herbalist enthusiast hobby she'd cultivated had afforded her early adult years with the kind of financial comfort she only could have dreamed of as a child, back when she survived on nothing but warm, buttery rolls and unclean water.

The world had not been kind to her parents, who had raised her the best they could on the pittance of a salary her father earned as a dockhand, mopping drunken sailor vomit on a nightly basis. That hard life had shown her though, that if she was to have any success in life, she would need to master a skill – a skill not many others could claim.

To be unique meant to have security. It meant that you were always needed and always payable, and Amelia intended to teach that hard-learned life lesson to her child in a not hard-learned way. Grimacing at the mere thought of that memory, she steeled her visage and shoved the last bite of bread in her mouth.

Amelia walked the familiar path toward Lumpy's garden, one hand resting on her swollen belly. The dirt road was still dappled with sunlight between the thatched eaves of her neighbors' homes, but something felt… off.

She couldn't name it at first.

It was the silence.

There were no children playing with hoops. No shouts from the smithy. Even the marketplace, which usually bustled with gossip and clattering pans, was subdued. A single bread vendor packed away his stall with stiff, mechanical movements, not even glancing up as she passed.

A dog barked once from behind a shuttered window, high-pitched and frantic. Then nothing.

The air was heavy—not hot, but weighted. Thick with something unspoken. She paused as a raven swooped low overhead, letting out a harsh caw that made her flinch. It landed on a lamppost and stared at her with oily black eyes.

Colson kicked suddenly, hard enough that Amelia winced and placed both hands on her belly. "Easy, sweetheart," she whispered. "We're just going to see Uncle Lumpy. Nothing to worry about."

But she couldn't shake the feeling that Marasol was holding its breath.

As she rounded the corner past the old well, she caught sight of an elderly woman—Mother Sira, the blind apothecary widow—sitting alone in the alley with her back pressed against the wall. The woman's empty gaze was fixed on the sky.

"Sira?" Amelia asked.

The woman didn't respond.

Amelia took a cautious step closer. "It's Amelia."

Still no answer—until, just as she was about to leave, the old woman muttered, "The harvest is coming early this year."

Amelia froze.

"I'm sorry?"

"The reaping," Sira said. "You hear it in the roots if you listen. The soil remembers."

Amelia opened her mouth, then closed it. Sira had always been eccentric, but this felt different. The way her voice rasped—like something foreign was speaking through her.

Before Amelia could ask more, the old woman simply turned her face away and folded her hands across her lap.

Amelia backed away slowly.

She didn't look back until the greenhouse's crooked roof finally came into view.

Lumpy's Greenhouse was the only establishment in a five-town radius that maintained a nursery of all the most important herbs Amelia needed to do her healing work, which is what brought her to Marasol in the first place. Lumpy was a man who took the nickname out of self-deprecating humor – his general body shape being somewhat of a mound, with rolls of fat cascading down that mound and lending credence to the name.

Being a caretaker of small herbs and various florals, his chosen career didn't require much physical labor and contributed heavily to his portly stature, accentuated by the fact that he could not refuse a halfway decent pastry – or really any baked good for that matter.

Lumpy's jolly demeanor could make even the saltiest sailor crack a smile and join in on a belly laugh. It was this characteristic that made Amelia spend so much time in his Greenhouse. Lumpy was just plain good company, and he appreciated the things that she appreciated.

In a town full of admirers, he was her best and only real friend. Sure, the townsfolk gave her all kinds of praise, love, and adoration for the things she'd managed to accomplish for them. But no one quite understood her love for herbology like Lumpy.

The large cowbell above the door jingled its' happy tune and startled Lumpy from a mid-day nap as Amelia walked in, shrouded by angelic light. He blinked at her groggily for a few seconds, unable to focus his eyes, and finally made out the large belly he'd grown accustomed to seeing in his shop once a week.

"Amelia, me girl!" he began cheerily, "Ye caught me unawares. Thank goodness fer that fancy new alarm system that sweet lad Grisham sold me!"

Amelia chuckled lightly. "Lumpy, it's just a bell. Did Grisham play you for a fool with his newest scam?"

"Nah, he's a sweet boy, lassie." He fired back, "I already telled ye that. Not a scammy bone in his tiny little underfed body."

The horticulturist folded his arms and assumed his most cross posture, forcing out a sarcastic grin. They both sat there, waiting for the other to crack first, both finally busting up with laughter at the same time as Amelia threw Lumpy an extra roll – which he happily scarfed down.

Amelia moved closer, eyeing the crates of tomatoes arranged along the left bench. "These are hideous. Lumpy in name and in nature."

"Better than those bland golden pears the guild keeps pushing," he muttered. "Lumpy's have character."

She grinned and plucked one up, running her fingers over its bumpy skin. "This one looks like it's scowling at me."

"Means it's ripe."

He reached into a small wooden drawer beneath the planting bench and drew something out: a chain, slightly tarnished, with a small jade charm shaped like a leaf.

"Here," he said, awkwardly holding it out. "Was my wife's."

Amelia blinked. "Lumpy, I can't –"

"You can." He pressed it into her palm. "She always said jade was for new beginnings. For protection. Thought your little one could use both."

Her throat caught.

He looked away, as if embarrassed by the sentiment. "Besides," he added gruffly, "You've put up with my groaning all these years. About time I paid you back."

Amelia wrapped her fingers around the charm and nodded. "Thank you."

He busied himself with rearranging a sprig of dill, but his movements were slower. More deliberate. She noticed a slight shake in his hand.

"Everything alright?" she asked gently.

Lumpy hesitated. "Just been thinking. About roots, and when to pull them up."

Amelia frowned, but he turned away before she could press.

"I need to replenish my stock of wolfsbane," Amelia started. "The villagers seem to be passing around some sort of lung infection. It's going around like mad!"

"Aye, seen the same," Lumpy replied. "Nearly half the town guard is home sick, so says me nephew. That poor boy's been running ragged, what with the Captain keeping 'im on shifts for the last week."

"Poor Latham indeed! I'll be sure to bring him some tea for energy and wellness support tonight. Throw some licorice root, ginseng, and echinacea in my order while you're at it."

Lumpy's stool groaned with displeasure as he shifted his weight to stand up and collect Amelia's herbs. "I assume ye be needin' fresh wolfsbane for the medicine and dried materials for the tea?"

"Please!" Amelia chirped with her sing-song voice.

"Go ahead and lock that front door so we can walk through the greenhouse and find the wolfsbane. Me tum-tum could use the exercise and me heart could use the company," the gardener said with a weak smile.

Amelia did as he asked, also hanging his *"On a break, don't come back later"* sign on the front door. She chuckled as she did so, not entirely understanding how he managed to maintain this business with as much as he didn't like to work or provide any semblance of customer service. Noticing that he was already out of sight, Amelia swung her obtuse belly around and waddled as fast as her pregnant feet would move.

She caught up to him in no time at all, even at her slower pace, due to the strain Lumpy's general obesity put on his ankles. He had barely even made it to the greenhouse door in the shop's back alley.

Hearing her coming, the man hurriedly unlocked the greenhouse as fast as his pudgy fingers would move and barely managed to pop open the door for Amelia like the gentleman he was known to be. "Me lady," he announced with an overly dramatic bow – which was really just a head nod and a hand flourish. The healer just giggled and tiptoed through the door.

Upon entering the greenhouse, one could not help but be in pure awe of the collection Lumpy had amassed. Rows upon rows of plants of every variety sat on tables in clay pots, reaching their stalks to the heavens and soaking in every bit of light they could. The horticulturist had decided to sort them in what appeared to be a "Pretty" to "Hideous" manner – though that meant nothing when considering the benefits and detriments of the plant life contained in this nursery. More often than not, the prettiest leaves and flowers were an indication of a deadly poison while the blander buds provided the most homeopathic benefit.

Amelia took it all in with a deep sniff, delighting in the varying smells and the general humidity of the environment; to her, it felt like a scented sauna, where she could spend hours relaxing and letting her worries melt away.

"Ye know," Lumpy began, "many of these plants are much like yerself."

Waking from her daydream with a start, Amelia just offered an "Oh?" in response.

"Aye. Beautiful, and fragile, while also dangerous and the best healing agent around if properly utilized."

"Lumpy! I'm married, you flatterer!"

"Bah, t'weren't meant like tha' and ye knows it," Lumpy shot back.

"I can't help but mess with you dear friend, you're the only one I can do it with! Frederick is always out working the road construction, so the most conversation I get is with you and my patients."

The shop owner gave a little pouty grin, accepting the teasing in stride, and breaking into his characteristic ear-to-ear smile. "Ye know how to make a lad feel important, ye know tha'?"

A slight commotion rang in from outside on the street, and Amelia reached across and squeezed Lumpy's hand, enjoying every single second of their friendship. The commotion got a little louder as what sounded like soldiers jingled past in their chainmail armor, but nothing could be seen through the fogged glass windows of the greenhouse.

Refusing to let go of her small hand, Lumpy continued, "I don' think I'm long left fer this life, me girl." Amelia perked up at that, instant alarm in her eyes. "I been feelin' it fer a while now. Me bones ache. Me muscles ache. Me eyes ache… and me heart aches."

"Lindall –" Amelia started, but was immediately cut off.

"Don' ye dare use me real name girl. Ye know be'er than tha'…"

"I'm sorry. I'm so sorry. I know she was the only one who used your real name." Amelia quickly apologized.

"Ye remind me so much o' her," Lumpy reminisced. "Yer beauty, yer joy, yer kind heart. The gods truly granted me a gift when they dropped ye on this earth. Because o' knowin' ye, I've had the heart to go on…" He paused, blinking back some highly uncharacteristic tears.

"But me plants need someone to take care o' them," he continued. Then he finally met her gaze and locked eyes, tears freely falling. "They need ye to take care o' them, because I have to go, lass. I promised her I'd take her ashes to the sea, and I won't be able to make that trip much longer – and I won' be makin' it back neither."

Unable to hold his fierce stare, she dropped her eyes, squeezing his hand ever tighter. "I don't know what to say Lumpy… of course I will keep an eye on your plants. And I will honor her memory, til my dying day. This place was as much your baby as this one growing in my belly," she finished with a strained voice.

Lumpy let go suddenly, and wrapped her in a tight bear hug instead, using what little burst of strength he could muster to spin her around. Like a little girl being swung up high by her daddy, Amelia giggled with pleasure thinking she had made his day one last time before he left.

But then she felt his arms go limp. Suddenly she was beginning to support his weight, and when she hooked her arms under his, her hand knocked against something wooden.

Slowly guiding him to his knees, she saw the hatchet protruding from the center of his back and laid him on his side. A direct hit to his spine – he'd been paralyzed the second he was hit. "What is going on?!" she cried.

"Run…" was all he managed to spit out, through the blood erupting from his mouth. He brushed her cheek gently, and smiled, the light fading from his cherubic face.

Lumpy hit the floorboards with a sickening crack.

Blood spread like spilled ink across the wooden slats, too much, too fast. Amelia dropped to her knees, slipping in it, her hands reaching for him even before she could form words. She pressed both palms against the wound in his chest, screaming in defiance for help, for healing, for anything.

"Lumpy—Lumpy, look at me—stay with me—!"

His eyes fluttered.

One hand reached up, trembling, barely able to find her arm.

She caught it, held it tightly.

"I'm here. I'm right here. You're okay."

But even as she said the words, she knew they weren't true.

His chest convulsed with each breath, shallow and rasping. There was a gurgle in his throat. His free hand curled and uncurled against the floorboards.

"Don't go," she whispered. "Please, do not go."

A flicker of focus returned to his eyes.

His mouth worked silently. She leaned closer, desperate.

"'Leaf…'" he breathed.

"What?" she asked, voice cracking.

"Leaf... still... green..."

Amelia's breath caught in her chest.

The pendant. Jade. Protection.

She clutched it around her neck as his hand went limp in hers.

Then the light left his eyes.

"No," she said, shaking her head. "No, no—"

She tried anyway. She searched with frantic panic in her eyes, for anything in the greenhouse that might staunch of the flow of the blood.

She knew he would have something, but there was nothing within reach. It was happening too fast. She smacked his cheek, hard.

Lumpy's body didn't stir.

The blood kept running.

Outside, fire spread toward the greenhouse.

Amelia collapsed against his chest, sobbing.

That moment, a giant-of-a-man dressed head to toe in animal hides burst through the greenhouse wall with a roar, and the sounds of battle and death raged in from outside.

The marauder chuckled as he shook shards of wood and glass from his shoulders and was quickly felled by an arrow through the back of his neck. Amelia screamed as his blood splattered her face, then looked past his falling body to see Lumpy's nephew Latham offer a quick salute before chasing down another threat.

Amelia stumbled out of the rubble in a haze, not fully processing what was happening.

All around her, screams echoed throughout the streets as men, women, and children were slaughtered and the marauders made off with wares of every variety. A group of empty-handed marauders spotted her, grinned, and slowly stalked her way.

Finally realizing the danger she was in, the healer bolted as fast as her swollen feet would carry her, but was caught in short order by the elbow as the five men surrounded her.

"The warlord appreciates your offering," the largest of the men stated simply.

Her face briefly contorted in confusion before she felt the butt end of a sword smack her in the head.

"He will make a fine warrior under our care," the same man stated matter-of-factly. "Assuming he survives the manner of his birth, that is."

Pain bloomed.

White-hot, blooming like firecrackers behind her eyes.

They dragged her down onto the street. Her knees scraped stone. She tried to twist away, but the hands were too strong. Calloused. Grimy. Fingers bit into her arms. Into her belly.

"No—no, please, not him—!"

A blow to the face. Something cracked. Her mouth filled with the taste of metal and ash. The world reeled sideways. She couldn't tell if she was screaming anymore.

She couldn't feel her legs.

"Get it out of her."

That voice. The one with the belt full of knives.

A hand grabbed her chin and forced it toward the sky. She saw clouds. Gray and thin. Marasol's sky.

Suffering from a severe concussion, she didn't even feel the pain as the men cut her open and offered a low whistle of appreciation for the male child she'd born.

Colson kicked once. A final, panicked flurry.

Then everything went still.

Something was torn. Not just her skin. Her.

Her body buckled.

She felt them pull him from her. Her arms, pinned. Her vision doubled.

And then—

And then she heard him.

A cry.

Brief.

Piercing.

Alive.

She reached for the sound with her mind, with her soul, with everything she had left—

But then came the cold.

Something deep and green, thick as rot, pulled itself from her core. Her mind stretched to hold it, but couldn't. Her thoughts folded in on themselves. She wasn't a woman anymore. Not a healer. Not even a mother.

She was a vessel.

Everything she'd lost poured out in that one burst.

Light and death and rage and love.

She saw Lumpy again for a moment—smiling through his tears. She saw her husband's arms wrapped around her during a spring dance. She saw a child she'd never get to raise.

Waking slightly from the concussed stupor, Amelia looked upon her son's face and used her dying breath to release a wail that hummed with dark energy. Winds began to pick up, howling like a pack of ravenous wolves, while the sun faded from view and an eerie green light surrounded the road where she lay dying.

With a sudden reverberation of bass, the glow exploded outward in all directions, and Amelia could hear the men's abrupt surprise before they were flung from where she lay. The explosion also affected her, knocking her slightly raised head forcefully back into the cobblestone of the road and rendering her unconscious.

Around her lay devastation, for blocks – the majority of Marasol. At the epicenter, the green glow continued, materializing as "living" light in the form of hundreds of serpents slithering towards Amelia's body. Rather than striking her as a snake would, the lights simply tunneled into her body.

The light faded.

What remained was not silence—but stillness. A vacuum where sound had been. Even the birds, once cawing madly from the rooftops, had vanished.

The central street of Marasol no longer resembled a town. Blackened earth fanned out in a perfect circle around Amelia's crumpled form—thirty yards across, scorched like the blast of an artillery shell. The cobblestones had cracked and curled. Windowpanes nearest the epicenter were blown outward, their glass embedded in walls like arrowheads. Doors sagged on one hinge. Banners fluttered from soot-streaked beams.

And in the distance, beyond the alleyways, a single church bell gave one broken clang as it collapsed—then nothing.

A man stumbled from the wreckage, one arm bent at a sickening angle, half his face burned raw. He dropped to his knees in the ash, coughing hard, eyes wild with terror. He looked once toward the figure in the center of the blast and let out a shaking breath.

"Witch," he whispered.

Then he toppled forward, unmoving.

***

Further away from the town, a patrol of armored riders paused at the edge of the forest path, having seen the sky rip itself open moments earlier. Their captain said nothing—just raised one gloved hand to signal caution.

The stench hit them first: scorched earth, burnt wood, and something else, something metallic and sickeningly sweet. Then the sight: Marasol, a town they knew at the edge of their Kingdom, reduced to a blackened, smoking crater. It wasn't a fire. It wasn't a conventional attack. This was... an eradication.

Their horses shied, whinnying in terror, sensing the lingering unnaturalness in the air. The men, hardened soldiers, stared with slack jaws, their faces pale beneath their helmets.

The youngest among them peered ahead at the ruin of Marasol.

"Who did this?" he asked, voice barely above the wind.

The captain didn't answer.

Instead, he reached into a leather satchel and retrieved a scroll. Unfurled it. Studied it. Then looked back up at the town.

Captain Borus, a veteran of a dozen skirmishes, felt a cold knot of dread tighten in his gut. This wasn't the work of bandits, or even a rival lord. This was... an act of God, or something far worse. Magic that could tear the world asunder was not a tale untold in their land, but it was a tale older than time. Older than most living members of society.

He'd dismissed them as superstition. Now, looking at the devastation, he wasn't so sure. 'Mark the place,' he commanded, his voice rough. 'Burn nothing. Touch nothing. This... this is not a battlefield. This is a wound. And we do not know what contagion it holds.'

They would return to The Nine, and report their findings. Magic was making a very public re-appearance.

Chapter 4
The Learning Curve

The nearby village of Bellanor was a particularly lively one. It was for this reason that Kel had never liked it – too noisy. Merchant's carts full of knick-knacks, furs, leathers, weapons, meats, and all variety of things careened down the main road; though, to call it a road was somewhat overkill.

Bellanor was nothing more than a collection of homes and businesses, laid out in what could be considered a mile-long rectangle with a cleared section of haphazardly buried flat stones collected from the coast serving as the road. This of course meant that any merchant stupid enough to hawk their wares here caused a ruckus as their wagon's metal-reinforced wheels clack, clack, clacked against the street.

Men, women, and children of all ages talked loudly over one another in an effort to get the best deals, sell the most inventory, and – most importantly – the juiciest gossip. Next to the lone inn of the village sat a brothel, whose ladies of the night continually called out in their sweetest high-pitched voices, like land Sirens drawing their victims in.

Across from the brothel was the ramshackle building that served as the village's school, for any child of the ill fortune to be born here. Immediately adjacent to the school was the local healer's cottage, led by quite the grumpy old man, who had become incredibly spiteful over his years of tending to the woes of these village folk.

As one of the few truly coastal population centers of Litharia, it still managed to attract visitors and permanent migrants, despite the general lack of order that would come from a more civilized location. And yet, with all of this hustle and bustle, Kel'rak had a major problem. He couldn't hear any of it.

How am I to sell this bull, if I cannot hear nor speak to any of these locals? He asked of Voidtooth.

"Worry not, Lambie, where there's a will, there's a way" it quipped back, imparting mental images of various common hand signals for everyday things like money, pointing, and joyful expressions.

Kel's eyes and mouth sagged into an expression of annoyance. *You think I can get a halfway decent price for a bull by acting like someone who has never been taught to speak?*, he thought incredulously.

"Fine, fine, how about this? We just… kill everyone and take all of their things!" the weapon implored hungrily, replacing the previous mental images with those of blood and death.

I will not kill innocent people, Kel fired back flatly.

"You never let me do anything fun," Voidtooth whined in what Kel decided was a very childish voice.

I do what killing I must to keep your power fed, but I will not kill innocent folk. The ex-farmer responded harshly. *Now are you going to give me a solution or should I start begging on the corner of the road with a sign, and hope anyone in this gods-forsaken village can read?*

It had been about a week since Kel'rak and Voidtooth had set out from what Kel affectionately labeled "Zaulyl Peninsula". In that time, the newly minted adventurer had come to realize that the dagger wanted one thing and one thing only – death.

Its' sole purpose on this planet was to kill and feed, and if it didn't get what it wanted in a timely manner it would nag and nag until he finally caved from the constant headache. That being said, he had learned some useful ways to employ magic in that short week.

In their hunt of a pack of wolves, the weapon had imparted the knowledge of how to manipulate his fear into a cocoon of darkness, shrouding the wolves' vision of him and making them rely on their sense of smell and hearing. Voidtooth, on the other hand, could feel their life energies in the dark, and directed Kel'rak in the direction of each of their throats.

As with the final kill of the herd of cows, the weapon savored the final kill – the Alpha – and consumed it wholly with its' acidic shadowstuff.

Another night, the dagger had shown Kel'rak how to enhance his physical agility and strength – fueled by his own hatred, rather than the weapon's energy – as they came across a tent of highwaymen. The ragtag bandits had a woman in bindings, discussing to the side what he could only assume were going to be the vile things they would do to her.

Of course, without the ability to hear what was being discussed, he couldn't confirm his suspicions; but it didn't take working ears to know nothing good would happen to that poor girl this night if he didn't intervene.

Taking the opportunity to both enact some justice and feed his weapon's bottomless pit, Kel'rak dashed out of the woods towards the campfire. His pure rage and hatred pumping his legs with more strength than ever, he closed the gap before the group even knew what was happening and opened three jugulars with a single backhanded swipe of his blade.

One of the remaining three men turned tail towards the woods and received a thrown Voidtooth bite in the base of his skull. Seeing their assailant now unarmed, the final two enemies stalked forward, each with a hand-and-a-half sword at the ready. But then Kel'rak charged forward once more, the same shining weapon impossibly in hand, first using his legs to launch himself into a spear tackle of one enemy with a forward stab to the heart, then rolling deftly on impact towards the final bandit and jamming Voidtooth up under his chin with a throaty growl.

In his blood-rage, Kel almost listened to Voidtooth's insistence that he just end the woman's suffering, but instead shook it off and cut her bindings before simply walking away without a word.

Reflecting still on that night, the ex-farmer finally reached the inn, tied up Sugar and the bull outside, and stepped into his temporary home. Inside, the scene wasn't much different than out on the street. Men of every age and background gathered around tables placing bets, regaling each other with tales of valor, and arguing over this farm issue or that – their booming voices reverberating in Kel's chest but otherwise making no sound.

The innkeeper had clearly been trying to flag him down while he was distracted, because when he looked back towards the bar, the portly man was flailing his arms and giving Kel'rak an explicitly angry look.

"What can I do for you, lad?" Kel imagined the man saying, trying to read his lips.

Rather than trying to talk back, Kel pointed first to his ear, then lips, and mouthed the word "deaf". Turning five different shades of red with embarrassment, the innkeeper pleaded a quick apology that Kel couldn't hear and disappeared to the back before returning with a board and some chalk. It read, "So sorry, I didn't know. Do you need a room?"

Nodding emphatically, he gestured for the board and chalk and wrote, "I have only my bull as payment." Once the innkeeper read that and made a disappointed face, Kel erased the message and started again. "Is there anyone here who can help me?" Again letting the man read, then holding a finger up, he erased and started again. "I will be swindled by these merchants without help."

Making a face like a lightbulb went off in his head, the innkeeper directed Kel's eyes towards the large hearth, where a thin looking man sat by himself drinking a warm beverage. "He can sign. Interpret." The man wrote.

"I don't know how" Kel'rak replied, sighing deeply.

"I'm sorry lad, that's all I know." The innkeeper wrote back. "Have a drink on the house."

Kel'rak accepted the mead with a grateful bow to the innkeeper and turned towards the fireplace. *How in the nine hells am I supposed to do this?* He thought.

Thinking back on it, he turned back to the innkeeper and pointed towards the chalkboard – which the man had otherwise already forgotten about – and was given an emphatic head nod, as if to say "Yes, of course, please just take whatever you need I'm so sorry!". Tucking it under his arm, Kel pivoted on his heel and started off with every bit of confidence he could muster.

The stranger looked up as he closed the gap, clearly the ever-alert type. With a clearly forced smile, he rose to meet Kel. As he stood, he offered what looked like a salute, while also verbally stating "Hello!" and offering a handshake.

The man held up his hands like upside down claws, shaking them back and forth, and started off saying "What can I do for you?"; however, Kel realized he was trying to speak in sign and quickly cut him off with a single raised finger and raised eyebrows, trying to say "Please hold" but also not be rude.

Grabbing his board and feeling highly uncomfortable, Kel'rak nevertheless pressed forward. He wrote, "The barkeep said you might help?". Again, the man offered those shaking upside down claws, saying "What?" and pausing to allow Kel to write again. "I don't know sign. I need help selling my bull."

The man pulled a stray strand of his shoulder-length black hair back out of his eyes and tucked it behind his ear, revealing a slight point on the tip. Seeing Kel's eyes widen immediately, he pointed towards the chalkboard and wrote down "Half-elf".

As though expecting that to be all the explanation necessary, he gave a toothy smile and handed the board back. Kel'rak had traveled most of the continent over his lifetime but had never so much as seen an elf. The citizens of the Kingdom of the Nine were a highly suspicious and secretive folk, preferring to stay within the security of their natural land borders: The Jester Crags, a massive crescent-moon shaped lake that surrounded their city, and a smaller mountain range beyond that which offered them favorable weather year-round by rebounding any of the nastier coastal weather.

Voidtooth perked up at the notion. It suddenly had an idea.

"While I like to think that an elf's essence is particularly delicious and would rather consume him, you now have the advantage you need, Lambie."

With an extreme exertion, Kel kept himself from visibly reacting to the sudden conversation in his head and managed to continue it without alerting the helpful half-elf. *I'll bite – what's the advantage?*, he thought with disdain.

"Even if magic had fully disappeared from the planet, as you claim, even a half-breed such as this should retain a measure of the natural magical affinity known among his kin," Voidtooth began. "This means he should not react poorly to the existence of a magical item, or its' abilities – if he hasn't already felt my presence."

Slow down, you're talking nonsense again. Magical affinity? Magical items? You mean to tell me there's more than just you?

"Of course there are more than just me, you twit." The weapon snapped back with irritation. "I am, however, one of but a few *sentient* magical items. So let's keep that bit to ourselves."

Done. Happily. But where exactly does this advantage come into play? Kel asked.

"A teaching moment, farm boy. Today, you start learning about other magics – ordinarily, we wouldn't bother with what I'm about to teach you, because few have the ability to master multiple emotions, but we will still draw from your fear for this opportunity." Voidtooth replied.

"Ordinarily, Peace is known as the emotion related to water- and nature-based…. *healing magics*." The weapon gave its' fake retching sound inside Kel's head again, rendering him temporarily nauseous. "However, when combined with a dark magic based on fear and the need to survive, it can be used to extract information – such as this strange sign language. You must both fear for your current situation and accept it peacefully within your soul as the next step in your destiny for this to work. Hold me by my blade, and offer him the handle, and I will demonstrate."

Realizing he had been standing there with a dumb look on his face for a solid minute, Kel'rak moved to do as the weapon instructed. He began to write, "Knowing your heritage, may I ask a favor?"

"I only offer favors to those I don't consider a stranger," the half-elf wrote back. "My name is Zekven Teluil."

"Kel'rak Zaulyl. Now we are not strangers." Kel wrote with a strained smile, hoping for the best.

Zek responded in kind with that overly large toothy smile. "How do I say that surname? And what can I do for you Kel'rak?"

"Think ZOW-LEEL." Kel wrote. Glancing all around to make sure no one else was reading over his shoulder, he continued, "It will sound weird…My weapon is imbued with magic. It will allow me to learn from you, so that we might communicate better."

The half-elf raised an eyebrow but gave no other visual indicator of alarm. "Do you intend to stab me?" he wrote with a slight grin on his face.

"Gods no!" Kel wrote with shock in his eyes. "In fact, I will be more in danger than you. You must hold the hilt while I hold the blade."

At this, both eyebrows went up, and Zekven responded simply with "Very well."

Kel'rak unsheathed his instrument of death and flipped it around so that Zekven might hold it safely by the hilt, while he grasped it by the flat sides of the blade. Once both men had a firm grip on the weapon, a cool dark liquid not unlike maple syrup oozed from the blade and began to circle around their combined grasps in a figure eight pattern, as though it couldn't decide which person to go to.

Finally, the darkwater slowed and slithered up the half-elf's arm, toward his temple. There on the side of his head, it swirled for a few seconds before sliding back down the arm towards Kel'rak and repeating the motions on him.

The moment that the darkwater met the side of Kel's head, he felt an influx of information unlike anything he could have imagined.

Signs and their associated meanings flashed within his mind's eye, proper grammatical structure rooted itself deep inside his brain, and meaning conveyed through facial expression left an imperative note in the forefront of his consciousness. He blinked, the rush of information leaving him a little dizzy, and let go of Voidtooth to stagger backwards into his chair where he accepted the needed support on his rear end instead of his feet.

Shaking his head to clear the cobwebs in his mind, the ex-farmer put forth an extreme effort to focus on the half-elf in front of him, whom was staring at the weapon in his hand as though it might explode.

I'll take that back now, Kel signed to Zek, with an alarming degree of expertise.

Wide-eyed and looking quite excitable, Zekven handed the weapon back hilt-first. *That is quite an artifact,* he replied with an emphatic expression on the "quite".

You don't know the half of it, Kel replied with a heavy grin.

Well, I suppose we can go sell that bull of yours now! I will interpret and let you know through sign whether he sounds as though you're receiving a good price. Zekven said, his smile every bit as toothy as before. *Then you can tell me more about this magic of yours over a pint you get me with all of that coin!*

***

A full coin pouch, a reserved private suite, and a pint of mead each later, Kel and Zek were sitting once again by the hearth signing back and forth merrily.

That poor farmer never stood a chance once you played the deaf guilt trip! Kel signed, tears in his eyes from laughter.

It helps to know how to lay it on thick, Zek replied with a foamy upper lip grin.

That reminds me, Kel'rak cut in with what he hoped wasn't too much honesty, *aren't you high folk a little too important and prideful to bother helping some random, deaf stranger you just met, with something as riveting as interpreter work?*

Wincing as though Kel's question had re-opened a papercut, Zekven signed back, *Let's just say I'm familiar with not really being accepted.* As though to accentuate his point, he tucked one half of his hair behind an ear again, putting on full display his half-breed heritage.

"Your delicious new acquaintance is hiding something," Voidtooth cut in.

Aren't we all, Kel'rak replied with a mental eyeroll.

"I don't just mean he has a past... while I was sending his brain the query for the bulk of sign language information, I met a block. There's something he is guarding tightly in that head of his." The weapon informed Kel'rak.

Ignoring the warning, Kel asked Zek, *What is there to be done around here for work?*

If you mean to ask me what sellswords are hiring, I've no clue, Zekven replied. *I generally avoid them and the village guard like the plague. Those morons don't appreciate good help.*

Ahh, so you're on the wrong side of the law? Kel signed back, bouncing his eyebrow playfully.

Zek chuckled with laughter that Kel couldn't hear, but which was infectious, nonetheless. *That's one way of putting it,* the half elf replied. *I think of it less as stealing and more of "borrowing without permission" from those who don't need what they have – usually those coming from the capital cities with all their riches in tow.*

Kel'rak eyed the half-elf with a new appreciation. *I would not have taken you for a master thief,* he replied.

Never judge a book by its' innocent-looking cover, my friend, Zek signed. *Though, I would hardly consider myself a master, just… talented.*

Feeling the effects of the mead starting to wane, having finished his pint a while ago and declining any refills – to the dismay of the flirty barmaid – Kel'rak suddenly shoved his tankard forward and grinned with a twinkle in his eye.

I could use to stretch my legs, he started. *I saw a wanted poster while we were outside – what say you to a short adventure? I haven't had company like yours in a long time, and I could use a partner who understands my newfound disability.*

Making a show of thinking about it, Zekven first rubbed his chin while leaning back in his chair and staring at the ceiling, then twirled a small strand of hair around his finger before shooting forward again with a loud clack of the chair legs, fire in his eyes.

Will there be loot? He replied.

A band of highwaymen robbed one of those new migrant families from Delmar, you tell me! Kel answered with a cheeky grin. *The wanted poster didn't say how much was stolen either. Likely they didn't even know how much wealth they had and won't miss a few baubles,* Kel'rak finished.

Notes From the Garden
What life throws at us

Marasol is a small town, but it is my small town now. My grandmother taught me everything, insisting a good healer was needed everywhere. I came here with a handful of dried herbs, a bag of clean bandages, and a head full of hope. Establishing myself wasn't easy; old habits, old prejudices, died hard in these parts.

Most days were quiet, filled with simple aches, coughs, and the occasional splinter. People were slow to trust a new face, especially one who didn't carry a family name known for generations here.

I spent hours at my little stand, patiently explaining the benefits of willow bark for fevers or lavender for restless nights. Every satisfied patient felt like a small victory, a tiny root sinking into Marasol's soil.

My garden, behind the small cottage I rented, was my sanctuary. Every morning, I'd greet the dew-kissed leaves, their vibrant colors a testament to nature's relentless push for life. It was there, among the chamomile and the valerian, that I truly felt at peace, felt connected to the very essence of healing.

But today, I delivered a lamb. I was only at that house because Mrs. Garamond needed a tincture for her jaw pain! I met her nephew, Frederick, at the market yesterday when I was setting up the medicine stand. Goodness, was he a dream. His blue eyes glinted in the sun, and when he smiled, I thought I might die.

He stood near the baker's stall, his laughter carrying over the din of the market, rich and warm like fresh-baked bread. He was speaking with old Master Grogan, probably about crop yields or the price of wool.

His hair, the color of sun-warmed hay, fell just-so across his forehead, and his shoulders were broad under a simple homespun shirt. When he turned, his gaze swept over the crowd, and for a fleeting moment, it snagged on me.

He wasn't even looking for me - obviously. In fact, he probably wouldn't have even noticed me, if it weren't for the sign over my stall. A slight frown creased his brow for a moment, then it smoothed into a curious, almost amused expression as his gaze finally landed on me, then on my mud-stained apron. I was covered in soil, having spent the morning in the garden selecting plants to bring with me.

Even my face was smudged with black mud stains. I felt like a wild creature pulled from the forest and in that moment I just wanted the earth to swallow me whole.

Ugh. I'm getting distracted.

The point is, I met him yesterday because his Aunt was in terrible pain from a jaw infection! This was it, my lucky break. I could feel it in my bones! Finally, the people of this town would take me seriously, if I could just help the lady.

If I could successfully treat a prominent member of the community, word would spread. The whispers of skepticism would turn into murmurs of trust. My livelihood, my very purpose in Marasol, hinged on this.

For the record, though, I am not happy she was in pain! My, I feel like such a horrible person for being happy about this. No, no, that's not right. It isn't the pain I welcome, but the chance to end it. To prove that my remedies, my knowledge, my hands, could bring relief where others might fail. It is the hope of being truly useful, truly needed.

Anyway, the path to the Garamond farm was well-worn, but I felt like I flew over it. When I arrived at the farm, I heard shouting from the barn. I recognized Frederick's voice from the day before, and heard a woman's voice as well.

He ran from the building with a bucket in hand towards a well, so I made my way in faster to meet him halfway. I absolutely put in more effort today, which I am POSITIVE he noticed, because when he saw me coming he tripped over himself and sloshed a bunch of water everywhere.

Back on topic, Amelia.

I made to hand him the bottle of pain reliever and give him the instructions for his Aunt, but he grabbed me by the hand and led me into the barn. There sat Mrs. Garamond, one hand on her jaw and yelling for him to hurry, while her other hand gently stroked the head of the mother Ewe! Her poor little bleats sounded like she was in so much pain.

The usual farm smells—manure, hay, distant woodsmoke— were present, but underneath them, I picked up a faint, metallic tang. Something was wrong.

The ewe lay on her side, panting heavily, and her large eyes glazed with distress. Her bleats weren't just pain; there was a guttural, desperate note to them, a sound of profound struggle. My healer's instincts, trained for human anatomy, screamed that something was terribly wrong with the delivery.

This was no mere tincture delivery. This was a life. Or two lives. An animal, yes, but no less precious in its struggle for existence. My heart pounded. I'd never assisted with a birthing, let alone an animal one, in my life. Every lesson from Grandmother had been about the human body, its intricate workings. But life, she'd always said, was life. And suffering, suffering knew no species.

A moment's hesitation. Just a flicker. The thought of my clean hands, the new dress I wore to get Frederick's attention. Then, the ewe let out another terrible, drawn-out cry, and all thought of propriety vanished. Grandmother always said a true healer didn't just know remedies; she knew compassion.

And compassion, in this moment, demanded action. I wouldn't stand by and watch a life fade simply because I was untrained. What life throws at us, indeed.

Frederick, his face etched with worry, explained what little they knew—the ewe had been in labor for hours, and the lamb was not presenting correctly. No time for squeamishness. I pushed up my sleeves, ignoring the mud and grime.

'Clean water, Frederick. And a clean cloth, quickly!'

My hands, usually mixing herbs or bandaging wounds, now moved to examine the struggling mother. It was messy, far messier than anything I'd ever done. The smell of birth, of blood and fluid, was overpowering.

I had to feel, to guide, to pull with a gentle but firm insistence. The ewe's cries escalated, and I whispered reassurances, words I'd hoped to soon speak to countless human patients, hoping she understood.

Then, with a final, desperate push from the mother and a steady, careful tug from me, it emerged. Slippery, tiny, and wet. A tiny, perfect lamb, bleating its first shaky cry. Relief, so profound it nearly buckled my knees, washed over me. Mrs. Garamond let out a sob of pure gratitude, stroking the mother ewe, who was already turning her head to lick her newborn.

Frederick, who had stood by, pale but ready to assist, simply stared. His blue eyes, which had sparkled with amusement at the market, now shone with something deeper—a mixture of awe and profound gratitude. 'Amelia,' he breathed, his voice rough. 'You... you saved them. Thank you. Truly.'

Recovering from his shock, he fetched fresh straw, and we worked in tandem, clearing the birthing fluids, ensuring the ewe was comfortable. My hands were still sticky with the mess of birth, my dress ruined, but I didn't care. The grit and grime were badges of honor, proof of a challenge met.

He offered me a clean cloth for my face, his fingers brushing mine. His gaze lingered for a moment, and in those blue depths, I saw something new – not just gratitude, but a quiet admiration. It was a look that made my heart flutter in a completely different way than before.

The embarrassment from the market was long forgotten, replaced by a surge of fierce pride. It wasn't the kind of healing Grandmother had taught me from books, but it was healing all the same. I had adapted. I had dived in. And I had saved a life.

What life throws at us, indeed. It rarely comes in the package you expect. Sometimes, it's jaw pain; other times, it's a struggling ewe on the brink of death.

But the lesson, I think, is the same. Don't hesitate. Don't stand on ceremony. Don't be afraid to get your hands dirty, to adapt, even if it's not the dirt you planned for. Because in those moments, in the unexpected, that's when you truly discover what you're capable of. That's when you truly become a healer.

EDIT: He asked me to dinner! It seems 'diving in' isn't just for medical emergencies. It's for the heart too, for the sudden, thrilling possibility of something new.

Chapter 5
The Realization

Wisps of smoke rose lazily from the burnt straw roofs of Marasol where fires from rampaging marauders once blazed. A few remaining embers still crackled their last spits of life among the homes of the dead.

The only sounds that could be heard in the corpse-littered cobblestone street were the carrion birds' mad cackles as they descended upon a rare feast they would never see again in their lifetime. Among it all, no other movement occurred – not even small rodents or house pets. Nothing was left.

Had anyone been painting the scene on the main road, they would have done a double take partway through, as a large pool of blood just sort of… disappeared. They then likely would have put their paint supplies down and gingerly tip-toed towards the previously gruesome scene, and watched as a dead woman's skin seemed to stitch itself back together.

The gaping hip-to-hip hole in her abdomen – a wound too grievous for any person to survive without medical attention – sealed completely. Her skin flushed from the pale bluish-purple of death, to a healthy and vibrant golden hue as blood rushed to the sun-tanned tissues.

Amelia awoke jolting upright like the spring on a mouse trap, gasping for air as though she'd just breached the surface of a lake after several minutes under water. In a way, she had; every cell of her body craved oxygen, after having begun to decay for the past several hours. Her brain was in a fog. Though she saw her surroundings, none of it made sense at first.

Everything was colorless, flattened by ash. Her eyes, still adjusting to light and movement, couldn't make sense of the smeared shapes around her—jagged posts where walls used to stand, hollow shells of buildings she once walked past every morning.

Slowly, her breath calmed enough for her to crawl forward a few feet, the stone beneath her knees warm from earlier fires. She blinked, hard, trying to clear the fog from her vision.

And then her mind caught up.

A child's stuffed bear lay ten feet away, scorched but still clutched in a small, outstretched hand. The fingers were skeletal. The arm was too small.

Amelia recoiled like she'd been shot.

Her breath hitched. The fog in her head lifted—replaced by a tidal wave of memory. That toy belonged to Lia, the tailor's daughter. Five, maybe six years old. Amelia had given her a peppermint after a scraped knee just last week. The girl had told her it was "the best day of her life."

That day was gone.

That life was gone.

Amelia clutched her chest, her heart pounding, every beat louder than the last. She staggered to her feet and turned—there, the remains of the mill, blackened to its stone foundation.

There, the street where lanterns once hung, now draped in smoke and limbs. There, the remnants of the healing garden she had cultivated with her own hands—now a smear of crushed herbs and char.

Her stomach turned. She fell to her knees again and heaved.

When it passed, she was shaking. She pressed her palms to the ground, needing the feel of something real, something solid. But even the cobblestones betrayed her—they were slick with blood. Her breath caught in her throat again, but she refused to vomit a second time.

She sat back and stared numbly at the skeletal ruin of Marasol.

Every home was either collapsed or scorched.

Every window blown out.

No fire crews.

No cleanup.

No survivors.

She was alone.

And somehow, that was the most terrifying part—not that she had died, not that she had come back, but that she had been brought back to this.

"Why me?" she whispered. "Why this?"

A gust of wind stirred a sheet of blackened parchment across the road. It skidded, caught briefly on the toe of her boot, and blew on. No answer came.

Tears blurred her vision again, and this time she didn't wipe them away. She let them fall.

Gone were the cheery baker's shop and the snooty cheese maker's home, replaced by a vision of the blackened and crumbled support beams that used to hold them together.

Gone were the sounds of children's laughter as they rolled hoops down the lane with sticks, challenging their friends to dive through. Gone was the clip-clop of hooves as horses strolled leisurely with their master's loads. And gone was Lumpy's greenhouse, reduced to ash and broken glass.

She felt, more than heard the next sensation, as she became fully cognizant of her surroundings. Amelia's head itched – no, her *brain* itched.

No, that's still not it, she thought as she closed her eyes and focused on the sensation.

Something was clawing at the edges of her consciousness. Multiple somethings. Many somethings. She tugged on her ears until it felt as though they would rip off and scratched at her scalp until it started to bleed, trying to get the feeling to go away but nothing worked.

Finally, she heard them. Dozens of voices! Pleading, begging for release. The healer's eyes darted around, trying to find the source of the noise, reeling with confusion. How could she be hearing so many voices when everything and everyone around her was dead?

"Where am I?"

"Let me go!"

"My son! Where is my son!?"

"I have to get back to my post before the captain knows I'm gone!"

So many voices. So much screaming that wouldn't stop. Amelia sprinted up and down the street, looking for any sign of life, any way to explain what was happening. More death. More destruction. More smoke and ashes.

Coming back to where she started, the healer paced in circles, crushing her head between her hands to keep it from exploding outwards from the pressure of hundreds of voices. Suddenly, her eyes found the corpse of one of the raiders that had taken her whole world from her. In a fit of rage, she ran over to it stomping on bone, guts, and genitalia, releasing all of her inner agony on the one thing she could physically see and blame; she was pulled from her trance, however, when she saw the tiny body laying nearby.

Her baby boy, her Colson, also lay dead on the street. She wept so hard she vomited.

Amelia scooped his tiny body up in her arms, ignoring the smell of rotting flesh and committing every single detail of his face to her memory. In that scrutinizing inspection, she quickly realized that no physical trauma had killed him. In fact, short of the more obvious signs of decay, there was no particular reason that he should be dead. He was pristine and perfect, as every newborn was. So why was her baby boy dead?

The memory came rushing back to her just then. Her dying screams of anguish, the vicious men who had cut Colson from her belly, his blood-covered body as they pulled him out, and the explosion of green light that had knocked her out.

The explosion of green light that had culminated in the release of her final breath.

It was her. She had done it.

She was the reason he was dead – the reason everyone was dead.

Yet here she was, healthy and fit as she'd ever been in her life. Choking back further tears, she set down Colson's body and tried to sort through the panic. Just then, she heard that evil man's voice again.

"Where am I?" his voice echoed the same sentiment as the others.

She knew beyond the shadow of a doubt he was dead, but she still heard him, clear as day. Amelia closed her eyes and concentrated inward, feeling for the consciousness stuck in the depths of her mind.

He was there, she could feel it. The longer she probed, the more she felt the souls of the people she'd come to know as friends. She felt their pain and confusion. She felt their sadness, and it only made her madder. There he was!

Though she couldn't see it, she was certain this consciousness belonged to the man who murdered her and took her Colson.

COLSON! She felt a younger consciousness nearby, one whose only thoughts were jumbled confusion, who couldn't tell the difference between the dark of a womb and the dark of this void. Trembling with elation, she called out to it in her mind, reaching out to him with all of her will.

Colson's spirit recognized its' mother's presence instantly, having spent his whole existence nestled comfortably inside of her. He sped toward her "arms" in her mind's eye, both of them radiating joy and warmth.

Amelia opened her eyes, feeling that same warmth in her chest. She brought her hands up, cupping around the warmth near her heart, and brought them back down again. They glowed with a faint golden light – tiny, but warm. She understood in an instant it was Colson, even though she didn't know how.

She could have sat there staring for hours, marveling at his inner light, but it quickly started to fade. It appeared his soul couldn't survive without a vessel for long. Amelia panicked, frantically searching the town, but there was no life to be found and she couldn't just put him in a dead body!

The healer's eyes searched high and low, looking for anyone, anything that might still be alive and intact enough to contain her son's spirit.

Finally, she heard the call of a raven on high. It circled above her, taking in the scene of the dead below, deciding where to begin feasting. With no other option before her, Amelia wasted no time, throwing Colson's spirit as hard as she could at the raven.

Her aim was true and Colson's light sped toward the bird, perhaps enhanced by magic, or just by desperation. The two collided, and the raven stopped its' circle of flight, flapping to and fro as if wrestling with a wriggling fish in its' claws. Finally, after what seemed like an infinity, Amelia watched as the raven leveled out, shook its' head as if to clear the cobwebs, and turned towards her.

It glided down to face level, flapping at a speed that allowed it to hover in one spot, and stared at her with an intensity she hoped would never stop.

He was still alive! She had saved him.

"Come here, sweet boy," Amelia cooed gently.

Colson acquiesced immediately, alighting on her shoulder and nestling close. His smooth feathers against her cheek tickled her senses, filling her with a sense of joy unlike any she'd ever known. He wasn't the child she'd born anymore, but he was still her boy. And she would protect him from any kind of danger ever again.

Amelia reached up to gently stroke his head and was startled by a sharp pain in her abdomen. A deep, one inch cut had reappeared on her stomach. She panicked once more, because she knew then that removing Colson's life force from her body had taken away some of the energy that had brought her back to life and healed her.

Was there no way to win?

The evil man's voice echoed in her head once more and her visage steeled. The rage returned as she searched through the dark library of her mind for the man who had caused all of this pain. This time, she knew what she was looking for, and she quickly found his soul hiding in a corner of her mind.

She felt, more than saw, his spirit cowering in her incorporeal presence. He didn't know that the dark, shadowy, humanoid shape in front of him was Amelia, but he knew nonetheless that it was dangerous. The dead raider tried to flee, running circles around the library of her mind, and Amelia's spirit chuckled with delight. She would enjoy this.

She gave chase, but only slowly, letting the man's spirit fully come to terms with the fact that there was no escape, before reaching out with a shadowy claw and anchoring it into his spirit's "shoulder". Just as she appeared as a humanoid shape to him, so too did he for her, so she couldn't make out his features as he cowered in fear, but she could feel it.

She reveled in it. No one would hurt her Colson and get away with it. Her shadowy form opened its' maw and consumed the man's spirit head to toe, converting his life force into a necromantic healing magic to close her re-opened wound.

Amelia, back in the physical world, shivered with delight as the wound closed up and she realized she had the power to protect them now.

It didn't hurt—not in the way a healing wound was supposed to hurt. Amelia had stitched enough people in her time to know what pain looked like, sounded like, felt like. But this was something stranger. Deeper. As the skin drew closed over her stomach, it brought with it a phantom sensation that defied any anatomy textbook. A pulling, yes—but also a threading. Not like a needle, but like something unseen was reaching through her to pull her form back into cohesion.

It wasn't cellular regeneration.

It wasn't healing.

It was rewriting.

She clutched at her sides, panting. Her skin buzzed, every hair tingling with static. A low vibration echoed through her ribs as if something ancient and half-buried were stirring awake inside her bones. Not pain. Not warmth. But power. Raw and patient and quietly aware.

For a moment, she wasn't sure the body that had risen was still entirely hers.

She looked down at her hands.

Same calluses. Same faint freckles across her knuckles. But there was something alien in the way her fingers curled when she focused. The motion felt too graceful, too deliberate—like her body had become a tool repurposed by something else.

She swallowed hard and looked away.

This wasn't the time to ask questions she wasn't ready to hear answers to.

The wound closed with unnatural precision, leaving behind only a faint pink ridge that faded as she watched. She touched the skin, half-expecting it to tear back open—nothing in her body felt entirely real anymore. Yet the flesh held, warm and solid.

The cost had been a man's soul.

She thought she'd feel more disgusted.

Instead, there was only… stillness.

No celebration. No horror.

Just silence where pain had been.

A small part of her—the part that had once wrapped children's ankles in clean linen and brewed willowbark tea for swollen joints—whispered that this wasn't right. That she should recoil. That she should feel shame for what she'd done, no matter how monstrous the victim had been.

But Amelia just looked down at her hands.

She flexed her fingers, remembering how they trembled when she'd delivered Colson, how they had gone numb as he slipped from her body during the raid. Those hands hadn't saved him then.

These hands might now.

What was one soul, one vile man's lingering remnant, when weighed against her child's safety? If her magic could protect Colson—if this power could preserve his fragile new form—then let the world burn around them.

If there was sin in what she had done, she would carry it.

Gladly.

The healer she once was might not have recognized the woman standing in her place now.

But the mother did.

And the mother was unrepentant.

As Amelia turned from the ashes of Marasol, the vault inside her stirred again.

The voices didn't scream this time. They murmured. Whispered. Grieved.

A single thought rose from the quiet chorus and pressed itself into her awareness—not like speech, but like memory returning in someone else's handwriting.

She closed her eyes.

And saw a cellar.

Scars

Cramped. Cold. Lit only by the flickering flame of a tallow candle wedged between two bricks. A boy no older than ten crouched in the corner, arms around his knees, a wooden sword clutched in both hands. His eyes were wide, unfocused. Dirt streaked one cheek. His mouth moved without sound.

Please. Please, let it stop.

Boots thundered overhead. Screams—real screams—cut through the floorboards like blades. A crash. A roar. Then silence.

He hugged the sword tighter.

"I'll be brave," he mouthed.

But no one came for him.

Amelia gasped and stumbled, blinking away the vision. Her legs trembled. The Vault receded into quiet again.

The boy's soul that she recognized as Cilian still lingered.

Small.

Fragile.

Waiting.

Not for judgment, just for someone to remember he'd been real.

She wiped her cheek and stepped forward—faster this time, unwilling to look back.

She walked out the front gate from the devastation of Marasol with her head held high, Colson perched on her shoulder, tuning out the vault of souls in her mind still calling out for release. She had accepted their deaths as a necessary means to an end and would use them as needed to keep her and Colson safe. Though she knew she should confirm her suspicions, she knew as well that her husband was surely dead, caught in the initial battle of the raid outside of Marasol.

She decided it was best to avoid the sight of the corpse of another loved one, and simply walked North, toward Flintlock Bay. She would find a new life for her and Colson. This time, she would protect them.

As if reading her mind, Colson gave a low throaty croaking call, and nuzzled her cheek once more. He took flight and Amelia smiled with content as she watched her boy literally soar to new heights.

Chapter 6
The Reveal

Kel'rak and Zekven stalked through the darkness, on their fifth such excursion in as many nights. They had quickly learned since their first meeting how to work best together; however, Zekven had primarily learned that to work together meant to work separately. Kel's deafness had become a bit of a problem on their first two jaunts, as he couldn't hear just how loud he was being.

When trying to sneak into a caravan of wagons or into a home in the middle of the night, not being able to hear the crunch of leaves, crack of twigs, or thunk of boots on boards is equivalent to walking around in broad daylight wearing a sign that says "I'm a thief" on it.

Fortunately for them as a pair, Kel'rak was a particularly deadly partner, and even once caught in the act was somehow always able to get out of a hairy situation.

Their first outing pursuing the bounty from the wanted board had resulted in Kel'rak taking on the entire band of highwaymen – Zekven noted eight total, with Kel taking down the first three in a matter of seconds with nothing but his dagger before the remaining five bolted. The way his new partner moved with a practiced ease in combat, he knew he had chosen well in teaming up with Kel.

A few questions gnawed at Zek's mind about the supposed farmer's past, but he shoved them down. At the very least, he never wanted to end up on the man's red ledger.

The partners returned the bulk of the loot to the owners after dropping a few pieces of jewelry off at the suite they were still staying in. No one would miss a few items that could be explained away as having been sold already by the highwaymen.

The reward from that adventure had provided them with enough coin to rent the room through the week and still have some left for incidentals.

By day three, the pair had learned that Kel should act as both lookout and muscle, while Zek was the shadow in the night. Kel'rak had even decided to act as a distraction, going as far as walking into the light of a campfire and striking up conversation with his handy chalkboard on the opposite side of the valuables to draw their victims' attention away from Zek's approach.

They decided after that, that it was their best tactic in a migrant caravan situation, because even if word started to go around that people's valuables had started going missing, Kel'rak – and Zek by extension since they were always seen together – would have plausible deniability.

Tonight, however, was a different story. Zek had picked up the scent of a new rich family that had made it into town before their newfound partnership and had already set up shop in a permanent residence. Not their typical kind of job, these new business owners bought and sold high quality adventurer's equipment rather than shiny baubles.

If the two men were going to continue in this line of work, Zekven knew they had to get some better gear than the basics they were operating with. The day prior, Zek had spent his time studying their habits: when they ate, when they went to relieve themselves, where the merchandise sat, where the back room was, when they closed up shop, and when they went to bed.

Confident that he could infiltrate the building easily enough, Zek had spent all of today looking forward to this job. The son was the key to the entire operation, as he seemed to manage the entire inventory while his parents did the sales work. He also never seemed to tire and made a shockingly small amount of noise for someone who lugged around large crates all day.

All of them lived in the same building directly above the shop, which provided Zek an opportunity he couldn't ignore. As he and Kel'rak approached the property, he signaled a stop at the edge of the tree line.

Once we're done here, we need to leave town, he signed, a serious expression painted on his face. *We won't be able to walk around town wearing this gear, or they'll know exactly who took it – at the very least, they will claim we bought stolen goods.*

If Kel'rak was disappointed, he didn't let it show. *So be it*, he replied quickly. Then, with a sly grin, he followed up with, *The life of an adventurer!*

They each clapped each other on the shoulders in what had become a kind of hype ritual right before executing a job, and Zekven pulled up his hood as he turned to leave. The agreed upon warning signal was for Kel to run out of the woods screaming about a wolf, directing attention to himself so that Zek could get out of there if things got too dicey.

The thief was perhaps a little too confident that he wouldn't need to worry about that though. He had his own tricks.

As he reached the side entrance to the shop, he pulled out his pick and got to work on the simple lock. It clicked over in a matter of seconds, making a little too much noise for his liking, but allowing him entry, nonetheless. Silently closing the door behind him, Zek turned to his work.

Directly ahead lay the storage room, while halfway down the hallway turned left towards the shop area and right towards the stairs going up to the residence. A simple setup for a simple shop.

Zekven padded forward, taking care to step lightly on the balls of his feet, and hooked left at the turn into the shop area. Along the bench lay a variety of tools, from small hatchets for wood chopping, to swords, bows, and other weaponry.

At the front door was an empty crate, alongside the family's dirty boots – including the boots of the son. They had an ornate inlaid design that resembled a fox tail, with comfortable fur insulation to keep the wearer warm and hold the boot snug to the wearer's calf.

Zek measured his own foot in comparison and found them too large for himself, tossing the pair of boots instead into the empty crate and moving on. They might fit Kel'rak, after all. He added a few throwing knives, a shortbow and quiver full of arrows, an exceptionally crafted leather tunic for himself, a climbing rope and hook, and a few other essentials such as flint and steel, waterskins, and dried jerky.

At the risk of making the crate a little too noisy to sneak out with, he also added a pair of silver bracelets in the form of serpents with green eyes and some other pricey looking pieces of jewelry. The emerald eyes seemed to gleam with an inner light, drawing his gaze.

He felt a flicker of curiosity, a pull he couldn't quite explain, but he shoved them into the crate, focusing on the task. They all sat on a high shelf and were the only items of their type in the whole store.

Moving on to the storage room, he rooted around the shelves looking for anything of value. Zek's eyes were drawn to what looked at first like a pair of ordinary short swords, but at second glance seemed made of a different type of metal each.

One was tinted blue with snowflake etching along the length of the blade, while the other was a light red with flames etched into the metal near the hilt. They lay near a pair of matching scabbards, each also with their own snowflake and flame inlays.

Zekven scooped them up, unable to resist the temptation of these fine weapons. The moment his hands closed around the hilts of the two short swords, a distinct sensation pulsed through him.

The blue blade felt cold, like mountain air, and a faint shiver traced his spine, as if a winter wind had just passed through the room. The red one, conversely, radiated a subtle, almost imperceptible warmth, a low thrum that spoke of contained fire.

These were more than just finely crafted steel; they were imbued with something primal, something beyond the mundane. His thief's instincts, usually focused on monetary value, now recognized a different kind of treasure: raw, untamed magic.

Into the crate they went, along with another new pair of comfy boots he found in his size, and another black leather armor set he found for Kel'rak. Confident he'd gathered everything of use, Zek lifted the crate full of gear onto his shoulder – groaning with the effort – and headed toward the side door. Just as he reached for the handle, he heard footsteps behind him. He froze, waiting to hear which voice addressed him.

"Finn?" the mother's voice started, every bit as sleepy as he'd expected. "I thought I heard a noise, is everything okay sweetheart?"

In a deeper voice, Zekven replied over his shoulder, "Just a late-night buyer ma! They paid extra for delivery."

He forced Finn's voice from his throat, a perfect mimicry, but his heart hammered against his ribs. The air was thick with the scent of sleep and old wood. Every creak of the floorboards, every rustle of the mother's nightgown, felt amplified.

He could feel the warmth of her presence just beyond the door, her sleepy sighs. It was a delicate dance, a tightrope walk over a chasm of discovery.

Finn's mother, sleepy but alert, felt a faint, almost imperceptible prickle of unease. Her son's voice was right, his words familiar, but something in the cadence, a subtle shift in the air around him, felt... off. A mother's intuition, perhaps, or a subconscious recognition of the unnatural. She shivered, pulling her shawl tighter, attributing it to the night chill.

"Okay darling. Please don't be long, I keep hearing rumors of highwaymen in the woods."

Her voice, thick with maternal concern, was a sharp reminder of the risks. He had to keep his own breathing even, his posture relaxed, even as every fiber of his being screamed for him to bolt.

"Sure thing ma, I'll be right back!"

He hoped his voice didn't betray the frantic beat of his pulse. He stepped out the door as the mother turned back up the stairs none-the-wiser, and trotted off towards the woods where Kel'rak lay in wait.

That was too close for comfort, he thought to himself. Reminding himself never to get that greedy again, he adjusted the crate on his shoulder and kept on going all the way to the meeting spot.

Kel appeared from the back side of a large oak and stepped into the moonlight so Zek could see his signs. *About time! I was beginning to worry you'd been caught. No one came or went though, so I kept waiting,* he started.

Told you I had it handled, friend! Zek signed back, setting down the crate with another groan, bracing his back with his now-empty hand as he stood tall once more. He looked now at his partner, his tell-tale toothy grin shining in the moonlight. But Kel'rak just looked him up and down in complete confusion.

What's wrong?... Zekven started. He looked down at his feet and hands, and noticed they were slightly bulkier, darker skinned, and hairy. *Oh hells...*

"I knew it!" Voidtooth shouted in triumph in Kel'rak's head.

***

About a quarter mile walk in silence later, the two reached a spot in the woods deep enough to avoid any outside suspicion. Kel'rak carried the crate this time, for fairness' sake, similarly setting it down with a groan when they both agreed they'd found a good enough clearing.

Zekven – now back in his half-elf form – wandered off without saying a word to gather up firewood, while Kel'rak took inventory of what was in the box, laying it all out for easy pickings.

He automatically knew the swords weren't for him, for he had no need with Voidtooth in hand. Setting those to the side, he found two pairs of boots and leather armor – one set of each plainly smaller than the other, Kel set those with the swords.

Along with those items for Zek, he placed the throwing knives and the bow and quiver. Deciding Zek probably had enough to carry at that point, he took it upon himself to put the climbing rope and hook in his pack, along with the remainder of the essentials. Not knowing what to do with the shiny bits, he left those laying out to discuss with his partner and started dressing in the new boots and armor.

The black leather armor was form fitting on Kel, not too tight but also not so loose that it would chafe. He tested its' flexibility by going through a few combat rolls, easily coming up from each without having to worry about adjusting the fit. This particular set also protected his shoulders with a pair of similarly stained epaulets, which rolled together like a collapsible awning when he raised his arms. Zek had chosen well for him, and regardless of their current awkward situation, Kel couldn't help but appreciate the man's eye for quality.

As Kel'rak removed his old worn leather boots to put on the newly acquired ones, Zek came back with the wood for the fire. Not worried about sound this far out into the woods, he simply dropped the bundle in his arms haphazardly and signed to Kel with emphasis on the last few signs.

If you could still hear, you would think I were cat calling you, friend. That armor suits you! He forced his signature toothy grin.

I think it suits an assassin, Kel shot back a little harsher than intended.

Forgive me, is that not what you are? Your skillset says otherwise, Zek tried to backpeddle.

Kel'rak just sighed and continued, seeming slightly depressed. *It's not what I ever wanted to be, but I can't deny that it's what I've become.*

Scars

The words tasted like ash, even if he couldn't hear them. 'Assassin.' It was a brutal, efficient word, devoid of the gentle rhythms of a farmer's life. A life he didn't even get to live.

He had wanted the feel of soil between his fingers, the quiet satisfaction of a well-tended field. Now, his hands were again accustomed to the slickness of blood, the cold weight of a blade. A life he had fled.

He had sought solitude, a life free from conflict, and instead, he had become the very embodiment of it. The irony was a bitter twist in his gut. He was dangerous, yes, but at what cost to the man he once was? This new skin, tough and unyielding, felt both like a shield and a prison.

He continued lacing the new boots, finger tracing the foxtail design in absentminded appreciation. *These are some high quality boots you found for me,* he continued, trying to convey sincere thanks through his expression.

Zek chuckled and signed back, *I have some suspicions they're not unlike that dagger of yours. Try walking around a bit, I want to test a theory.* Zek noted that the clearing they had chosen had fallen sticks and dried leaves all around.

Kel'rak looked up curiously and stood, testing the ankle support and comfort. He took a few steps around the clearing, feeling debris crunch under his feet. But Zekven's eyes told him his suspicions were true.

You just made no sound! Zek signed excitedly.

I did what? Kel replied.

Those steps you took should have made enough sound to wake a sleeping bear. I heard nothing! Those boots are indeed magical.

Kel'rak bent over, scrutinizing the craftsmanship with more detail. If that were true, he supposed a mark of the fox did make sense, as they were stealthy creatures. Excitement gathering, he broke into a sprint running full speed at a nearby oak tree and launched himself skyward, up into the branches. Zekven followed behind, but lost Kel in the branches, who dropped behind him and tapped him lightly on the shoulder. Kel'rak caught Zek's reflexive elbow jab and gave a hearty belly laugh. He had really made no sound!

Zekven offered up a genuine grin this time and laughed with his partner, thankful they no longer had to worry about that problem. *You really got me!* he signed happily, acting out what would have been his own death were he an enemy.

The two men wrapped a friendly arm around each other's shoulders, already over the awkwardness, and got to the task of setting up their campfire. Once it was roaring and they were munching on some exquisitely spiced, smoked, and dried jerky, Kel'rak asked the question that had been burning in his mind for well over an hour.

So what was that about earlier? The different face, I mean. He signed, somewhat apologetically.

Zekven hung his head low with apparent shame and signed back, *Shapeshifter.*

Voidtooth's suspicions confirmed, it echoed in Kel's mind, "Changeling. He is a Changeling. A magical creature, which your idiot history books claim don't exist anymore."

Trying his best to hide his surprise, Kel signed back, *So you can just change into whatever thing you want? You could turn into a horse and spirit us away from here?*

Scars

Unfortunately, it only works like that for folks that use magic to shapeshift – you might call them a Druid. Us Shapeshifters can only change forms into something of a similar body type; that is to say, something humanoid. He explained through slow and deliberate sign.

Please don't think I was hiding this from you with ill intent, Zek signed, still apologetic. *I've chosen to live the life of a half-elf, because I know what it's like to live the way they do... never fully accepted by either elves or humans, always just kind of tolerated.*

It was a life lived in the margins, always observing, always adapting. Elves saw the human in him, too rough, too quick to anger. Humans saw the elf, too aloof, too strange, with eyes that held ancient secrets. He had learned to blend, to become what was needed, but never truly to belong.

Choosing the half-elf form wasn't just about convenience; it was a defiant embrace of his own liminality, a quiet rebellion against a world that demanded rigid categories.

Realizing his concentration-face while trying to make sure he was reading the signs with proper understanding looked like he was angry, Kel raised his hands with innocent assurance.

I only wanted to understand better. You have to know that it was weird seeing someone I don't know signing to me as if they knew me! He chuckled.

Zek flashed a smile up at Kel, *I'm sure! But it definitely came in handy back there. That guy's mother woke up and caught me walking out the door. I had to lie about a late-night order on the fly and do my best to mimic his voice.*

With newfound appreciation for his partner, Kel responded, *That certainly explains your lack of surprise at the existence of my dagger! I thought for sure all magic was gone from the land for the last century, yet everywhere I look it seems to be popping up.*

It was a dizzying realization. The Reckoning, the great purge, had been preached as absolute, final. Yet, here it was, bubbling to the surface like a forgotten spring. First Voidtooth, now Zek's shifting form, and these enchanted items. The world, he realized, was not as dead to magic as he had been taught. It was merely dormant, and now, for reasons he couldn't fathom, it was stirring awake, promising chaos and power in equal measure.

Zek's eyes flashed with pleasure as he looked over to the short swords he had nabbed. *You don't know the half of it…*

***

The two short swords, the boots, the serpent bracelets—they had sat on the high shelf for months, gathering dust. The shop owners, Jasper and his wife Fearne, had always found them... difficult. Not just heavy, but with a strange, almost unsettling aura.

Customers would often pick them up, then put them down with a shiver, claiming they felt 'cold' or 'unlucky.' Jasper had dismissed it as foolishness, but even he felt a strange relief when a thief the night before had, unknowingly, relieved him of their presence. They were just 'hard to sell,' he'd told his wife.

Chapter 7
The Call

A woman's scream rent the night air. It was somewhere close, but he couldn't quite make out the location. She screamed again, clearly fighting against an aggressor. Sometimes muffled, sometimes throaty and full of rage and determination. Every time the woman's voice sounded, it seemed to come from a different direction.

He turned to and fro, scanning the various alleyways as he sprinted down the main lane, searching for any visible altercation. No such luck.

Reaching the end of the road with no sign of a struggle aside from the woman's screams, eyes wide with adrenaline, he turned a one-eighty and sped back the way he'd come. He ran and ran, legs pumping like a mighty elk, spiriting him down the road that never seemed to end. And still, the woman's screams continued.

No matter how far he went, her screams sounded as if they were right by his side, fighting an aggressor he'd never be able to stop. Even more curious, no candle lights came on in neighboring windows. Not one person seemed to care that a woman was in extreme duress.

He skidded to a stop, hunched over and doing his best to catch a breath. The victim screamed once more, this one clearly the result of severe pain. He bolted upright, the blood curdling sound tensing his spinal cord like a string pulling tight a collapsible wooden thumb puppet.

Suddenly, a hand grabbed him on the shoulder from behind with a grip like iron, and he spun around to meet the threat –

Kel'rak awoke with a growl like a feral beast, Voidtooth in hand dripping with caustic shadow, and nearly opened Zekven's jugular from ear to ear before seeing the absolute terror in his only friend's eyes. As he did, his grip on Voidtooth crumbled, the weapon dropping to the ground with a thud and reappearing at the sheathe on his right hip in a puff of black smoke.

Kel'rak crab-walked backwards about five paces before a stray stick jabbed into the palm of his left hand and he collapsed in a heap of pain and sobs, clutching tightly at his chest where his lungs couldn't seem to get enough air to support the panic attack.

As Zek slowly approached, worry plain on his face, Kel looked back up and waved him away with shame in his eyes, refusing to fully make eye contact.

"Night terrors," Kel shakily signed. "They started about a year ago and have been getting worse of late."

Zekven knelt beside the poor man and gave his knee a reassuring pat. "You're okay friend. Just breathe. You are in good company and the sun is coming over the horizon."

Kel'rak responded with a weak smile, still panting heavily. "You're too kind. I nearly killed you!" he signed apologetically.

"Think nothing of it Kel," the thief fired back, "we all have our demons. I just couldn't sit and watch you squirm around the way you were, it was clearly a very traumatic dream."

Mimicking his friend's words the week before, Kel signed back, "You don't know the half of it."

***

As Kel sat against Sugar, eating his breakfast following the nightmare while her warm chest rose and fell, he had a thought. *Voidtooth?*

"Yes, Lambie?"

Please stop that.

"Nay."

Fine. I wanted to ask, can you send me from one location to another?

"Like a teleport spell?" the weapon asked with incredulity.

In a way, Kel'rak replied. *I need to get over a wall.*

"I know what ye intend to do Lad, I'm in your head," It replied. "Ye might think I could do what you ask, because of the way you cannot be rid of me –"

Poof, Kel interrupted.

"Aye. Poof," Voidtooth replied with more than a little bit of irritation. "Alas, that is due to our magical bond. I do not have the kind of magic to do what ye ask."

Kel'rak let his disappointment show on his face. *Oh, okay –*

"But YOU do." The weapon interjected.

Watching from the other side of the campfire, Zekven noticed his friend's facial expression change once more to hope and excitement, bearing witness to an internal monologue he couldn't begin to understand. He lay down slowly, arms reaching up and hands behind his head, masking his own internal monologue from his partner and wondering what was going through the man's head.

What do you mean I have the magic? Kel replied, subconsciously scrunching his face in confusion.

"I told ye when I first explained magic. It's not finger wiggles. It is your control over your emotions and the creative process inside your mind. Your magic manifests however you need it to, assuming you can think it up. Take our informational extraction spell, with your nimble-fingered imposter friend over there. Knowing the way two different magics worked, I put together those two feelings of fear and peace and combined them to create something beneficial to the situation."

So you think that I can do something similar to get myself over or through a wall?

"Knowing the force in your head that is driving you, I know you can," Voidtooth finished.

The weapon left it at that, going uncharacteristically silent. It wasn't entirely sure he could pull it off because the mixture of magics required would branch outside of his emotional affinity, but having filtered through his memories it knew he had excellent control of his emotions.

Kel'rak ruminated on Voidtooth's advice as he slowly ate at the fried eggs Zek had made for them. The way he saw it, Voidtooth was a very literal being that spoke in specific words, for a specific reason. There had to be a hint in what it chose to say. "Your magic manifests however you need it to..." it had said.

It had also specifically stated the magic it had drawn from related to fear and peace. In that exchange, the magic had the intent of withdrawing information from a source; but, what if he could push information to a source, or more specifically, to a location? In the end, a person's body is just another piece of information in the vast space of existence.

He also thought about the nature of the emotions necessary to complete the exchange. In the former instance, Voidtooth had instructed him to fear for his current plight and then accept that what he needed to accomplish was the next necessary step in the journey. Those straightforward instructions had been easy enough to follow, and he felt they had the essence of what he should follow for his experiment. But how to modify the magic to fit his need?

The more Kel'rak thought about the problem, he realized his issue was not just one of fear, but desperation. Without being able to do this magic, he could never hope to accomplish his goal; however, it went beyond desperation. He realized this was an issue of passion. An all-consuming goal that drove his every action, whether he realized it or not.

He imagined the same black smoke that Voidtooth created every time it reappeared from another location and used that as a focal point for his efforts.

Setting the eggs aside and sitting up straight, the assassin closed his eyes and focused on all these necessary components, breathing deeply. He knew from sitting across from his companion that Zekven sat against a shaded tree with gnarled roots arched like a cat about fifteen feet away.

Eyes still closed, he took another deep breath and exhaled a cold shadow, which raced towards the location of his choosing. There it coalesced into the vague shape of a man Kel'rak's size, in a balanced standing position on the top of the root.

Zekven cracked open a singular eye as he felt the cold shadow pass him by and bolted upright as the shadowy form took shape above him. With an alerting cry to Kel, he fell backwards in a desperate attempt to put space between himself and the apparition.

The changeling, a master of physical transformation, gaped at the shadowy form of Kel'rak with a primal terror that transcended his usual bravado. His own magic was about bending flesh, about mimicking life. This was about bending *nothingness*, about creating something from pure shadow. It felt wrong, a violation of the natural order he understood.

He stumbled backward, his hand instinctively going to his own throat, as if to ward off an unseen threat. This wasn't just a trick; it was a glimpse into a power that was ancient, terrifying, and utterly alien to his own kind.

Behind Zek, Kel'rak inhaled deeply once more, feeling a sense of forward inertia as the cold shadow re-entered his lungs. Opening his eyes finally, the farmer-turned-assassin looked back across the campsite to where Sugar lay with her head up, eyes and ears alert. As she offered up what he decided to take as an approving whinny, he grinned ear to ear in victory.

Moving as if to pump one fist in the air to celebrate his triumph, Kel'rak lost his footing on the root he now saw was mossy and slick, and felt the same desperate feeling resurface as he shadow-stepped across to where Zek now sat staring up at him in outright confusion. Voidtooth only passed feelings of approval and adoration.

Bubbling with mirth at his own success, Kel'rak helped his friend to his feet and signed, "Don't bother waiting up for me tonight, I have business to handle in Delmar. We will hole up at the Troll's Breath Tavern, I know the innkeeper there."

***

Stepping with the slightest swagger, he walked straight up to the wrought iron gate that separated the poor from the rich, bathed in the light of the full moon. Its sheer stone walls stood ten men tall, too difficult for any normal man to scale without breaching equipment and an army giving him a distraction.

But Kel'rak Zaulyl was a normal man no longer. A light chuckle erupted from his lips, strengthening into a cackle as he considered the irony of this futile wall.

The Captain of the Guard heard the commotion from below, and walked towards the edge of the wall, wondering what buffoon would possibly disturb the peace at this time of night. However, as he reached the edge to peer over, the cackling abruptly stopped. There was no one below. No visible movement for as far as the eye could see.

I must be losing it, he thought. *Too much time spent covering for that pile of giant's dung they call a guardsman.*

As the Captain began to turn away, the laughter suddenly started again, but closer this time - too close. The poor officer had no time to react before a curved, inky-black blade found its perch in his jugular.

"Oh, but this is going to be so much fun!" Kel'rak exclaimed, watching in wonder as the shadowstuff that leaked from his dagger ate away at the Captain's flesh, soon leaving nothing more than a pile of blood and armor. Feeling quite invigorated, the assassin turned away, practically skipping towards the keep like a child at play.

Kel'rak swept through the castle like a poltergeist, riotous with laughter the entire time, reveling in his ability to teleport through the shadows of the halls and leaving piles of blood and armor where guards dared to interfere. As he rounded the final corner, the assassin came to an abrupt halt, realizing how close he was to his goal.

The door to the laird's private quarters lay just in front of him – guard-less, he noticed, realizing the raucous laughter had probably attracted every guard in the castle. Trying his best to overcome his glee, Kel'rak forced down the laughter and touched his dagger to the locking mechanism, asking Voidtooth to release some corrosive shadow.

Literally biting his tongue to keep his mirth in check, he silently padded into the room by enacting his boots' magic and closed the door behind him.

He found it interesting that the laird still lay fast asleep. *How easy it must be to sleep deeply when you live in such luxury and safety*, he thought with extreme sarcasm, moving towards the bed.

Kel'rak went about his work methodically, gently but firmly tying the laird's wrists and ankles to each bedpost with strips of his own silky sheets, then sheathing his inky black dagger. From his left hip, he drew a new dagger – plain in appearance, but with a serrated edge on each side.

Hardening his visage, Kel'rak swiped his dagger across the laird's cheek, waking him from his no-doubt whore-filled dreams and inciting an instant panic.

"Good evening, laird of this heavens-forsaken land!" Kel'rak began, not caring that he couldn't hear his own words. "Don't fret, you can scream as much as you would like! I've already killed all of your guards; no one will come for you."

Despite the assassin's words, the man seemed frozen in his panic and remained silent. Irritated, Kel'rak continued with his planned monologue. "You see, tonight I am to be your judge and jury. Tonight, you pay for all of the terrible things you have done to the women of this land."

"Do you see this blade in my hand? I have specifically enchanted it to cause pain, but not to let you bleed," the assassin stated with a grin. "You see, I feel it's fair to feel all of the pain that all of the women you raped and left for dead also felt, whilst similarly restrained and unable to die." The laird suddenly began to thrash about, trying with all his obese might to free himself of his bonds.

Kel'rak began jumping with elation. "Yes, yes! There's the proper amount of fear we were looking for!"

Twirling his instrument of pain in his fingers, he continued, "For our first case, the accused stands guilty of the rape, torture, and murder - *of my wife!*" the murderous maniac finished with a growl, as his dagger planted itself firmly in the laird's manhood.

***

Troll's Breath Tavern was famous for its rough and rowdy crowds. Townsfolk came here to unwind, mercenaries came seeking payouts, and even the local guard showed up to down a Troll's Breath ale or two. There was an unspoken understanding that whatever happened in the tavern, stayed in the tavern.

Kel'rak liked it that way. It made endless cheap entertainment, bar fight after bar fight, to help relax after an eventful night of torture and murder. The wooden wall groaned as he reclined against it, finding a comfortable spot in his corner of the tavern, where no one could ambush him.

He had never had been fond of the Troll's Breath ale – its sole purpose was to make the imbiber drunk as fast as possible. It was true, there was ne'er a finer liquid courage in all the realms; however, the very aptly named drink tasted about as pleasant as a rotting onion and left behind the foulest of breath. And as much as he would like to forget his pain for just one night, the assassin instead ordered the only red wine the tavern offered and sipped thoughtfully. He hoped his wife's spirit was satisfied with the justice he had served.

Truly, tonight's events had been all about her – he did not feel better about it at all. His wife was still gone. Nothing could bring her back. At least by his actions tonight, her spirit might rest peacefully in the afterlife. Kel'rak continued to sip his wine over the next hour, the only existence of calm in an otherwise chaotic storm of people.

***

As Kel'rak the Vengeful opened the door to the room he and Zek had rented for the next few days, he glanced over to his partner's cot and saw a shadowy figure standing over him.

It turned its' featureless face towards him, and Voidtooth panicked inside his mind, "On your hands and knees, NOW!"

With an exertion of willpower, it forced his body downward going as far as forcing him to place his forehead on the squeaky, vomit-stained floorboards.

"I was disappointed when I came in here only to find the Changeling," the velvety-smooth voice began – curiously, inside Kel's head. "But you… are a curious creature," it finished with an appreciative tone.

"I can find a few uses for a man of your abilities."

Kel'rak dared to look up at the intruder, which simply waved a hand at the rousing Zekven, who slumped back down to sleep. Kel stayed on his knees but sat upright to better examine this clearly magical thing that had so easily bested Zek.

It took a few steps closer to him without so much as a quiver of the floorboards, somehow simultaneously thrilling Kel's senses while also terrifying him to the point of paralysis.

"You don't cower in fear – even at the insistence of your... weapon," the voice continued. "I appreciate that in my Chosen."

Kel'rak scrunched his nose in confusion and tilted his head towards the figure.

"You put on an impressive display this evening, Master Zaulyl. Some hundred and twenty years ago, I - along with the others - gave up the idea of bothering with humanity. But you just might help to heal that ancient scar."

Seeing Kel's eyes go wide at the realization of who this thing was, it continued, "You created magics that haven't been seen or used since humans started killing off magic wielders." The shadowy man appeared to look him up and down as if in appreciation for a finely crafted item.

"You mastered control of your desperation, your passion, your fear, your anger, and your hate. Hells, you infused your own magic into another weapon and managed to figure out soul projection in a single day! Yes...you will do," the Baron of Shadows finished, as it gently touched its' palm to his chest, just above his heart. The touch instantly rendered him unconscious, sparing him searing pain as the cold-burn of that touch left a handprint.

"I will be watching, Champion," it spoke into his dreams. "Call upon the Baron should you ever need me."

Chapter 8
The Retribution

Heavy booted feet left these, Amelia thought to herself.

With her background as a healer she was never one trained to track game, but the tracks in front of her were left by large men in a hurry as sure as the sun rises every day.

She had come upon them about ten miles outside of Marasol, where the road her husband's team had been working on came to its end and became grass and dirt tracks worn down by wagon wheels and horse hooves.

These tracks were the closest thing the woman had seen since leaving the town, indicating where the marauders may have come from. She followed them with ease, the prints not yet erased by time as the weather had cooperated with her. The trail of footprints went for many miles along the dirt road, unerringly Northward towards her eventual destination.

This single purpose guided her, keeping the grief at bay, each step determined. Though she had left her past behind her with adventure in her eyes, it was not lost on Amelia that she had no clue what her next step should be outside of getting to the next destination.

Flintlock Bay was a couple weeks of travel on foot, and the quiet was enough to drive a person insane. Colson's company with his cute squawks and chitters were only able to keep that quiet away for so long. Without other companionship to distract, the grief returned posthaste. So when the tracks conveniently showed up, she leapt upon them like a bloodhound.

If these truly were from the same group of men that had ransacked the town, she had some aggression to get out. She felt it, like a slithering grime, beneath her skin. The power of her hatred was tangible, living – and it begged for release.

This 'grime' was no mere sensation; it was a living entity within her, a coiled viper of frozen fury thrumming just beneath the surface of her flesh. It wasn't cold, not precisely, but a negation of warmth, a deep, abyssal chill that seeped into her bones from the very core of her being.

When her anger flared, it pulsed and constricted, a viscous, burning current that coursed through her veins, tingling at her fingertips and behind her eyes. It spoke to her, not in words, but in a low, guttural hum, a promise of retribution that resonated with every beat of her shattered heart.

This power, born of grief and hatred, was wild and untamed, a primal force that yearned for expression, begging to be unleashed against those who had inflicted such unimaginable pain. It was a terrifying companion, yet in its raw, destructive potential, she found a morbid sense of purpose.

At the end of the third day of walking, the footpath diverted from the main road. Amelia had honestly lost track of how far she had travelled, with the smoking ruins of her home far beyond her line of sight. To her right lay the Edruvian river, running in a winding path from Flintlock Bay to Marasol, then further Southeast to the reclusive Kingdom of the Nine. To her left was a dense forest – the forest towards which this diverted footpath now led.

Amelia absentmindedly reached up to her shoulder to scratch the feathers on Colson's chest, the large birdboy warbling with content at his mother's show of affection. She cocked her head to the left at a slight angle, noting a depression in the tall grass leading toward the woods.

Enough men had walked through that grass to leave a semi-permanent depression, but not recently enough to worry her much as to the possibility of them lurking about.

This appeared to just be the point where they came to and from the main road to whatever hideout they had in the forest. Not that it would do them much good. The woman's eyebrows furrowed with both anger and determination as she stalked towards her prey, like a hound dog with a fresh scent.

As Amelia entered the forest, the air grew heavy. Not just with the scent of damp earth and pine, but with the palpable weight of her rage. Trees she once might have found peaceful with their gently flapping leaves seemed to shy away from her in fear, their clawed branches trying but failing to give her more space. Squirrels fled at the mere sight of her, hurtling upwards to their hollows at breakneck speeds.

Unseen by the woman herself, the very ground beneath her feet blackened and cracked, the blades of grass and other leafy undergrowth withering with her passing. Every bit of life that came into contact with her seemed to enter a rapid state of decay, either drying into fragile husks or melting into sludge.

Even the wind, formerly creating a light rustle in the foliage overhead, seemed to cower away and leave the surroundings eerily silent.

The forest, usually alive with the rustle of unseen creatures and the chirping of birds, fell into an unnatural hush as she passed. Even the insects seemed to cease their buzzing, as if holding their breath.

\A deer, startled by her approach, didn't just flee; it bolted with a desperate, almost suicidal speed, crashing through the undergrowth as if pursued by an invisible predator. The very trees seemed to twist away from her, their ancient roots recoiling from the blight she carried.

The silence was profound, a vacuum where life had once hummed. Each step Amelia took was accompanied by a faint, brittle crackle, like dry bone snapping, as healthy green sprigs beneath her boots shriveled to ash. The vibrant emerald moss on ancient stones turned a sickly, shimmering grey, then dissolved into a putrid, viscous sludge that seeped into the soil.

A metallic, almost ozone-like tang permeated the air, sharp enough to make her eyes water, overriding the familiar scents of damp earth and pine. It was as if the very vitality of the forest recoiled from her presence, leaving behind a wake of unnatural stillness and decay.

She didn't consciously direct it, but a deep, chilling awareness settled in her bones, an understanding that this grim transformation was an extension of herself.

She followed the tracks easy enough, as they became an eventual path, worn into the ground over time by consistent footfalls. Her eyes scanned the trunks around her and the boughs overhead for danger, her heightened emotional state keeping her on alert. Once the path became visible enough to see from a distance, she broke from the trail and stepped into the overgrowth. Dried twigs and brambles tore at the hem of her skirt, but she did not care, for she was of a singular focus.

Colson alighted from her shoulder with a soft caw as she entered the brush, unable to keep his balance as his mother bent and twisted through the bushes and branches. He followed by air and tree, flying or hopping from perch to perch.

An observant scout may have noticed him following a specific path while looking down, but if they did, none took action.

The spirit of vengeance that was Amelia saw the ginger head of a man pop up from a bent posture, seemingly stretching out the soreness of a long watch. His face was filthy, appearing as though he'd gone unwashed for several days at the least. His vibrant beard and hair gave away his position at a glance, but he was not making any attempts at secrecy as he groaned with displeasure from his aching back.

Amelia glanced about, nervous at first that she had stumbled into the camp proper, but soon realized the man was nothing more than a guard - a lone guard at that. She grinned at their unfortunate lack of real security... well, unfortunate for the man in front of her.

She snuck around to his left, thinking to strangle the man and dig her nails into his flesh, ripping his lifeblood out the way they had ripped Colson from her. But she never got the chance. Though he was distracted and generally unaware, the unmistakable sound of a branch cracking under her feet gave her away when she got within arms reach.

The magic that had left a trail of death underfoot betrayed her, sucking the moisture from the branch she had stepped on and rendered it brittle.

The guard's eyes went wide as he reached for his weapon, turning about with speed Amelia hadn't expected from the man. She retracted her hands involuntarily, gasping a deep breath as she fell backwards onto her rear end and raised an arm to deflect what she anticipated to be a strike; however, the attack never came. Her eyes closed with fear, she first felt the air about her grow colder.

Opening her eyes, she saw the man kneeling before her, both hands clutched around his throat. His eyes were bulging from his head, the veins on his temples straining to push the blood to his brain. A faint wisp of water vapor erupted from his lips, joining the larger ball of air and mist that spun in front of him.

As his throat constricted, his bulging eyes, in their last moments of awareness, saw not just a woman, but a flicker of green light, a cold flame that stole his very breath. A half-forgotten tale from his childhood, of spirits that sucked the life from men, flashed through his mind, a terror far deeper than the simple fear of death.

Amelia watched in horror - and satisfaction - as the man's lips and fingers first turned blue, then purple. Unable to take a breath, he collapsed in a heap, dead at her feet. She looked down at the corpse, a blank stare pasted upon her face as she finally noticed the ground around her.

A rough circle about ten feet in diameter surrounded her and the dead man, the ground either blackened with death, or rimmed with frost. She bent down to inspect the man a little closer and saw ice crystals had formed around his eyelids and on his tongue.

Though the situation was grim, she smiled nonetheless. She had managed to use the power again. She still did not have control of it, but neither was it a one-time fluke. She would figure it out, and when she did, she would make every single one of them beg for mercy.

***

Scars

Emhoff leaned his head back, reveling in the heat soothing his aching muscles. The wood stove heated bath was a rare luxury, one his group had hauled back in one of the many wagons gathered from the most recent raid. As the warlord of the community it naturally went to him for first use.

As one who did not participate in the fighting, did he necessarily need it? No. But it was the principle of the matter.

He had only attained the power granted by his stature by maintaining his position through strength. Whether that be strength of body, or strength of presence, it mattered not. He knew that strength in all aspects was what would keep him here, so that was what he did. First pick of the spoils was his right, regardless of whether he needed anything or not.

Laughter broke out among the camp, catching Emhoff's attention by its' tone. He craned his neck, stretching his view over the edge of the tub and around his tent flap, and saw a lone woman standing within the walls of the spiked barricade encircled by no less than fifteen of his men.

She stood at ease, her posture indicating her utter lack of amusement, with a curious blackbird hunched on her shoulder and peering back and forth with twitchy movements at the men gathered 'round.

The warlord sighed at the interruption to his relaxation, but still raised his arms overhead and pulled himself out of the steaming water. The corded muscles of his body flexed involuntarily at the contradictory feeling of the cool evening air. He wrapped a thick rug around his waist and cinched it in place with a belt, grabbing his signature double-bladed axe from its resting place nearby as he made his way over to the circle.

Emhoff gathered his confidence and barked out, "What has the forest brought us today, brothers?"

The gathered men glanced back at their chief with grins on their faces, opening a gap for him to step into, his body now steaming with heat against the night. He rested his axe upon his right shoulder and cocked his head to the left, sizing up the diminutive woman.

She was a full three heads smaller than him, covered in raggedy clothing that was torn in a hundred different places. He supposed she had stumbled her way North from the sacking of the town, following the cover of the forest for safety and finding none. Her hands trembled, presumably from the chill of the night. He doubted it was from fear, as one would expect of such a waif, given her overall posture he had first noted from afar.

The warlord stepped forward on calloused bare feet, exuding every bit the beastial hulk his seven foot stature could give off. He raised a hand palm skyward, as if to reach for her chin.

"I wouldn't mind sharing the warmth of a bear skin with one as pretty as y–," he began, but was cut off.

Her hand lashed out, palm flat and glowing with a sickly green light. As it connected with his abdomen, the power contained within exploded outward, launching the bear of a man backwards some twenty feet to land in the dirt. His weapon went flying, all thoughts of holding onto it gone as he tumbled through the air.

Emhoff rose in one fluid motion, uncaring of his nakedness as he glared hatred at the woman for the embarrassment, the rug that had covered him still falling to the ground. It did not even register in his mind that what just happened should not have happened. She had shamed him in front of the entire community.

None of his challengers had done that and lived. Nor would some filthy wench who tricked him.

His men just stared at him, dumbfounded. It was infuriating. Did he put together a band of idiots?

"Kill her!" he roared, pointing with fury at the woman. The marauders erupted into motion like a wave cresting a cliff, going from baffled blank stares to brandished weapons and cries of outrage in the instant their leader called the order.

Amelia inhaled deeply, her rage fueling her intent, as every man around her halted in his tracks. To a person, they opened and closed their mouths, trying and failing to take in air like a fish out of water. As the woman sucked air in through her mouth, so too did the men around her lose their very breath from theirs.

It appeared in the same frosty mist she had first seen from her prior victim, each man's lips cracking with ice as the dark chill left their bodies.

A chilling void opened within her, drawing in not just the cold night air, but a desperate, invisible essence from those around her. She felt their straining lungs, their panicked hearts, the sudden, sharp terror that blossomed in their eyes as their very life force seemed to thin and dissipate. It was a ghastly, profound hunger, and for the first time, she felt truly *fed* by the suffering of others, a dark satisfaction curling in her gut even as her own chest filled with their stolen air.

They clawed at the air, swinging wildly in their attempts to grasp at something, anything. Two of the men beat on the backs of their brethren, trying to force the lungs of their comrades to take in air. Yet another stumbled towards a tree, needing something to lean on as the strength in his legs gave out due to oxygen deprivation.

They grasped at their throats, their eyes wide with bewilderment. This wasn't a blade, or a fist; it was an invisible force, an unseen hand squeezing the very life from their lungs. Some stumbled, others thrashed, convinced they were suddenly afflicted by a terrible, unknown plague. Their fear was pure, unadulterated terror of the inexplicable, a horror that transcended any battle wound.

One of the first men to spin around and charge at Amelia seemed to make the connection first, seeing the mist move towards her as she stood with pure, calm, hatred in her eyes.

He grabbed the shortsword from his belt with trembling fingers and shambled towards her, his only intent to get close enough to draw her attention. To distract her from whatever she was doing. But his foot caught on a raised root, and he collapsed forward with his sword raised high.

He fell to the ground on a sharp rock, piercing his chest with the full momentum of his fall and opening a hole in his already failing lung. His sword, however, continued its downward arc, the blade connecting with the side of her calf and drawing a deep red line.

Amelia screamed in pain and surprise, and the magic broke. The icy power gathered in front of her rocketed forward in a cone. The man on the ground lay unaffected, now breathing, but bleeding profusely and with only one working lung. His comrades on the other hand – their screams were fuel for nightmares. But they were abrupt.

No, their screams were not abrupt. They were severed. The power she unleashed was less a sound, more a shattering force, a thousand unseen razors rending flesh from bone. It wasn't just skin that peeled away, but layers of their very being, exposing the raw, glistening muscle beneath, tendon snapping and sinew tearing with sickening efficiency.

The air itself became a fine mist of crimson, reflecting the moonlight in a grotesque, shimmering veil. The stench of iron, of hot, living blood, filled her nostrils, a perverse perfume to her shattered senses, mingling with the last, choked gasps of their dying breaths.

The injured man watched in horror as the power sliced and flayed the skin from his friends' bodies, their exposed musculature standing in poses of pure silent agony as blood gushed from the exposed flesh.

Emhoff stood behind the group of men, unaffected by the blast itself, but now covered in the bloody skins of the men he once ruled. Those skins, thawing from the blast with a sickening rapidity, squelched to the ground in a pile of slop around him. His own body, still fully nude, was painted red.

Bits of flesh, hair, and even some chipped teeth were embedded in his hair and thick beard. The taste of copper filled his mouth and he spit out gobbets of liquid, not realizing he had taken it in during the blast. He retched, unable to keep his disgust at bay.

He had done some violent and disgusting things in his time as warlord, but this didn't come close. When people called things a bloodbath, they didn't mean it literally. But having just left his bath and now feeling the full-bodied embrace of a different kind of liquid, there was a whole new meaning to the phrase.

Amelia approached the pathetic man as he knelt on all fours with a shocking amount of disdain in her heart. The initial blast had shocked her, sure. She had even felt a slight twinge of guilt upon seeing the state of the men surrounding her. That feeling evolved, however, into a dark sort of joy as she observed the group collapse to the ground and die a death of pure pain as their exposed nerve endings touched the dirt of the forest floor and felt the bite of the night air.

But this man? This pathetic, overgrown manchild, was the man they had claimed her baby for? The reason her baby was no longer a baby, but a bird?

The disdain transformed into a cold, hard fury that eclipsed the fleeting guilt she had felt for the others only moments before. This was *him*. This bloated, reeking beast, covered in the remains of his subordinates, this was the face of the cruelty that had ripped her world apart. The man who had likely ordered the unspeakable, who saw women as playthings and lives as spoils.

Her memories, vivid and agonizing, flashed: the gentle warmth of Colson in her belly, the simple joy of mixing herbs, the healing touch of her hands that once soothed pain.

All of it shattered by men like *him*. The thought solidified into an unyielding resolve: there would be no mercy, no quick end. Only the slow, agonizing dissolution he so richly deserved for every innocent life he had defiled, especially hers, especially Colson's.

The rage overwhelmed her.

She gripped his face in both hands and squeezed. Those same tendrils of slithering grime underneath her skin oozed from her pores, flowing over her unblemished skin and onto Emhoff's face with an immediate sizzle.

It ate into his flesh like acid, melting the skin and muscle from his face, encapsulating his head fully.

It entered his mouth, nostrils and ears, dissolving him from the inside out.

Scars

The behemoth of a man went slack under her hands, his weight pulling him out of her grasp as the flesh from his neck-up gave way to the top of his spine and his skull. She turned away with satisfaction as the bone itself pitted under the magic's acidic effect.

She glanced over at the dying man who had struck her with his blade, then down at her own bleeding leg. She limped over to him, kneeling at his side and held a hand to his chest.

"I must thank you," she started, "for showing me what it took to get a grip on this power."

The marauder pissed himself in fear.

"Come, join the others. If you're nice, I'll let you stay for a while, while one of the others heals me."

As she finished that sentence, she flexed her fingers over the wound on the man's chest, and a green light glowed. His back arched as she pulled a golden thread from his body, and his eyes clouded over with white.

She crushed the golden thread into her own chest, the light disappearing as she heard his voice join the cacophony already in her mind's Vault.

As she walked away from the massacre to continue her Northward trek, a small army of emerald snakes with golden eyes slithered out of the men she had murdered. Each absorbed into her body as it came into contact with her heel, the gash in her leg stitching itself together with each step.

Chapter 9
The "Rescue"

Having rushed Zek out of the city of Delmar to avoid the potential of any retribution related to Laird Delmar's death, Kel looked over his shoulder once more to confirm he no longer saw the parapets of the castle on the horizon and took a deep calming breath. They had galloped out of the city's main gate headed East, turning South at the fork to follow Hell's Peaks.

That had kept the city in view longer, but Kel reasoned that if they headed North towards Fairbourne instead, word of the Laird's death might precede them and bring unwanted attention to two unannounced and well-armed travelers.

Zek was the first to break the communication dam. "I'll assume the sounds of those war horns shortly after we exited the wall had something to do with your 'business'?" he signed with a slight snicker.

Kel offered a nervous laugh in return as he seemed to shrink into himself a bit. "We will call it *unfinished* business."

"I've found there's no such thing as *finished* business, my friend."

That last response made Kel go quiet again, as the screams of Lair Delmar echoed in his mind. The newly minted assassin had thought that by exacting his revenge in honor of his wife, the night terrors would stop; but they hadn't. If anything, the nightmares had gotten worse since their stay at the Troll's Breath Tavern.

Scars

His chest now bore the mark of a god! The resulting burn left him wincing at every step Sugar took, as his shirt bounced up and down across that tender skin. He had neglected to strap on his fine leather armor that morning, choosing instead to strap it to the saddle, left to bounce against Sugar's rippling flanks.

His partner took note of every single one of these otherwise minor details. Since the night Zek had appropriated their gear, Kel rarely took it off. When he did it was generally only to wash himself up and then to clean the gear, before tying it all immediately back on. He wore the armor as if it were a second skin, seeming to take comfort in the simple fact that should someone get the jump on him, he had time to react in kind.

Zek noticed too, the not-so-hidden winces of pain every time Kel thought he wasn't looking. Something bad had happened to his partner during this "business" of his, and he wasn't being very forthcoming, but past life experiences had taught him that asking the question would just result in explosive anger, so he just dropped it and continued to ride in silence.

The pair rode for another few miles along Hell's Forest, under the shadow of the mountain, before deciding to stop for the night. The sun would be down within the next couple of hours, and they still needed to get deep enough into the woods to shield the light of their campfire from view of the road. As they crossed the threshold of the forest and the last of the sun's rays were blocked by the thick boughs of the elm trees, the light ricocheted from the emerald eye of the serpentine bracelet on Kel's left wrist. The two men had been able to hock most of their wares to a few merchants before leaving Delmar, but none had wanted to take the pair of bracelets.

Having offered them to Zek, who said they weren't quite his style, Kel'rak conceded the point and put them on his own wrists rather than to keep them jangling inside his pack. He immediately felt a magical emanation from the jeweled pair of snakes but hadn't had the time to reflect on that feeling since beginning their flight from the city.

He resolved to do just that before laying down for the night. Any extra edge he could gain through the use of magic seemed to be worth the effort since Voidtooth entered his life, like a mutually beneficial parasite. It had allowed him his revenge, a thing he never thought possible.

It had provided a solution to his newfound deaf identity, in the form of his sound dampening boots and the all-important skill to communicate in sign. And most importantly, it had made him dangerous.

Already, he knew the possibilities were limitless with his magic, assuming he could master his emotions.

From nearby, a sudden call cried out as Kel and Zek's mounts cantered along the trail; female – and young – if judging by the tone. It was followed by a raucous laughter from several male voices.

Zek'ven signaled to Ken what he had heard, and without so much as a sidelong glance at Zek, Kel'rak spurred Sugar on through the trees, taking whipping branches to the face and arms and caring not at all about anything but the young girl in distress. He could feel Sugar's powerful legs pumping underneath him but knew by the look on Zek's face it wouldn't be fast enough.

Desperation fueled him, and he passed his own temporary strengthening magic to Sugar, spurring her on faster than she'd ever run in her life.

Coming up on a clearing, Kel'rak was soon enough able to discern the situation through the tree line as he rode. A group of ten men circled around a young woman, prodding her with long sticks and making lewd gestures.

As Sugar exploded out of the tree line, Kel'rak spotted another – very small – person emerging from the trees closer to the surrounded woman. It was a young girl – bald except for a single brown topknot, who couldn't have seen past her fifteenth winter – sprinting with full abandon towards the group of men with a large birch staff in hand.

She made no sound as she ran, taking the group by complete surprise as she used the staff to vault herself inside the circle. Though the men were caught off guard, some recovered quicker than the others, and started to tighten the noose.

The young girl spun the staff around her like an extension of her own body, the holes in either end of it creating a distracting whistling sound that further put off the men. After the nearest assailant stopped his forward progress to reassess this tiny defender, she abruptly stopped the twirling and planted the butt-end of the staff in the man's groin, lifting him slightly off the ground with surprising strength before retracting and smacking him across the temple with the momentum of a full spin behind the strike.

The man fell to the ground unconscious, making not a sound.

Seeing their comrade down for the count, the remaining nine men decided it best to bull-rush the girl all at once, coming at her with all variety of sharp weapons. They never stood a chance.

Her attacks became a dance of spins, flips, vaults, and rolls. She never spent longer than a second focusing on one target and never stopped moving. As the girl would land in one position, she would jab a man away with a prod to the sternum, and the next she would come up from a roll to whip another in the face.

And so it continued as Sugar and Kel'rak rode in from the far side of the clearing, with the assassin slowing and watching in amazement as the girl flung each assailant from the circle with ease.

He had seen skilled fighters, men who moved with brutal efficiency, but this was different. This was not just practiced combat; it was a fluid, almost impossible grace. Her movements seemed to defy the very laws of physics, a blur of motion that left his eyes struggling to keep pace.

It was a dance, yes, but a deadly one, performed with a precision that hinted at years of rigorous, almost spiritual training. It was a kind of power he hadn't encountered before, so different from the raw, visceral force that surged through him with Voidtooth.

Just as Kel got within speaking range, the girl dispatched the last man, sending him spinning two feet away to the ground. She finally noticed Kel's approach and resumed a defensive stance in front of the woman she'd rescued.

"Halt! Turn around, lest ye wind up like these dolts!" she exclaimed.

Kel raised his empty hands from the reins, making it plain he was not one of them, as Zekven trotted up alongside him and translated to sign. "I was only coming to do what you've already accomplished, young Master…"

"Shawna," she replied, "of the Temple of the Jade Dahlia."

A monk? Kel thought to himself, as Zek interpreted his next words to sign. "Master Shawna. You're quite the warrior for one so young."

Shawna turned her back on him, making it clear she no longer felt this unannounced deaf man to be a threat, and consoled the other woman whose shoulders were still bobbing from her silent weeping. "You're safe now, lady."

The woman looked up then, and flung her arms around the younger girl, wailing with embarrassment and telling Shawna repeatedly how much she appreciated her help and how she wished she were strong like the girl. The young monk turned bright red at the attention, finding the young woman who appeared to be a few years her senior to be quite attractive, and held her back at arm's length to assure her that it was no trouble at all.

"At least allow me to tend to your wounds," the young woman, who identified herself as Samarra, insisted.

"I'm not hurt!" Shawna said as she spun a complete circle with her arms open wide, further assuring Samarra that everything was indeed okay.

Within the same breath, Kel'rak noticed one of the men rising quietly – axe in hand – to attack Shawna from behind. He drew Voidtooth from its' sheath and brought his arm up as if to throw the dagger at the attacker; but, on the up motion, the emerald eyes of the serpentine bracelet on his throwing arm briefly flashed with deep green light as the snake came to life and launched itself at the man.

It grew in size as it flew through the air, landing upon the man's chest and quickly coiling around his neck, squeezing with enough might to turn his face purple in a matter of seconds. The magical garrote loosened only after he stopped thrashing, slithering back to Kel'rak and leaping to his wrist, where it became once again a piece of nondescript jewelry.

Kel could only stand and watch in stupefied amazement as the event transpired, bringing his right arm up to eye level to inspect the bracelet with a new appreciation.

A choked gasp tore from Samarra's lips, her eyes wide with a terror that mirrored the dying man's. Shawna, who had just been in the midst of her triumphant stance, spun, her staff snapping up defensively, her fierce expression replaced by utter shock and a flicker of primal fear. They had seen violence, yes, but this was something else. Something unnatural. Something that defied their understanding of the world.

Shawna had just dispatched a man with practiced, physical grace, same as always, but she stared at the serpent bracelet with a bewildered frown. Her world was one of balance, of honed body and disciplined mind. This... this was a violation of all natural laws. A piece of jewelry, *alive*? It was an abomination, a trick of the darkest arts, and a shiver, cold and unwelcome, traced its way down her spine. Her training had prepared her for men, for beasts, but not for inanimate objects coming to terrifying life.

Shawna also looked back to Kel'rak with new appreciation, covering up her own shock, having dismissed him simply based on his disability. "Quite the bag of tricks you have, Master Assassin!"

With Zek continuing to interpret, Kel simply shook his head and responded, "I am no master."

It was Zekven's turn to interject. "This is Kel'rak Zaulyl, and I am Zekven Teluil. We mean no harm and only came to provide whatever assistance we may, good ladies." He finished with a bow and a toothy grin. "Our path takes us South through the woods to the river, and Hell's Ferry."

Kel cringed slightly at the amount of detail Zek was offering up to these strangers, but he reminded himself these two young women were just that – young women, with no affiliation to Laird Delmar or his guards.

"Would you mind terribly if I tagged along?" Samarra started. "I assure you, I am a skilled healer!" She finished with a sidelong glance at Kel'rak, who she'd noticed wincing a few times whenever he bent forward.

"Nor am I as helpless as I just made myself out to be," she added as she hung her head in shame.

Shawna glanced back and forth between the two men and the beautiful woman she'd just rescued and gave her head a rough shake to clear the cobwebs.

"Well, I guess I'm coming too!" she exclaimed, her prior fierce expression melted away and replaced by an ear-to-ear smile indicative of her youth. "You klutzes are going to need another night guard, and my training allows me to function on just two hours of sleep!"

As Zekven finished signing that last statement, a thought occurred to Kel'rak. "What is a monk doing so far from home, anyway?" he asked with sincere curiosity.

Shawna blushed at the question and fidgeted, drawing a circle in the dirt with her staff as she spoke.

"The Master of Flowers has sent me on a journey of personal growth," she stated calmly, belying the irritation buried within. "Master Halani believes that I *can progress no further until the storms inside my mind match the calm river flow of my combat art.*" As she finished the quote from her master, she jabbed her staff into the drawn circle with further unexpected strength, driving it several inches into the ground and leaving it standing perfectly straight as she crossed her arms and tapped her foot angrily.

It was almost like she was daring one of the other three present to defend Master Halani's stance; rather than doing so, Zekven plopped a hand on her shoulder and smiled disarmingly.

He turned back to Kel'rak now as he both spoke and signed, "I think we have more than enough provisions to add these two gentleladies to our posse? And I'd really rather not leave a young lady in the woods by herself. I may be a rapscallion, but I am not without my honor!"

Kel could only chuckle in response and turned towards Sugar to lead her to Samarra. He reached out for the young woman's hand and guided it to Sugar's muzzle, making soft shushing sounds and sneaking Sam an apple from his pack.

"You'll be her new best friend," he promised. "Just be sure to lay your fingers flat or she might decide they look like delicious carrots!"

Samarra's face lit up as Sugar walked up close and nudged her outstretched hand to get at the apple. A soft snort of approval escaped the mare's lips as she took the juicy snack and crunched it down in three bites. Zekven offered to do the same for Shawna with his much younger colt, but she held her hand up while shaking her head and smiling.

"I need no mount but thank you," she stated simply.

Zekven eyed the tiny girl's frame with skepticism, but if he had a critique, he kept it to himself. The new team of four set to work stripping the assailants of anything useful, rounding up the unconscious ones Shawna hadn't outright killed into a back-to-back sitting group resembling a wildflower, with their legs splayed outward to prevent the entire unconscious band of would-be sexual predators from falling over and loosening any of their bonds.

Samarra insisted that Zek and Kel drive a large stick into the ground between all of them, so they would have something to rest against. Neither man could wrap their head around how she could possibly still care for their well-being, but they respected her wish – for which she rewarded each a tight hug and an ear-to-ear smile.

Some time later, with the monk walking next to Sugar and Sam, and Kel walking next to Zek, the group started off out of the clearing heading South. Just inside the treeline, Shawna broke the awkward silence with a question.

"Samarra, why *did* you care so much about them? They meant to do countless bad things to you!" she exclaimed, Zek interpreting on the fly.

"My daddy always told me that we should treat others with kindness, and that's something I intend to do, even to my enemies," Sam responded flatly.

Shawna started to reply about how she could respect that, when Sam continued in a huskier voice, "though they deserve to burn for eternity." Zekven was looking towards Kel'rak to interpret and didn't see, but Kel could have sworn he saw a faint red glow coming from Samarra's direction as she spoke the second time.

Shawna instead responded with a single "Aye", plodding on with eyes averted and head down. As if that confirmation were a command word, a scream and a bright orange flash erupted behind them from back in the clearing.

The screams were not human, not anymore. They were the raw, animalistic cries of men consumed by an agony beyond comprehension, a sound that scraped against Kel'rak's very soul. The air behind them, which had been crisp with the scent of pine and damp earth, now reeked of burning flesh and scorching wood. Zekven stumbled, his jaw slack, his eyes wide with a horror that transcended his usual roguish charm.

Only three heads whipped around at the conflagration. Shawna froze, her head snapping back, her body rigid with a fear that was alien to her. They were transfixed, utterly paralyzed by the bloodcurdling sounds of men being cooked alive.

But Samarra, her face a mask of serene detachment, merely continued her soft hushing noises, her hand a calming presence on Sugar's flank, urging the mare forward.

With Zekven and Shawna transfixed on the bloodcurdling screams of the men being cooked alive, Kel'rak slowly turned back towards Sam with a raised eyebrow. The faint red glow from Samarra, the way her voice had changed, the sudden, impossible conflagration behind them... It was another piece of the puzzle, a terrifying confirmation that magic wasn't just returning; it was manifesting in unexpected, potent, and often horrifying ways.

Chapter 10
The Wanderer

The early morning sun peeked over the crest of Amelia's forehead and into her closed eyes, waking her with gentle warmth as if greeting a close friend. She woke from her reverie with a grin, as she had done every morning these past six weeks, feeling the rhythmic rise and fall of Colson's breaths as he slumbered peacefully at her navel.

She reveled in the peace of mother nature's gifts – from the soft moss acting as that evening's bed to the babbling brook she bathed in, to the bounty of plant-based foods the expert herbalist knew to be safe to eat, she had everything she needed to thrive.

The same could not be said for her short-lived stay in the town of Flintlock Bay.

***

Here she was quickly met with dirty looks, though it was not for her lack of clean clothes, or her lack of a decent hairbrush and therefore disheveled hair; rather, it was the black bird upon her shoulder. Flintlock Bay was loudly and proudly *not* a pirate city, but neither was it necessarily a law-abiding city residing under the rule of any kingdom.

Her waters harbored whoever had the coin to pay the port fee, which also meant her population was the rough 'n tumble sailor type – rude, obnoxious, and superstitious to boot. Paired with her current appearance, it wasn't long before the whispers of "witch", "hag", and – somehow – "she-devil" floated through the air behind her.

The fear in Flintlock Bay was a palpable thing, a thick, suffocating blanket that pressed in on her. Shopkeepers averted their eyes, their hands twitching towards hidden charms. Children, bolder than their parents, would point and shriek, then flee behind skirts, their cries of 'witch!' echoing down the narrow streets.

An old woman, her face a roadmap of wrinkles, spat on the ground as Amelia passed, then made the sign of the crossed fingers, a desperate attempt to ward off evil. It was a collective, ingrained terror, passed down through generations, now reawakened by her very presence. None of it was entirely unexpected, but Amelia was surprised by how much their words affected her.

Until recently, she was beloved by many; praised even, by those she served. Until recently, she was naught but a healer. But now? What does one call a woman that consumes the life-force and souls of others to maintain her health, and manifests her fear, grief, and hate to reduce entire towns to rubble and ash?

She could come up with no other term than witch and it terrified her. Nor had one-hundred years without magic apparently done anything to silence those with the fear born of superstition and old folk tales. Amelia hadn't even *done* anything to anyone, she just looked the part, and that was enough.

Amelia the Witch spent about two hours in town. Just long enough to find the local herbalist and sell several bundles of rare plants she had picked up along the road from Marasol.

The money she earned from her sale was enough to buy a new outfit from the tailor down the street, complete with thigh-high black travel boots from the leatherworker next door. She wore her new white linen pants tucked into the boots, to keep the fine leather from chafing her raw calves. This, she accompanied with a loose-fitting dark red blouse, to accentuate her auburn hair.

To stave off the cold of the oncoming winter – though, this far from the Crags and so close to the coast, it was less worry – Amelia spent extra on a fur-lined black cloak with hood. The way she saw it, if everyone was going to call her a witch she may as well look the part. Of course, none of this would have been possible with Colson on her shoulder, so she had sent him off to hunt while she shopped.

The leatherworker was kind enough to throw in a small dagger that strapped to the side of her boot, providing her with a tool with which to harvest meat from any game she managed to trap. Without having to buy a weapon, Amelia had enough left over for a hearty meal and a single night's stay at a local tavern; however, she quickly learned that word of her arrival had spread through town like wildfire.

Colson had ridden along on her shoulder since leaving the shops, having tired his wings while hunting for an entire hour, which left Amelia sticking out like a sore thumb. She was turned away from three different inns in different parts of the town over the course of the next hour.

As she shambled up to the fourth and final location atop a hill overlooking most of the town and the bridge that crossed Flintlock Channel towards Fairbourne, feet leaden with the weight of rejection, she paused before opening the door just long enough to give herself a once-over.

Deciding she looked presentable-enough, Amelia took a deep breath and moved to enter, but was stopped by a quiet, "Pssst". The witch whipped her head around – sending Colson hopping with squawking annoyance to her other shoulder – to the sight of a young stableboy, no more than ten winters old, beckoning to her and disappearing behind the corner of the building.

Amelia followed without hesitation, not really worried about an ambush. The townspeople had already proven themselves too afraid to be within ten feet of her.

Rounding the corner, the witch just caught the sight of the stableboy talking to a portly woman by the lantern at the back door, before returning the woman's cheerful high-five and running off to the stable with a steaming muffin and an apple for the only horse boarded that night. Suspecting the woman to be the innkeeper, Amelia painted on her best smile and strode confidently toward the door.

"Hail, and blessings upon your home!" the witch began.

"May the stars guide your feet," the innkeeper responded as customary. Though she kept up her most cheery business-woman face, it was not difficult to note the once-over she gave Amelia and the longer-than-a-second stare at Colson. "You are the newcomer to town that I've heard much gossip about today, yes?"

"Yes ma'am," Amelia answered with a slight curtsy. This she followed up with an innocent tone, "I've not had the best luck finding a suitable room since finishing my shopping."

"Can't imagine why," the innkeeper replied with a knowing smirk and another glance towards Colson. "It's like this lass – even if I felt I could risk the unbroken look of my common space by givin' ye a room, I've got none this evening…"

Celia's smile, though warm, was strained. Her eyes darted nervously to the busy common room, then back to Amelia, a silent plea for understanding.

"It's not just the rooms, lass," she'd whispered, her voice barely audible. "Folks here... they remember the stories. They fear what they don't understand. And a raven... a black bird... it's a powerful symbol, one they associate with ill omens, with dark magic."

Amelia could feel her face scrunching up with frustration as she started to protest, but the woman held up a finger and continued.

"That being said, I understand the troubles of being a woman in a strange town better than any. I can give ye a warm meal, and I've already sent young Thomas to clear and wash a stall in a tucked-away corner of the stable for a measure of privacy. This time of year is light on road travelers and heavy on sailors arriving off the sea, so I have the stable space but no more," she finished with an apologetic smile.

Her offer of the stable stall was a quiet act of defiance against the prevailing fear, a testament to her compassion, but it also underscored the deep-seated superstition that gripped the town.

"That is more than I could have asked for," Amelia grinned, "and I appreciate you sticking your neck out for me Miss….?"

"Celia."

"Miss Celia," she finished, reaching for her coin purse.

Celia waggled a pudgy finger Amelia's direction, scolding her with a look like a concerned mother. "That's not necessary, but thank you," she said firmly while grasping the young woman by the shoulders. "By the stars," she exclaimed, "ye really need that meal! Go find Thomas and I will be back with some warm bread and beef stew."

Amelia laughed to herself breathlessly and shook her head in exasperation as Miss Celia hurried off, switching from her gentle mothering voice to a loud yell at her kitchen staff for an order of stew and warmed cider for "Thomas' break!".

The witch turned her head towards her baby boy and stroked the feathers on his head gently, promising as she walked toward the stable to request Thomas bring him enough straw to build a hasty nest for their first truly restful night since leaving the desolation of Marasol.

A healthy and muscular young brown horse with white spots glanced backwards at her with half an effort as she walked into the stable, dismissing her entirely with a snort as it returned to what was a peaceful slumber. Thomas' head popped out of the stall on the end and he waved her down with a gap-toothed smile before disappearing back inside.

"A-a-apologies miss," he stuttered, "I'm n-nearly d-done but the floor will need to d-d-dry. I thought I h-had more t-time." The boy was clearly stressed and received more beratement than compliments, but he had done a grand job in such a short time.

"There is nothing to apologize for young master, you've done a weary heart a fine service," Amelia replied.

"I have set a small table and chair inside of the stall for you miss, they are already d-dry and ready for you."

Amelia gave the boy a tight hug and a kiss on the head before dismissing him with her thanks once more and her request for Colson's straw. She settled slowly into the plain wooden chair, accepting its' begrudging creak as an echo to her own aching joints complaints, while Colson alighted on the table with a gentle scritch-scratch from his scrambling talons.

"We are finding a way, sweet boy. We are finding our way."

***

As she lay remembering her time in town, she remembered also leaving some of her only remaining change in her stew bowl for young Thomas and smiled once more to herself. She could survive on next to nothing, so Amelia expected her small token of appreciation for his effort was of more value to him than it ever could be to her.

Doing her best not to disturb Colson's sleep, Amelia popped her head up from her resting position off to the side of the main roadway and stared off into the distance. It was clear that she would never be accepted somewhere like Flintlock Bay, and she doubted the nearby major city of Fairbourne would be much better – their populations being largely the same kind of folk.

That left her only direction being South, towards the small crossroads village of Three Corners and the citadel of South Peak. It would mean back-tracking by a considerable amount, but Amelia didn't really mind. She had yet to find her new reason for life, only knowing she wanted to live it out with her baby boy.

During her inner contemplations, she began absentmindedly stroking Colson's silky head and back. He rolled over and arched his back into her touch, but otherwise stayed asleep.

Thoroughly enjoying his satisfied mid-sleep coos, Amelia was spurred on to more vigorous head scratches, pulling out a feather in the process. While a slight surprise, this wasn't an entirely new concept to the woman, who had secretly been pocketing his "baby feathers" as they fell out every now and then – a curse of emotional proportions for a mother unable to save her baby's first tooth.

What was shocking were the other four feathers that came out with the next two gentle strokes down Colson's back.

Panic set in as Amelia accidentally pulled out yet another two feathers – this time, from his left wing – while trying to rotate Colson to his belly. The seven follicles that housed these feathers emanated a faint green glow, warranting further inspection.

This only pushed the witch into a deeper panic attack because the inspection of the affected area revealed rotted skin and a greenish flame that emitted cold rather than heat. Now fully hyperventilating, Amelia bolted upright, rousing her baby violently which resulted in a mild burst of about 10 more feathers as he flapped his wings to hop away. The more feathers came out, the more intense the green flame seemed to become.

Colson squawked, not in pain, but in surprise as more and more feathers dropped from his body to be replaced by cold flames – cold flames he could not feel. Amelia rushed to her baby's aid and cradled him in her arms. She did this partially to comfort him and partially to prevent any more feather loss until she came up with another idea.

The witch's attunement to the dark energy coursing through Colson's body came with a certain amount of understanding, grounding her once more as she hugged him tight and absorbed all the information she could.

Scars

Colson's soul was proving to be too much for the small body of the raven. This, she knew by instinct. The purity and sheer potential power of a "newborn" soul was far too strong of a force to be housed within the small avian form. Still cradling her boy in her arms as he got colder and colder, Amelia scanned her surroundings with the voracity of a dog with a fresh bone, which – incidentally – she saw.

Evidently used to human interaction, the stray glanced her way while still chewing on its bone, seeming to feel unthreatened by the woman.

The dog appeared to be some sort of wolf mixed with a hound. It had the tell-tale floppy ears of a hound dog, with the wiry fur of a wolf. It was just as large, with paws that seemed to grasp the bone of its' prey as if they had opposable thumbs. The powerful jaws splintered the bone with ease, cracking into the delicious inner marrow with gusto.

Not seeing a better option, Amelia reached deep within herself to the now-familiar well of souls contained within. Having been liberally crushing the souls of the raiders, but still not willing to destroy the souls of the townspeople of Marasol, she plucked one of the two remaining souls of the raiders from the pool. Like feeding a cricket to a lizard, she "dragged" the panicked soul from her forehead to the focal point within her chest and devoured the life energy of the raider, feeling its essence fuel her power once more.

The stray wolf-dog, usually bold around humans, sensed the shift in the air. Its ears flattened, a low whimper escaping its throat as the cold, green light pulsed from the glowing raven. Its instincts screamed danger, a primal terror of something fundamentally *wrong* with the world.

It backed away slowly, its hackles rising, a guttural growl rumbling in its chest, torn between its ingrained trust of humans and the overwhelming, terrifying aura of raw, dark magic emanating from Amelia.

Guided by her fear, the witch hovered her claw-like hand over Colson's raven body and seemed to vacuum his soul from the vessel. She "caught" the soul in her grasp – the rotted body collapsing to the ground in a pile of broken mush – and flung it at the wolf-dog's face.

Though alarmed by her sudden movement, it didn't seem to see the energy flying at it and so it held its ground in perfect position for Colson's soul to enter the fresh vessel. Amelia waited, biting her lip with worry as Colson fought to take control of the body. Any bystanders within view would have thought the dog to be covered in fleas or some other irritant, the way it flailed, rolled, and scratched throughout the possession.

The battle of wills ended as abrupt as it had begun, with the wolf-dog-that-was-Colson lying paws up on the ground and pausing its thrashing long enough to realize he had won. It seemed Colson learned from the memories of the body he possessed upon victory, as – as with the raven – he rolled over without delay and up to his four feet as though he weren't used to only being on two.

Her baby boy loped over to her, assailing her with wet kisses on her face and barreling her to the ground with joy. Again feeling his warmth instead of cold, Amelia let herself feel joy instead of fear once more. She snuggled into his fluffy body, reveling in her boy's love.

This was how a mother should truly feel. As a raven, Colson had done things no other human child could lay claim to –

flying, being the chief item. But his affections had come at the cost of the nip of a hard beak, or the accidental scratch of a sharp talon.

Now, there was only warmth. Now, Amelia could truly feel his closeness without worry of being accidentally injured. Though the wolf-dog body was dangerously equipped with both tooth and claw, they were far less dangerous under the careful guide of her boy.

Already, she could feel that this vessel was better equipped to handle the inner fire of Colson's soul; however, she could still feel that it would not be enough. Sure, it would last longer, but it would not permanently hold him. She needed another solution – one that wouldn't keep her continually pulling and pushing him to and from bodies.

Given that the raven's vessel had provided about six weeks' worth of viable time, she guessed she had about two months before they would need to begin the search for another body; a bigger body. More worrisome than that, she doubted she wouldn't need to use the remaining raider's soul for some random need before then, which left her with the guilt of needing to consume a soul from Marasol in order to keep her baby alive.

There was no need to worry about that right now though. She had time. Shoving the dark thoughts from her mind, Amelia instead just let herself be happy. She scratched Colson's big, fluffy head and shoulders, grinning ear-to-ear as his eyes rolled into the back of his head and his tongue lolled out to one side.

Yeah, we'll figure it out lovey, she thought to herself. *We have time.*

Chapter 11
The Secret

As a four-person troupe, Kel'rak and the others made it all the way to the river without incident. He wasn't sure whether that was due to the presence of himself and Zek as two dark-clad men of violent presence, or due to Shawna's endless stream of a mouth.

Had he not witnessed her martial training firsthand, he would never have believed that the kid was telling the truth about her background – everything he knew about monks related to self-control and the concept of listening rather than speaking. This kid would not shut up.

He suspected it had more to do with her clear attraction to Samarra than anything, whose voluptuous curves held the teen girl's gaze whenever the self-titled healer wasn't looking.

"…you haven't *lived* until you've seen the Temple, Samarra!" Kel saw his partner sign as he tuned back into the one-sided conversation.

"Is that so?" Sam replied, only halfway paying attention, and seeming to wrestle with something else internally.

Stopping at the river bank to scoop up a mouthful of the flowing water, the monk continued, "I swear! The whole place is built into the side of the mountain, which you would think would be so boring. But it lives up to its name!"

Zekven paused in his translations for a second and asked, "Do you mean to tell me the place is covered in dahlia flowers that are all the same color?"

"In a manner of speaking," Shawna said, stepping her sore sandaled feet into the cool water and sighing with relief. "The walls are adorned with dahlias carved from actual jade stones. There's one for every initiate the temple has trained over the centuries… mine hasn't made it up on the wall yet."

Samarra finally dismounted from Sugar, patting her gently on the rump, her sweet full-faced smile returned once more. Removing her travel boots and rolling the bottoms of her trousers up, she joined Shawna in the water and placed a hand on her shoulder.

"It sounds beautiful!" she replied, earning a look of glee from Shawna.

The team settled into what had become a routine of making camp for the coming evening. Zek and Shawna went to gather firewood while Samarra set to work on building their simple tents. Kel'rak, rather fond of his alone time, wandered off into the woods to set small game snares and hopefully find a deer they might harvest into some jerky for the rest of their trip. He absentmindedly rubbed Voidtooth's pommel with his thumb as he walked, feeling its' never-ending hunger weighing on his mind.

The assassin found that he didn't know what to do with himself when there weren't things to kill. Even with Zek around to translate, being social wasn't exactly in his wheelhouse, and his deafness made conversation awkward at times.

Instead, when he wasn't paying attention to the translated talks, he spoke internally with the weapon. He thirsted for knowledge, and the nefarious tool was all-too-happy to oblige so long as it meant it might feed soon. He asked a lot about the Baron; however, this particular topic was a little bit of a fight to get Voidtooth to talk about. It clearly feared the specter that it called a god.

He didn't quite get it. He doubted a god would downgrade themself by using a moniker such as "Baron", the fifth and lowest rank of peerage. That would imply that there were four stronger beings above him; that is, if gods even abided by the hierarchies of man. It very well could just be an endearing and smarmy title meant to make his faithful follow him blindly.

But that didn't quite make sense either since the gods disappeared from Litharia long ago. Sure, there were the handful of people across the continent that either spent far too much time in libraries and obsessed over the old religious texts, or that maintained the faiths within their own homes as a tradition, but not to the extent that a neat title would warrant any kind of attention from the population at large.

Kel'rak was able to gather from the weapon that the gods were once men and women who attained their godhood through mastery of their magics, which explained the Baron's shadowy form – he quite literally became that which he sought to master. This led to a feud between the gods to determine which magic, and therefore which facet of life's emotions was the strongest. Ultimately, there was no victor.

No single emotion's manifestation of magic proved stronger than another, when wielded by a master. When the gods figured out that they could mix magics by twining together different emotions, a full-scale war broke out. Litharia became their battleground, an island nation cut off from the rest of the world where the gods could do battle without wiping out the entirety of intelligent life.

Their battles raised the mountains from the very earth, forming both Hell's Peak and the Crags. Elemental beings of fire and water clashed at their command. The winds howled and flashed with green light as living beings just ceased to exist. The elves of the Nine lived under the constant threat of explosive doom that rained from above, cut off from the rest of civilization.

From among their ranks, another god rose to power, a master of all magics. Her utter control of her emotions was like a beacon for the warring gods, who realized they had become blinded by their irrational civil war and had destroyed the homes they loved.

Rather than using her mastery to overpower the other gods, Nithana insisted she could teach them to accomplish what she had.

She ported them away to another dimension entirely, ending the conflict but leaving the rest of civilization to pick up the pieces. Some gods, like the Baron, had sat out the war in its entirety. They resurfaced only once the other gods disappeared, offering to tutor the uninitiated in the magical arts, so that together they might drive the leftover forces of destruction from the face of the realm.

This worked for a time – these gods guiding the learning of many men and women who had the power to eradicate those threats.

But the scarred memories and skepticism of those that remained did not easily forget the past. Once most of the monsters were driven out, the only monsters that remained were those with the power to overthrow the common man, and thus began the Reckoning.

The weapon's words tore at the very fabric of his understanding. The Reckoning. Not a glorious victory of man over magic, but a desperate, terrified retreat of beings who had grown to realize they were destroying everything they had ever cared about.

His entire life, every lesson, every sermon, had been a lie. Magic wasn't gone; it had simply withdrawn, leaving humanity to wallow in its ignorance, clinging to a false sense of triumph. The realization was a cold, bitter taste in his mouth, a new scar on his perception of the world.

So the Baron and the other gods gave up. They called through the cosmos for Nithana's guidance and she whisked them away. That was the last Voidtooth had felt its connection to the Baron, until that night in the Troll's Breath.

Kel'rak knew just through Zek's existence that magical beings hadn't been eradicated as once thought, so he also knew there had to be other magical beings in the realm.

Which begged the question – why did the Baron choose him, with all the other possibilities? He didn't get to finish the thought path, as he wandered back into camp with a brace of conies in hand, where a fire seemed to crackle in anticipation of the meat that would roast and drip its fats over it.

Samarra took the carcasses to dress and clean them in the fresh water of the river, in preparation for the night's meal. Shawna, true to form, continued to blather on about something that Zekven translated into sign as "breathing techniques". Full from having foraged as he hunted, the assassin elected to slink off outside the firelight and drop into slumber, his thoughts and dreams full of epic magical showdowns.

***

He awoke a few hours later, stretching the stiffness of laying on the packed ground of the forest floor from his back. Zek lay a few feet away, his shortswords in hand and ready for combat at the slightest disturbance. Near the embers of the fire, Shawna slept slumped over in the spot she'd been sitting when he left the group to their conversation.

Outside the firelight, by the gently burbling river, sat Samarra. She sat in a meditative pose at the water's edge, legs crossed and back rigid. Under the direct moonlight, she should have glowed with a white radiance, but instead seemed bathed in the orange light of sunset.

As the assassin circled his approach from her right side, he began to understand why. Though she sat in the white light of the moon, her eyes burned with a deep red glow – more like smoke than fire, but intense, nonetheless.

Though his boots muffled his every step, her head whipped right towards him just as he caught view of her eyes. Rather than speaking, she pointed to his left wrist. Puzzled, he glanced down to the snake bracelet, the only adornment on that arm and the matching twin to the one on his right. It flashed a dim green light for half a breath, and he flicked his gaze back to Samarra, who only nodded and smiled an uncharacteristic sultry smile.

Removing the bracelet from his left wrist, he tossed it over to Samarra, who caught it without looking and casually let it slither upon her own wrist. As she turned away from him once more to stare at the river, he "heard" her voice – no, not Samarra's voice, but a newer voice – inside his head, the same way he heard Voidtooth.

This voice, husky and dripping with seduction, said only, *Samarra is asleep darling. Have you come to play with me?*

Kel'rak did his best to show no emotion, but he was caught off guard. *What do you mean she is asleep? Am I not talking to her now?*

What could only be described as a "tsk tsk" sound played in his head. *So much power, yet so little knowledge,* the female voice said. *Our girl is tired, so I took the night shift. I do so enjoy the quiet moments where she doesn't babble. If you're not here to play, I'd like to ask for my quiet time back.*

You can't just drop a statement like that and expect me to not ask what in the hells you're talking about, miss…?

Samarra's head tilted to the left and the voice in Kel's head went silent for a moment, as if she were in contemplation of how much to say. *Alizarra – and the hells are precisely what we should be talking about! A much more entertaining place than this dreadfully scream-less borefest that you call the Prime Material Plane.*

Wait… do you mean to tell me you're some sort of demon? Kel'rak replied.

Alizarra's husky voice dropped into a low growl at what was apparently an insult. *THE demon, which you will remember from here on out unless you want me to rip your manhood from your flesh.*

Kel'rak backed up a step and raised his hands in a show of peace and surrender before Alizarra continued, *I have commanded the succubi of the Abyss for centuries.* She scoffed, an irritating sound when made out loud, and even worse inside one's head. *I try one simple damned possession, fail, and boom! I'm stuck here.*

How exactly are you stuck here? And where is "here"? he probed.

Samarra's head snapped back in his direction and gave him a look that said he was the dumbest person she'd ever met. *Here! In this body, in this Plane,* she answered.

Kel'rak swapped mental pathways and found instead his connection to Voidtooth. *Are you hearing all this?*

"Aye."

And?...

"I heared o' it happening before, but never seen it," the weapon replied.

Are you really going to make me ask you to complete your thought, he responded with irritation.

"Don't get yer knickers in a twist, I'm getting to it!" Voidtooth shot back. "A failed demonic possession is rumored to occur when the demon attempts to subdue a repentant soul who has committed to righting a past wrong – a really bad wrong."

So she's not lying to me then, Kel said.

"Nay, she's tellin ye right," it replied.

Careful how much you talk to that thing sweetheart, you will start to look a tad crazy, Alizarra passed along their link.

Realizing he'd managed to let his face tell the story of his internal discussion, he tightened his resolve and shut off the communication with the weapon.

So if you're a demon – why are we still alive?

Much as I miss a good torture, you're more useful to me alive than dead. That and little Miss Priss seems to like you all a lot, which works out for me – less energy I have to waste saving her ass from danger.

Her casual mention of 'good torture' and 'ripping manhood from flesh' was a stark, chilling reminder of the gulf between their worlds. Humans, even the most depraved, usually had some pretense, some twisted justification. Alizarra offered none. She simply *was*.

Her honesty was more terrifying than any lie, for it revealed a mindset utterly alien to his own, a being who operated on a scale of morality he couldn't even begin to comprehend. He felt a profound sense of unease, a new kind of fear that transcended the physical.

Why would you care? Kel asked.

Well, you see, I'm in a bit of a predicament – if the girl dies, I die. So it's in my best interest to keep her alive and well. Unfortunately, she ended with a small harrumph.

And do you both share memories, or…? He finished with the feeling of a question.

Or are you going to have to relive this entire conversation with her tomorrow? Yes, that one, you poor thing. You poor, delicious, thing. Alizarra finished with a purr.

Not interested, he responded as dryly as possible. *So, if you can keep Sam safe, what kept you from roasting those pricks from when we met, before Zek and I ever reached the clearing?*

I was asleep, obviously. Keep up – for an assassin you sure are slow.

Making a show of rolling his eyes, Kel'rak sat down next to Alizarra at the water's edge, assuming the same pose. *Is this information that you need me to keep from the others?* he asked, closing his eyes and focusing on the slight vibrations he felt in the grassy bank from the running water.

He wanted to make it clear that he didn't view the demon as a threat and was even willing to partner with her. The way she had casually cooked the bandits alive, he took a wild guess that his best bet right now was to exude an air of confidence, as though he felt her an equal.

Do whatever you want, darling, you're a grown man. But be prepared to come to our aid when your friends turn on us. The demon also closed her eyes, thereby reducing the red glow emanating from her face to a pair of wisps of red smoke coming from the corners of her eyes.

Before taking off the bracelet that created their mental connection and handing it back to Kel, she reached over and grasped his forearm with more strength than should be physically possible for Samarra's thin frame and said, *keep us safe, and I'll keep you safe. Now, since you're awake – and dreadfully boring – I'm going to go lay us down somewhere soft.*

Kel'rak took the bracelet back, mentally commanding it to slither back onto his left wrist, and watched the woman who was also part demon slink away towards the firelight. The world just seemed to be getting bigger every day. It was a lot to take in, for someone who until recently had just been a farmer intent on living out his days with his cows.

If gods were once men, and demons walked among them, then the world was a far more dangerous, far more unknowable place than any history book had dared to suggest. The thin veneer of civilization, the comforting illusion of human control, felt suddenly fragile, ready to shatter at the whim of ancient powers. His simple farm, his quiet life, seemed like a distant, impossible dream, a relic of a world that no longer existed.

He made a kissing sound, calling Sugar over to him, and leaned against her body for warmth as he realized it suddenly felt a lot colder by the riverbank without Alizarra around. He gave it just a few more days before the first snowfalls finally made their way down to ground level from the mountains – a thought that might make traversing the great lake of South Peak a little less fun, even on the relative safety of Hell's Ferry.

***

Kel'rak's guess proved accurate, with the season's first flurries beginning to fall as the troupe rounded the last bend to the quaint village of Hell's Ferry.

The residents here were a motley sort, consisting mostly of rogues and misfits of all backgrounds. It was a safe area to lay low, speaking relatively, as the village was too deep into the woods to warrant check-ins from the ruling city of Delmar and too far across the safety of the massive Lake Calisharra to worry in the slightest about investigation from the law based in South Peaks.

Capitalizing on this reputation, the village maintained a healthy trade tax between the two cities, in the form of fenced goods. Each boat that sailed to her docks of course bore legitimate cargo, usually for the purposes of keeping the residents fed and medicine provisioned.

However, her real profits were from the many high-priced art pieces that floated unannounced from thieves based in both major cities, who paid for safe passage of these goods to their clientele in either location. None of this was why the group had made their way here, though.

Hell's Ferry was so named because before it was a bustling port of chicanery, it was…well, a ferry. At the base of Hell's Peaks, it was the fastest direct route from Delmar to South Peak, regardless of the safer route along the paved roadways that circumvented Lake Calisharra and added many many miles to the trip.

At roughly two-hundred fifty miles long, and just shy of one-hundred miles wide at its widest point, the lake was second in size only to the mysterious wonder of water that surrounded the Kingdom of the Nine. Just to get all the way around it on foot was a three to five day journey, two by horse.

The ferry however, took a direct route from the village to South Peak proper. With its sails filled with the cool downdrafts from the mountains, the nautical adventure usually only took the better part of a day, allowing its riders to rest and relax while floating across the crisp waters of the mountain runoff.

The companions trudged up to the gate, ready for the journey through the trees and the dirt to be over with. A lone guard stood post, leaning back against the log wall on his right foot with the left propped up at an angle to keep balance. He appeared to be counting coins from his coin purse, whether from unofficial gate tolls or from last night's paycheck, they knew not. Hearing them approach, he stuffed the coins back in and cinched the tie tight, grabbing his spear that had been left to similarly lean against the wall to his right.

"Oi, state yer business!" he bellowed.

Zekven calmly waved back his companions and stepped forward. "We are simply escorting these young ladies through the woods on our way to find passage across the lake."

He finished his statement with a flip of a silver coin to the guard, whose eyes flashed greedily at what he saw as tonight's after-shift ale number five flying through the air towards him.

The guard deftly caught the coin from the air, snatching it in a movement so smooth one might think he was simply swatting at an annoying fly.

"I didn't see nuthin'," was all he said as he leaned back against the wall in the same comfortable position as before.

Samarra gasped and chuckled as she realized the implication of Zek's statement, as Shawna cocked her head to the side and thought about it for a minute. She raised a finger to her chin, scratching at it in absent-minded thought until it finally clicked. Her eyes each grew wide as her body stiffened in realization.

"You made him think we're whores!" the young monk exclaimed, pointing an accusatory finger Zekven's way.

The rogue waggled a finger in a "tsk tsk" motion and said, "Now that's no way for a monk of the Jade Dahlia to be speaking, even of the ladies of the night." He finished the last bit with a grin that broke into a belly laugh as he threw his head back and planted both hands firmly on his hips.

Eager for this role as glorified bodyguard to be over, Kel'rak rolled his eyes so hard it was almost audible, and his gaze landed on the village's inn. Heavily patting Zek full-palm on the shoulder to get his attention, he pointed in the direction of the building and made a beeline for the door. The ferry be damned, it could wait.

Scars

He hadn't slept on a real bed since they bolted out of Delmar and his back felt like someone had been beating him with a cane. By the time Zek and the girls had made their way inside, Kel'rak was already communicating via chalkboard with the innkeeper requesting: two rooms, four meals, and heated water for their washbasins.

He fished around his coin purse and found two gold coins, tossing them onto the counter and writing a final, *"One more, if you ensure we're not bothered,"* on the chalkboard. The thin, greasy man swooped up the coins with a quick look around the room to make sure no one else had seen the riches, and nodded affirmation back to Kel'rak.

A third gold coin arced from the assassin's hand into the innkeeper's apron pocket as Kel'rak turned away with a pitcher of ale in hand, and jerked a thumb back at the counter to the four mugs he'd left behind. Zek let out a deep sigh of content as Samarra hurried to the counter to scoop up the mugs.

The group found a table by the roaring hearth, where they all doffed their cloaks which were covered in the snow that had begun to fall in earnest just before they'd reached the building. With any luck, by the time they finished their drinks and meals the cloaks would be dry enough to stow away in their rooms without risking the stench of mildew. Kel'rak broke the silence first.

"So," he started, wincing as Zek hurriedly patted downwards to indicate that he was nearly yelling and adjusted his volume accordingly, "where will you ladies be heading off to after our rest tonight?"

Samarra shifted nervously, drawing Shawna's attention. "I... can't say with certainty," she mumbled. "I feel like I still owe you all my life, but I haven't even been of any use. And YOU won't even let me see whatever that wound is that pains you!" She pointed an accusatory finger at Kel'rak, who jumped back at the sudden outburst as Zek translated to sign on the fly.

The assassin recalled the way Alizarra had roasted the group of bandits and shivered, playing it off as residual cold chill from the outside. "I already told you, I'm just a bit sore from being on the road for so long," he insisted.

Shawna kicked her feet up on the table and made it clear she was so comfortable she felt like she owned the place. Teenagers… Kel'rak thought to himself.

"I for one have no intention of walking away from you two, if you'll have me," the monk chimed in. "The grandmaster sent me on my journey, and I have the feeling it's meant to be in your company."

"We live our lives taking from the rich and smiting wrongdoers where our conscience guides us, young monk," Zek said, raising his right eyebrow slightly. "Does that fit within the moral code of a disciple of the Jade Dahlia?"

"More or less," she answered with a backhanded wave, as if shooing his prattling away.

"If Shawna is staying with you, then I am too!" Sam said. "And from now on, if you get hurt, you better well tell me damnit!"

Zekven shot Kel a look that said *"You'll live, you baby."* before raising his glass in toast to their merry band and draining it in one go.

The assassin just looked on with apathy as the companions toasted, glancing to the side at Samarra – who was staring straight at him with smoking red eyes and a smirk while the others' glasses were raised.

I'll live, but it should prove interesting, he thought to himself.

Chapter 12
The Storm

The four adventurers each took deep breaths of the brisk glacier air flowing down off the mountain pass, their ferry bouncing with the gentle waves kicked up by the wind.

Though, to call her a ferry didn't do her much justice, as the journey across the massive lake necessitated a sea-worthy vessel such as the "Lady of the Lake", the once-combat-worthy longboat they now rode upon. With her one huge sail full of the powerful icy gale, she glided across the water as fast as a horse at full sprint.

Though the others had fought him on it, Kel'rak insisted that they take the first vessel out of town, so that they might make it to South Peak at a reasonable enough hour to find lodging. He regretted that decision now, under the intense light of the cloudless sky and sun.

The assassin had gotten used to getting around in the dark of night, and the shaded ground of the forest during the day. The direct sunlight, on what may as well be an open ocean for all he could see surrounding him, was like an oppressive weight he couldn't shake. It left him feeling exposed, vulnerable, and fidgeting his fingers over the intricate details of a carved onyx figurine of a horse he had bought back at the village.

"Use that, lad." Voidtooth chimed inside his head.

I'm sorry? he replied.

"Ye'd think ye would be used tae my responses to yer thoughts by now, Lambie," it chided. "I telled ye tae use that fear. Use the vulnerability, to cloak yerself in the shadows."

The dagger imparted a vision of the shadows from the large sail bending away from their current sun-oriented position to cover Kel'rak in the comforting darkness. He turned away from the others on the vessel, grinning as he focused on doing as his weapon suggested.

Harnessing the fear, he willed the shadows upon the deck to wrap around him like a thick blanket. His shoulders slumped in relaxation, feeling immediate relief, and he let out a deep sigh. Zekven, who had been pestering the ship's captain about the finer details of nautical life, noticed the area around his companion get darker out of the corner of his eye and paused mid-thought. The rogue tuned out the captain, who was all too happy to blab about his prized ship to any interested party, as he watched Kel's mannerisms.

The way he seemed to be nodding along to a conversation, but wasn't actually speaking to anyone. It had been happening more and more of late, with the assassin beginning to appear just a tad loony. Zek made a note to keep one eye open around his friend, just in case he was for some reason close to having some sort of existential crisis or mental break.

It was a silly thing to be bothered by, but Zek would almost bet money that his friend's physical aspects were changing as well. Since they'd met, the once-tanned skin of the ex-farmer seemed to grow paler with each passing day. Whether that was a trick of the direct sunlight they were now under or not, he was unsure of, but he knew something was going on with his buddy.

And he would be there to pick up whatever pieces he could when it all came tumbling down.

***

Shawna was ironically the only member of the party who didn't manage to hold down their breakfast (and lunch). Her monk martial training proved entirely useless, her skills tied to movement on solid ground, not to finding her balance on rocking waves; however, by the time the first city belltower rose above the horizon, she had showcased her mastery over her body by finding her sea legs.

Kel'rak couldn't help himself. At Shawna's expense, he began pounding out a four-count rhythm and started up the verse and chorus he used to whistle while working the field of his new homestead up North:

Oh, I was a lad just fresh to the sea,
With a heart full of dreams, and a spirit so free,
The waves they did rock, the ship heaved and swayed,
I stumbled and fell, feeling quite dismayed.

Yo-ho-ho, as the tide did roll,
I held onto the rail, finding sea legs of old,
With the salt in my hair and the wind in my soul,
I became a sailor with stories untold.

The old salts around, with weathered, tough skin,
Said "Lad don't you worry, you'll soon fit in,
It takes time young sailor, to learn the ropes well,

Afore ye know it, ye'll have stories to tell."

Poor Shawna burned a bright red, the Captain having joined along as the rowing crew stomped out the continued beat. Zekven swept Samarra up in a dance, skipping along the limited deck space with abandon.

Kel'rak felt... joy. He beamed with pure radiance at the sudden realization that he hadn't felt this way in many years, as he looped one arm around the shoulders of the monk.

His happiness literally radiated from him, his joy magically boosting the moods of all on board the Lady of Lake. Shawna's stomach settled and the sallow look under her eyes was replaced by her normal healthy, tanned skin. The assassin himself no longer shied from the sunlight, accepting its warmth and basking in it – until he realized what he was doing.

He scrunched his face, the joy interrupted by confusion, as he didn't understand how his affinity for darkness could allow the presence of light. That confusion created fear of the unknown, as lightning crackled overhead and ominous clouds appeared from nowhere and everywhere all at once. The wind howled as the crew and his new friends ducked for cover.

Kel'rak pivoted towards Sugar, who until this point had weathered the venture across the water as the picture of calm, standing proudly at the prow like she knew her magnificence should be captured as the ship's figurehead.

The storm Kel had accidentally summoned gained in intensity, throwing waves half as tall as the ship's mast at its occupants. Samarra and Zek only just reached Shawna in time and tackled her to the safety of the deck as one such wave crashed down upon the rowers, throwing two of the six men into the lake.

Kel shadow-stepped just behind Sugar's space after the rush of water passed, hoping to secure her in place with a stronger lashing to the stern. The mare finally succumbed to her own fear though, thrashing side to side and kicking backwards in her attempts to free herself from the claustrophobic space.

One such kick connected with the outer edge of the assassin's shoulder, dislocating the arm and sending him spinning through the air to land against the mast. Already under so much strain from the storm winds, the wood cracked upon impact as Kel'rak slumped to the floor, writhing from the fiery pain in his shoulder.

He heard the splintering wood and rolled out of the way on pure instinct – but Sugar had nowhere to go. The forty-foot tall mast and equally wide sail fell like a mighty mountain pine. Caught by the heavy rope used to raise and drop the sail, instead of slamming down upon the deck it instead swung in a wide arc, the wood connecting broadside with Sugar's ribs and sending her tumbling over the edge into the water.

Kel'rak shadowstepped once again across the deck and leaned over the side in a desperate attempt to grab her reins, knowing full well he did not have the strength to drag her back up. He watched in abject terror as the waves tossed the hull of the ship into direct contact with her face, the last look from her eyes one of pleading horror. The impact knocked Sugar unconscious, and she sank like a boulder.

The assassin screamed his desperation to the skies, his fear replaced by grief, breaking apart the magical storm in a matter of seconds.

He tore at his eyes, his arms, his clothing, until he felt the onyx figurine in his pocket. Feeling the approval of Voidtooth in the back of his mind, he threw all of his grief into what would become Sugar's watery grave below, begging her to come back to him.

What came instead was a silver-blue figure, seeming to gallop through the water, both corporeal and not at the same time. As it breached the surface, it did not break through in a massive splash, but instead seemed to jump out of the water and land back upon it as if it were solid ground.

Kel'rak stared, open-mouthed, at the perfect outline of his Sugar. Only, not her. He realized this was her soul, given form by his magic. He begged for her to come closer, choking through snot and tears as his companions looked on similarly mortified. So she came closer, her hooves passing directly through the rail of the hull and stepping firmly upon the deck.

Kel reached his hand out, feeling a physical connection with her nose as she gently pushed back against his hand – a cold connection, not unlike what one might expect when a ghost passes through one's body. He wrapped his arms around her neck and hugged her tight, his shoulders rocking with sobs, begging her forgiveness.

As she too, seemed to lean into the hug, her corporeal form began to fade into a mist. Kel'rak panicked as his arms passed through the space where her neck used to be and his eyes burst open just in time to see the silver-blue mist seeming to vacuum into the onyx figurine.

He knelt there at the prow for the rest of the journey to the harbor at South Peak, Zekven standing at his side in an attempt at comfort while Sam and Shawna both knelt with him and smothered him in hugs. Somehow, he'd never felt more alone.

The captain, a man who had weathered a hundred gales, stared at the sky with a look of utter bewilderment. This wasn't a storm; it was a *reaction*. The wind howled with a malevolent intelligence, the waves rose with impossible speed, and then, just as suddenly, the fury evaporated, leaving behind an eerie calm.

He crossed his arms, muttering prayers to forgotten sea gods, his gaze fixed on Kel'rak with a chilling suspicion. This man, with his strange, silent ways, was somehow connected to this unnatural event.

***

The captain - rightfully - demanded whatever coin the group had left that hadn't fallen overboard during the storm as payment for the damages to the ship. He eyed Kel'rak specifically throughout the exchange, as though he expected a demonspawn to appear on the man's shoulder at any second. But the assassin just stared at his feet in apathy as they all emptied their coin purses, not really giving a damn what the sailor asked for.

He hadn't been able to call Sugar back. He could feel the connection to her spirit within the figurine, but it was weak.

He let his friends lead the way after they disembarked, focusing with all his might on the connection with his sweet Sugar. Zekven stoically weaved through the crowds, picking a few well-to-do pockets as he did so, gathering enough coin for the entire group to stay somewhere nice for the night. He waggled his full coin pouch to the rest of the group and asked an elderly merchant to the side of the road if they knew of any nice establishments nearby.

"Can I interest you in some lucky rocks, young man?" the old crone replied.

The woman clearly was implying her information wouldn't come free, and Zekven couldn't help but chuckle. He leaned down low and inspected the "lucky" rocks. They looked suspiciously like the dusty rocks from the road they now stood on.

"Lucky, eh?" He picked up one that was speckled through with red dots and asked, "How much for this one?"

The woman's eyes went wide and her tongue flicked out to lick her lips like a lizard, before saying, "Five silver pieces!"

Zekven raised his eyebrows at the ludicrous price but pressed on nonetheless. He could steal more coin. "How's about I give you the five silver for the rock *and* information on a nice safe place to stay?"

She snatched the coins from his outstretched hand as he pocketed the rock, and - while counting the coins - said, "The Cedarstout, down the street four blocks, turn right, then left, then it's on your left. Best beds in the city."

Zek tipped an imaginary hat at the old bat and set off at once, hoping to get some much-needed alcohol in his friend's system at once. The rock merchant's directions proved true, as the group weaved through the crowds and managed to find their destination without further issue. The place was charming, in a hospital sort of way.

Unlike the average adventurer's tavern, it was *clean*. So clean as to be suspicious. If one were to listen to rumors, they would hear that the owner of the establishment intended it to be that way.

As a former adventurer themselves, the owner and proprietor of The Cedarstout prided themselves on providing a home-away-from-home feel to their clientele. They knew the harshness of life on the road and understood the need for a feeling of utter calm and safety at the end of a long road. It was just that feeling that they strove to perfect - and a feeling that was needed now more than ever for Kel'rak, whose mind was flipping through the memories of the last few years with Sugar on repeat.

The assassin wandered off away from the group to find the darkest corner possible - a feat entirely impossible in the white-painted great room of the inn - as he fiddled with the figurine that held Sugar's soul. He habitually picked a spot that allowed him to sit with his back to the wall, but sat with his face in his hands as a few tears found their way down.

Zek's eyes followed his friend away from the bar and watched him slump into a chair looking more defeated than he'd ever seen the man. He left Shawna and Samarra at the bar with that evening's barkeep, a motherly woman who was showering them both in compliments and insisting that they take her up on the bath charge for their room, for which she would waive any extra costs for hot water, rose oil, and other pampering devices.

Zekven slunk up to the table awkwardly, not quite sure how to handle the situation. Flipping a chair around backwards so that he could lean against its back, he propped his arms up and rested his chin there, waiting in silent solidarity for Kel'rak to speak up.

The pair stayed in silent contemplation for a few minutes, with the assassin eventually leaning on one elbow and balancing

Sugar's figurine on a point so that he could spin it round and round, watching the light catch every single intricate detail of the carving.

Finally, he spoke up. "She was the last thing Cecilia ever gave me."

Zekven raised a single eyebrow in response, but otherwise stayed quiet, letting his friend say what he needed in his own time.

"My wife..." Kel'rak clarified. "Her name was Cecilia. And Sugar was the last thing she ever gave me."

"The last thing I still had from her," he finished with a croak.

Sitting up to full height and making a grand gesture, thinking to be a light-hearted source of strength, the rakish rogue responded in sign supported speech with a hearty laugh, "Based on what I saw you do on that boat, I'd argue you still have the horse!"

"Do I, though? I don't even know for sure that I can bring her back out, if she's even still in here," Kel snapped, dropping the figurine and gesturing violently as it toppled over. He quickly dropped his anger and scrambled for the small statue, righting it once more as though he thought it might break from any small impact.

"Even if I can," he continued, "I still don't have *her*. She's gone. Never again can I sleep against her side, feeling her warmth and her huge rising chest. Touching her was like the first moment of touching a piece of ice, before it feels so cold that it burns - not quite freezing but still the absolute absence of warmth." Kel'rak pressed his thumb and forefinger against the inside edges of his eye sockets and top portion of his nose, fighting off a migraine from his internal stress.

"Beyond that, did I even truly save her? She should be among the stars now, with her herd. It was selfish, what I did. I couldn't let her move on, so I trapped her. It's like I'm just becoming a darker person the more I learn to use these abilities…"

"Now that's not true!" Zekven cut in, with increasingly sharp sign, silencing his friend before he said anything else self-deprecating. "I felt that magic on the ship. I felt the warmth radiating from you! It was like a wave of pure happiness. I suddenly felt like I had the strength to fight an entire war by myself, like when you suddenly start moving so fast I can barely see you and blood just kind of starts flying. It was like you gave that to me. That can't possibly be a bad or dark thing, my friend!"

He ended the final sign with emphasis on the sign for friend, holding the linked fingers tight as though to show the strength of their building bond.

Kel'rak smiled at the rogue as he considered the implication of his articulation. He and Zekven had become like brothers, inherently sticking up for and defending the other in any given situation. They felt as though they could fight back to back against an army and win. The men trusted each other with their lives.

But Sugar had also trusted Kel with her life - and he had failed her. Nay, he had killed her. Instead of unleashing fear upon his enemies, he had set his own fear on his poor, sweet horse.

"Aye, I may have shown that I could do a good thing," he started. "But my own unfamiliarity with my abilities killed her. It was *my* fault," he emphasized.

"You cannot be–"

"I do. I do believe that Zek," Kel'rak finished the thought for him. He pulled Voidtooth from its' sheath and laid it upon the table. "This is the only thing that continues to make sense to me. This weapon and its particular ability to draw out my natural affinities, are the only thing that make any sense these days. I know that I am a dark person, and I have come to accept that."

Zekven moved to protest once again but the assassin held a hand up to silence him.

"Sugar's sacrifice - for thinking of it as such is the only way I will stay sane - showed me that I can do so much more than I thought possible. But I fear I will drag you all to the Abyss with me while I figure it out..." said Kel'rak, his eyes and voice trailing off to hide his shame.

The young women of their group signaled to both men that they were heading upstairs to take the innkeeper up on her offer of baths, both practically giddy at the idea that they would soon sit entranced by pure relaxation. Kel'rak watched over his shoulder as they left, and could have sworn he saw the flash of red indicating Alizarra's presence as she glanced at him with pity while following behind Shawna.

Great. Even a demon pities me. How pathetic must I seem, he thought to himself with a mental sigh as he slumped back once more in his chair.

Zekven found himself at a rare loss of words regarding how to handle Kel's depression. Rather than trying to further console his friend, he stood from the table and clapped him on the shoulder. "Let's take a vacation to the pits then," he signed with a big smile. "But only once have we slept on a gods-forsaken comfortable mattress and washed the grime of the road from our bodies! Then, we will see what we can't find for work in this new city."

The rogue slowly wandered through the tangle of chairs and tables and made his way back to the bar, securing their room for the night with the money he had lifted from a few purses before eventually heading upstairs himself. The only remaining patron in the room, Kel'rak felt the intense loneliness creep in once more.

"Worry not, Kel'rak, husband of Cecilia, son of none, and father to none. You are my Chosen, something I do not pick idly and a blessing which I may only give out to a single living being," the voice of the Baron echoed into his head, catching the assassin off guard with its voice that sounded like the constant low rumble of thunder on the horizon.

Though he did flinch at the intrusion, to his credit he did not flail around like a terrified toddler or otherwise signal to anyone else that anything was amiss.

"While it is indeed abnormal to display complete control of the full range of one's emotions - and therefore the full range of magics - I daresay I would hardly be a competent god if I had not correctly inferred the breadth of your potential."

"...I beg your pardon?" Kel'rak asked.

The assassin felt a pang of irritation from the mental link. "Me god. You, strong destiny. Use big magics, kill many things.'

Did I just get sassed by a god? he thought.

"Yes."

Shit. "Sorry, your….Baron…ness? Highness?" Kel replied over their mental link.

"Don't apologize," it replied. "Powerful people don't apologize, they just get more powerful and make people fear their retribution. Now, stop worrying about the complexities of dark, light, good, and evil, and just go rest. I think you will find there are many tools to test your strength within this city," the Baron finished, its voice trailing off as the unexpected mental link was severed.

The absence of the divine connection left Kel'rak with the realization that the brand upon his chest was itching, and he wondered if that might be an indicator to prevent such a surprise in the future. He snatched up Sugar's figurine and bounded up the stairs, all self doubt forgotten as he rushed to find the rooms Zekven had secured.

J.A. McCoy

Zaulyl's Log
In Moments of Doubt

With Cecilia's death, the numbness consumed me. The world went silent. I wanted it to end. I wanted to fade into nothingness. It wasn't merely sadness; it was a cessation of all feeling, a dull throb that absorbed every other sensation.

The world became muted, colors bled out, sounds softened to an indistinguishable hum. I walked through days as if through a fog, the faces of others indistinct, their words mere echoes. My body moved, breathed, ate, but it felt hollow, animated by nothing but the lingering habit of existence.

My wife had been the sun around which my small world orbited, and when she was extinguished, the cold, boundless darkness of space consumed me.

With Sugar's passing, I recognize that now as the foolish whinging of a man who thought he had nothing left to lose. To think I was lost, truly lost, when I simply fled. Fled from the pity in their eyes, the awkward condolences, the impossible expectation that I should just 'move on.'

I saw it as freedom then, a rightful escape from a world that had betrayed me. Now, I see it as childish, a tantrum of a man who refused to face his pain with anything but abandonment.

I thought I had nothing left to lose, but I lost something far more precious: my own integrity, my connection to those who might have held me when I couldn't hold myself.

Looking back, I think she would have been disappointed in me. Nay, I know it. I left everything we had ever known, ever built, for my own selfish desires. As if the people who cared for us, wouldn't care for me in my time of need. My neighbors, who had shared our hearth on cold nights. The old widows Cecilia visited with baskets of food. My fellow soldiers, who had fought beside me.

I simply walked away, severing every tie, convinced my grief was a unique burden that no one else could possibly comprehend or alleviate. The very bedrock of community, of shared humanity, I discarded like a broken tool. Cecilia, who cherished kindness and loyalty above all else, would have seen that as a profound failure.

I deserved to grieve - I absolutely did. But abandoning everything was the wrong way to go about it. To assume that my pain negated my responsibilities to others, that it justified leaving them to wonder, to worry… that was the selfish core of my despair.

It wasn't bravery, or freedom. It was cowardice wrapped in self-pity.

With Sugar, I have another chance to do it right. I will miss my sweet girl, but I will not let the grief paralyze me this time. I can still feel her warm, gentle nudges against my leg, hear the soft nicker of her approval when I found a particularly sweet patch of grass. Her spirit, now a faint thrum in the onyx figurine, is a constant, subtle reminder of what I've lost.

But this time, the pain does not consume; it fuels. It hardens my resolve, rather than softening my will.

I have found a new family, a new purpose, I think. These people rely on me, and seem to care for me. I will not abandon them as I did the rest.

They have become anchors in a world that still feels adrift. We have shared laughter, fear, triumphs, and exhaustion. We have eaten together, fought together, watched each other's backs.

They look to me. For guidance, for protection, for leadership, even if unspoken. Zek trusts my judgment. Shawna watches my back. Samarra... Samarra sees more than she lets on, and still chooses to stand by me. Even a demon, for some reason, is relying on me to keep her safe.

This reliance, this unspoken bond, has given me a new compass point. A purpose that isn't about escaping, but about defending. A purpose that forces me to engage, to be present, to live.

Somehow, for some deluded reason, it took the intervention of a god to teach me that. I sat there, numb, spinning the figurine, the world a blur of apathy. He... They....It? Completely disregarded that paralytic I had come to know as a close friend. He simply waved aside my numbness, as if it were a wisp of smoke. His gaze, piercing and ancient, drilled into me, and for the first time in what felt like an eternity, I felt seen.

Not as a broken man, but a man defined by his scars. He didn't offer sympathy; he offered a challenge. He pointed to my potential, a fact he poignantly reminded me I would be wasting if I let the grief consume me again.

Certainly, no small amount of credit should be denied the voice in my head - that of this dagger. It, too, recognized the potential and helped me to unlock it.

But even the dagger prostrates itself before the Baron. The Baron who chose ME. He saw the fire beneath the ashes of my despair – the raw, untapped power I had only begun to understand. He didn't just see a man with a magical dagger; he saw the man behind the dagger, the one who could truly shape its power, not merely be consumed by it. He saw the resilience that made me uniquely suited for... something greater.

He looked past the glowing blade, past the whispers of fear, and saw me. Kel'rak. The shepherd, the husband, the man who had lost everything.

He saw my capacity, my scars, my untapped resilience. And he chose me for a purpose that transcended my petty revenge against Delmar, a purpose that stretched beyond simply surviving. He chose me to defend and protect those who are still here, those who have yet to face the horrors to come.

I am learning, day-by-day, that there is always more. This isn't facile optimism, not a denial of the deep, tearing agony that comes with loss. It is a truth forged in the crucible of despair. The pain, the sorrow, the moments of utter desolation – they carve deeper channels in the soul, not to empty us, but to allow more to flow through.

There is always more potential, more energy, more capability than the day prior. Even once a man has drained himself digging a trench, he might lay down to recuperate and find more of himself the next day to dig a little further. That trench digger, utterly spent, might find not just renewed strength, but a new efficiency in his movements, a deeper understanding of the earth itself.

He might dig not just further, but smarter, because he knows the cost of depletion.

Even when a forest is felled by loggers, life blooms once more with time. The logging leaves behind a barren landscape, stumps like broken teeth in the earth.

But given time, the roots, unseen and tenacious, will send up new shoots.

The forest will not be the same, perhaps wilder, perhaps tougher, but it will live. It will thrive. It will carry the memory of the pain, but it will also carry the promise of renewed growth, a testament to life's unyielding will.

For certain, different pains require different amounts of recovery, but the scars leave us more resilient. Scars are not just the marks of healing; they are lessons etched onto the very fabric of our being. They remind us of where we've been, how we've been broken, but also of how we've mended.

They are the toughened skin, the deeper roots, the more resilient wood. They are the proof that we survived, and because we survived, we learned. We learned to absorb the blow, to bend rather than break, and to rise with a quiet, fierce determination.

We bounce back harder. We don't just return to what we were; we return stronger, sharper, more aware of the knife's edge of existence. The world may try to fell us, to consume us with grief, to blind us with despair. But each blow leaves us with a deeper understanding of its force, and a greater capacity to withstand the next.

We become not just survivors, but inheritors of a harder-won strength. And that strength, I now understand, is a gift to be wielded.

A god told me directly that I am more than the sum of my parts. I am more than my affinity for the darkness. I can do more than the dagger would have me believe. Yes, it is a conduit for that which I feel the deepest, but I will no longer let it tempt me, let it guide my hand. I will not let the doubt hook its creeping

Scars

tendrils into my heart and crush my potential. I will not allow the grief of loss to paralyze me again.

I will fill those deeper channels with more - ever more - and let my scars tell my story. I am more than the sum of my parts.

Chapter 13
The Job

Zekven awoke with a jolt of pain as his heavy sword belt was tossed onto his blanket-covered hip. Squinting through the initial fog of the first few seconds within waking up, his face scrunched in confusion as he looked around the room.

He knew he had heard Kel'rak come in around the same time he was drifting off to sleep, and it didn't look like anything was out of place from last night - save for the sword belt laying across his body. The assassin confirmed for him that it was indeed the early morning hours as he flung the curtains open, allowing a flood of blinding sunlight to cascade over Zek's still unadjusted eyes.

Hissing in pain and flailing over backwards, he cursed in Kel's general direction and swore payback when he least expected it. Shortly thereafter, he remembered the man couldn't hear his tirade.

This left him feeling more than a little foolish, humbling him in an instant, so he waited for the assassin to turn around before signing "What in the bloody hells is going on?" with all the exasperation he would muster.

Not bothering to sign back, Kel'rak responded aloud, "It is a new day, in a new city, with new contacts to be made. And we need money."

He said this last bit as he waggled their once-more empty coin purse at his bleary-eyed friend.

"Well that was quick," Zekven replied in sign supported speech. "What turned your mood around, oh gloomy one? Find a nice maid to frisk in a dark alley?"

The assassin looked genuinely offended.

"Ah…right…sorry…"

"We've not made it this far by holding onto regrets, my friend," Kel'rak began. "The time to mourn has passed. It is still early morn, and I believe I saw a job board just inside the door when we came in. With any luck, we can have some funds to buy our companions some breakfast before they realize we are gone."

He finished this last statement with a forceful jerk as he tightened the last strap of his leather armor onto his chest, staring at Zek expectantly as if that was all the explanation necessary for him to jump to his feet like some sort of zealot.

Groaning, Zekven threw his sword belt back at Kel'rak – who side stepped the clumsy throw, letting the belt fall to his mattress – and rolled over back to sleep. The assassin just shook his head at the rogue and drew the curtains closed once more, letting his friend rest as long as he needed.

For now, he would hunt.

Rounding the corner as he came down the stairs, the common room was about the same as he had left it, with the exception of one additional patron from last night's stay enjoying a plate of breakfast.

His stomach howled as the smell of it carried across the room and from out of the kitchen. Piled high with sausages, flapjacks, and some smaller kind of bird's eggs – and paired with a glass of fruit juice – the steaming plate was the most delectable thing he had seen in weeks.

Determined to make it back in time to enjoy a full platter of the same, he made a beeline straight for the job board he had seen before.

While there was plenty of honest work to be had, his was the business of violence, not toiling under the sun and biting winter wind. Finally, his gaze fell upon the kind of work he had hoped for - a bounty. The words "dead or alive" further excited him, as it made the job easier. Without having to bring the individual in for questioning, he could finish up the job quicker, higher payment be damned.

The artist who had sketched the picture of the criminal in question had created a marvelously detailed piece, from the upper portion of the torso covered in fine clothes to the perfectly manicured light brown hair and beard. The target in question was undoubtedly a rakish man who had managed to use his charms to talk his way out of one-too-many situations, and the tactic had caught up to him.

Kel'rak glazed over the reported charges hefted against the man, not really caring what his crime was. At the end of the day, it was all the same, and he was now an assassin - like it or not.

Ripping the page from the board, he held it up to the new barkeep on shift before taking a piece of writing coal and asking in the blank space on the page "Where would I go to collect this bounty?" pointing once more to his ears to indicate his deafness.

The barkeep looked over Kel'rak skeptically at the revelation of his disability, but if he had more opinion on the matter he kept his mouth shut, instead writing "Magistrate" on the backside of the bounty sheet and doing his best to provide signs meaning to leave the front door of the inn and walk two blocks to the West.

Scars

Confident that the barkeep was not messing with him, he nodded his thanks before turning around and walking completely silent out the front door. The barkeep, a man who had seen his share of strange folk, felt a sudden, inexplicable chill as Kel'rak moved. There was no sound, no scuff of boot, no rustle of cloth. It was as if the man simply glided, a ghost in the morning light.

A shiver traced its way down his spine, and he instinctively clutched the amulet around his neck, muttering a silent prayer. He couldn't explain the feeling, but it was the kind of unnatural silence that made the hairs on his arms stand on end, a premonition of something deeply wrong.

He felt better once the unsettling, silent man was gone, but the memory lingered, a cold knot in his stomach.

As fate would have it, there was a fantastic chance that Kel'rak would indeed get that breakfast today.

Opting to walk in the direction opposite of the Magistrate's office, because what criminal would willingly walk to the home of the law, he spotted his target within minutes. The young man was trying to get a five finger discount on the city square's fruit merchant, distracting the older woman with his physical looks and honeyed words.

The criminal had had a wardrobe change, different from the clothes in the sketch, but undeniably still *him* in their base level of extravagance. The assassin let the scenario play out, vowing to gather up and return the woman's stolen food after all was said and done.

As his target departed the city square, he stalked him from about a hundred feet away, staying only just in view of the man at all times so as not to spook him unnecessarily. The man cut through several alleys, winding along what seemed to be a predetermined path, before reaching a plain red tent held up by nothing more than a taut line spanning the width of the alleyway.

The tent seemed too small for an entire adult man to comfortably lay in, much less sleep inside of - an issue double-downed on once his target fully disappeared from view.

Must be some kind of trap door or otherwise well-placed means of escape, he thought to himself.

Kel'rak entered the alley his target had disappeared into with Voidtooth palmed against his wrist, concealing it from view as he crept up to the tent, danger sense on full alert to the potential for ambush. But as he reached the tent flap and peered inside, his suspicions were confirmed by the sight of a sewer grate with the telltale scrapes on the ground indicating frequent use of the entrance.

Releasing the tension in his body from the held breath, Kel'rak tried a new technique with his magic. Recognizing and embracing the fear one should naturally feel from needing to enter a dark sewer without their sense of hearing, his eyes began to leak black smoke, which coalesced into two separate tendrils of semi-solid matter that quested down through the bars of the grate into the unknown below.

Gliding down the two primary support bars of a metal ladder into the murk of the sewer, the smoky tendrils reached the bottom and detected no immediate signs of life. Kel'rak - while removing the grate and beginning to climb down the ladder - sent each shadow sentry down opposite directions of the tunnel in search of his target.

The sentries passed various mushrooms and mud, but he noted a general lack of any standard sewer waste. This was a closed off, meticulously chosen home base. The man was smart, if an asshole.

He immediately enacted the magical silence of his boots as he stepped down the last few ladder rungs, making each step as quiet as if it had never been taken and ensuring he wouldn't give his target any forewarning of his coming.

Just as he made it to the sewer floor, the shadow sentry he had sent to the right encountered a dead end with another ladder leading up out of the underground maze. It had passed a few smaller tunnels only big enough for lesser amounts of waste from the buildings above ground and the rats that might scurry through and come across no life, so he dismissed the sentry, focusing instead on the one he had sent to the left.

Thanks to the enchantment upon his boots, he no longer crept along, instead striding confidently through the tunnel after the sentry and relying on it to be his eyes in the dark as it cleared the way for him.

Finally, a rat here and there. Where there were rats, there were food sources. Keeping the sentry about fifty feet ahead of him in the darkness, he continued forward through the bends in the tunnels, still passing minor tubes as before.

Just when he was beginning to get frustrated with the entire maze, he saw some pale light ahead around a right turn in the tunnel. He slowed down and directed the sentry to float up to the ceiling and it came around the corner, peering into the open space beyond.

The space he saw through the sentry's pseudo-consciousness was a colorless hub to the sewer, with all of the various tunnels connecting in this one room, a main drain tunnel located at the base of a slight decline in the floor.

The light Kel'rak had initially thought to come from the sun in the world above actually came from a hooded lantern placed upon a pole on the edge of a small, but lavish encampment. To the best of the sentry's abilities, there was no one present but the assassin's target, laying back in his cot and licking his fingers clean of the sugary fruit he had recently finished.

Dismissing the second sentry, the assassin took a circuitous route along the right-hand side of the room to avoid the thief's field of view. He mimicked a stealthed stride, not for the sake of sound, but to minimize his visible profile.

Internally questioning whether this was too easy or if magic was really just this overpowered, he struck. Voidtooth plunged hungrily into the thief's neck, drinking in the man's essence and cutting through the skin like a hot knife on butter. The most grisly of the work complete, Kel'rak summoned more of Voidtooth's corrosive shadowstuff to clean his hands of the gore and to remove the dripping blood from the severed head as he walked back the way he had come, gripping the head by a tuft of the once-manicured hair.

As the assassin turned the corner of the tunnel that would take him away from the central hub, a green light appeared, completely unnoticed by him. It first seemed to emanate from the chest area of the decapitated body, leaking out through the neck area, but emerged fully from where the heart was located.

Floating upward about four feet into the air, the soul of Nalgren Durre did not move on to the afterlife, but down another dark tunnel to the awaiting hands of a black and crimson-clad woman.

Rather than joining the soul vault inside her mind, Nalgren's soul was offered to the drooling mouth of a massive wolf-dog, who lapped it up like a drink of water. Amelia's eyes stayed glued to the tunnel entrance though, still entranced by the display of magic the assassin had made. She wasn't alone.

Amelia's eyes, sharp and discerning, tracked Kel'rak's movements with a chilling familiarity. She saw the subtle shift in the air around him, the way he seemed to bend the very shadows to his will. She recognized the cold efficiency of his kill, the effortless way he commanded his weapon.

He was like her, a creature of necessity, forged in the fires of loss. A kindred spirit in the growing darkness. The world might call him an 'assassin,' but she saw the true power beneath the surface, a reflection of her own burgeoning monstrosity.

***

Kel'rak emerged from the sewer, head in hand, and quickly realized the general populace would likely balk at the open carry of such a prize. His eyes fell upon the fabric of the tent that covered the sewer grate, which he greedily cut a large piece from to fashion a sack, using both the fabric of the tent and the cord that held it aloft.

Rising to his full height, Kel'rak slung the sack over his shoulder as though he were carrying naught but personal belongings, and made his way back through town towards the magistrate's office.

The entire ordeal had taken no more than an hour, the sun only now beginning to fully crest the horizon. He was making fantastic time, and suspected he could be back in time for breakfast, as promised.

Kel stuck to the alleyways he had traversed on the way to the hidden camp, waiting to emerge into the main thoroughfare until he reached the marketplace, which was now much busier than the hour prior. The magistrate's office was only a short walk, taking naught but ten minutes from the market at a leisurely stride. He didn't want to draw any attention to the bundle in his hands, after all.

The assassin decided to knock instead of just barging in, given that it was still the early morning hours. He waited a few heartbeats before he felt the dull vibrations of weighted feet approaching from the other side of the door. The door itself was jostled a few times, as he assumed bolts were being undone, before being opened by a frazzled looking soldier in plate armor.

"What is the meaning of such an early disturbance?!" the man Kel'rak determined to be a Captain, based on the insignia, demanded.

"Good morrow, Captain," he began cheerily. "I apologize for any inconvenience I've caused you by arriving so early, and for the accommodation I will have to ask you to make for my deafness. I have come to collect a bounty."

The Captain glowered at him with a single raised eyebrow, taking note of the tell-tale signs of tone-deafness in Kel'rak's speech that indicated his spoken truth, before simply gesturing that he come in.

The room they entered met the same aesthetic of every military structure Kel'rak had ever seen in his life from before his wife's death and his subsequent self-exile to the peninsula. It was simple, clean, and brown - boringly so. Except, that is, for the Captain's desk which was strewn with various papers and reports from the goings-on of the city.

The officer waited for Kel'rak to sit before doing so himself, wincing at the unintentional screech his armor made as one plate shifted over another. He would have to oil it later. Noting once again that Kel'rak didn't respond as one with working ears would, he nodded, pleased with the accidental confirmation that the man was not just trying to swindle him.

Raising his gauntleted hand to rub the sleepiness from his eyes, the Captain picked up the pile of wanted posters on the left side of his desk and arranged them for the assassin to choose from. Kel'rak placed his red bundle on top of the poster for Nalgren and untied the sack. The Captain's eyes went wide and he jerked back involuntarily as the pained face of a man who had died from his head being sawed off was revealed in all of its splendor.

Kel'rak sneered at the Captain's response, tying the bundle around the head once more to spare the weak-stomached soldier any more discomfort.

The officer reached for a paper and quill, writing out his name to be "Captain Remillard" and gesturing to himself then writing "Fifty gold pieces", before offering a hand to shake on the accepted bounty. Kel'rak responded in kind, shaking Captain Remillard's hand with a deceptively strong grasp before taking the proffered pouch.

As Remillard passed the pouch, he held a finger up to ask that Kel'rak wait before leaving and wrote, "In the future, if you *must* kill the target, please leave the body at the scene and inform the Officer On Duty of its location. An agent will investigate the site to confirm the kill, and we will send payment to your place of residence."

"Of course, Captain," Kel'rak replied, rising from the chair with a smile. Over his shoulder as he headed for the door, he said, "As further assistance to the Magistrate, if you head to the sewer entrance about five blocks South of here, you will find a large piece of red fabric" - he motioned to the sack on the desk once more - "covering the sewer grate. Entering the sewer from there, hang a left and you will eventually come to the central sewer drain where the target was camped. I noted that this entry-tunnel was utterly dry of any refuse. I suspect your office will make a lot of homeowners happy by unclogging their drains..."

Kel'rak stepped once more into the morning sunlight, closing the door to the Magistrate's office behind him, feeling quite good about his work. He made his way back to The Cedarstout Inn, reversing the effect of his magical boots, instead making them clack loudly against the cobblestones as he strolled down the lane.

While he could not hear the sound, he could feel the vibrations in his heel as he walked, and he knew many eyes were on him.

Several of those pairs of eyes watched him walk in with a bundle, and walk back out with a large pouch of coin. These folk watched this sort of thing happen daily, and knew the look of a dangerous bounty hunter when they saw one.

The whispers followed him like a second shadow.

'Did you see him? Went in without a sound, now he's waking the dead!'

'They say he doesn't speak, just... knows.'

'Yes Muriel, I know just as well as you what was in that sack. There was no blood! No man could do that alone.'

'It's unnatural, I tell you. He's got the mark of the old ones on him.'

The fear was a subtle undercurrent, a growing unease that permeated the market. They didn't understand *how* he did it, only that it defied their understanding of normal men, and therefore, it must be something dark, something to be feared.

Though Kel'rak couldn't hear the rumor train begin to spin its wheels, he grinned as he saw the many homeowners, shopkeepers, and other citizens begin to whisper among themselves.

***

As it turned out, this easy bounty would set the group up at the inn for several weeks, with just five gold pieces affording the four of them their rooms and services - with the works - for an entire week. Kel'rak was already seated at the same table he had been at the previous night, greedily scarfing down biscuits and white gravy with sausage patties when Zekven, Shawna, and Samarra finally came down the stairs.

He greeted his friends with cheer and waved over to the barkeep, signaling that his party was ready for their food. Three more steaming plates were brought and set in front of them. All three people just stared at him, dumbfounded.

"I did some perfectly legal work this morning for the city," he said, still sitting there with a stupid grin on his face.

He was happy again, accepting it this time. He embraced that happiness and spread the warmth of his aura to his friends subtly as they each took the first bites of their food. They swore up and down that it was single handedly the best biscuits and gravy any of them had ever had in their lives.

The awkwardness of the initial shock passed and they spent the morning chatting about nothing and everything, from rumored locations they all wanted to visit in the city to things they hoped to see at some point in their lifetimes, as Zekven happily translated everything to sign. He was just content that Kel'rak seemed to be past the events of the day prior.

When their plates were all empty and their stomachs full to the point of bloating, they all sat back in near unison and breathed deep sighs of contentment. Just then, the door to the inn opened to the late-morning sun and a woman entered the building.

A large grey dog entered with her, whose head she gently stroked and pointed off to the side to indicate where it should stay. It laid down just inside the door and to the right, finding a nook of shade where the sunlight couldn't quite reach between the inner floor and wall.

The woman first looked to the bar, and then snapped her eyes to the group of four as she made a bee line for their table.

"For an assassin, you're a surprisingly easy man to find, sir," she said with a surprised tone.

Zekven translated this, to which Kel'rak responded, "I'm sorry but I don't think we've met before, miss…?

"Oh my, I am so sorry. My name is Amelia," she said while extending her hand.

Kel'rak accepted the offered handshake and Zekven cut in, introducing everyone present before saying, "What can we do for you Amelia?"

"Well," she began awkwardly, shifting from foot to foot and wringing her hands together, "I was investigating a bounty, one Nalgren Durre. In following his trail, I came to his encampment expecting to be able to make my arrest, only to find him slain."

Zekven, Shawna, and Samarra all quickly glanced Kel'rak's way before turning their attention back to Amelia. Kel'rak just smiled through it all, not caring in the slightest that his friends now realized how he had made his "perfectly legal" money.

"Naturally, I went to the local magistrate to see if anyone had collected the bounty, hoping that I might still collect it for myself in the event that Mr. Durre's death was a murder of other origin. But the Captain on duty there said that the bounty had just been collected within the hour. When I asked him who you were, should I want to also hire you, he just said that a man with a shaved head wearing black leathers had collected the bounty without giving his name or location. It didn't take long to question the citizens outside to find where you'd gone - you didn't exactly... hide it," she finished in a meek expression.

"So, you're here to seek revenge on a sniped bounty?..." Zekven asked, surprised the woman would be bold enough to do so.

Her eyes opened wide, her fear and embarrassment on full display.

"No! No such thing sir!"

Samarra reached over to push another chair out for Amelia and gently touched her hand, smiling sweetly and offering the seat. The woman glanced over her shoulder once to check on her dog, who was snoring loudly even from across the common room, before accepting the seat.

"I only wanted to ask, would you be interested in hunting something more dangerous than a common thief?"

Chapter 14
The Mountain

High up on the upper third of Hell's Peaks, Winter was in full swing. The skycutter mountains were blanketed in the pure white of fresh undisturbed snow, even her needle-like pine trees coated in the frozen glitter of the season, eliminating all other colors from the terrain. The bulk of her residents were either hibernating for the coming months, or blended into the changed landscape as well as a ghost in a deep fog.

The truly observant might notice the black-speckled snowy owl diving through the air to catch its prey, or catch a glimpse of a pure-white fox prancing through the snow as it tries to pierce the thick layers to catch a mouse. But by and large, it was a desolate place to be.

It would continue to be this way for the next four months, having only just entered the coldest period. The island continent was provided with a near-constant atmospheric push of moisture from one direction or another, and Hell's Peaks were located at essentially the geographic center of it all.

Many among the enlightened races believed this to be an unlivable hellscape, hence the naming of the mountain range. Some even believed that their souls would be banished here if they lived an unworthy life, a location not exactly the common understanding of eternal torment, but rather eternal dismay.

An everlasting lack of joy.

One enlightened being, on the other hand, enjoyed the peace this superstition provided her. Having made her home somewhere between the lowest point of snow and the peak of the second-to-last mountain in the range, Pyrwineth the Eternal had lived over five centuries free from the ravages of time and the many crusades of men and gods alike.

In her cavern, built deep into the mountainside, she enjoyed a life of luxury. The snow could not reach her, the fearsome winds lost their bite, and the occasional snack even wandered in of its own accord. She never had to hunt, forage, or otherwise leave her home as everything was provided to her.

The warmth of the innermost sanctum even rose to the furthest reaches of the ceiling, creating an evermelt from encroaching snow in an upper ventilation shaft that dropped water into a pool for her to drink from.

Even the elusive dwarven race deep in their mountain tunnels had never bothered her, as she had chosen a spot above the main level of their city, the upside down pyramid that it was. They lived their lives in the eternal quest for precious metals, their inherent avarice leading them further and further down into the earth – not up.

Well… there was that one time, when a small party of young dwarves had come up the mountain in search of juniper berries and winter spices for their meadery. Pyrwineth had decided that day that she didn't care much for the taste of dwarves. Their meat was too dense and gamey. Like the difference between chewing a perfectly cooked fish and chewing a well-smoked piece of jerky.

The flavor wasn't bad, but the entire process was just too much work.

Of all the many comforts of her home though, she was most proud of her collection. Art, in all of its many forms, adorned every available space of the innermost cavern. Paintings of every size, medium, and theme were hung from the walls. Portraits of every major ruler throughout the history of Litharia were grouped by region and society.

The works of every well-known – and some less – poet and musician lay written upon unrolled vellum on desks made from the finest carpenters known to the annals of history. An instrument of every known kind lay encased and displayed in a box of glass on the rear wall, shined, polished, and otherwise maintained to pristine condition. Among her favorite treasures were row upon row of deep cherry red bookshelves which lined the floors and covered seventy percent of the open space in the two hundred foot radius cavern.

They were filled with historical, religious, informational, and otherwise fantastical texts written by hundreds of different authors throughout the eras.

She walked down the aisle of two such rows now, her fingers trailing along the spines of the books, the sensitive skin of the fingertips tingling from the varying textures of their bindings. Her collected written works numbered in the tens of thousands. She had read all of them, twice over, and knew the exact location of each novel.

Stopping suddenly, she pivoted left and grabbed the book on The Reckoning, penned by Brother Karthemere of the Holy Church - the only major organized religion to have survived the disappearance of the gods. In this most recent crusade driven by humankind, the main target had been magic users of their own race; however, magical creatures of all kinds had been included in the hunt, either forcing them to flee this plane of existence or hide in holes such as the one she now resided in.

Pyrwineth waved a hand as she turned back the way she'd come, causing the book to float in front of her and allowing her to study as she walked. She flipped through the pages absentmindedly as she meandered back to the main living space, another huge cavern adorned with plush bear skins from end to end, filling the floor with eclectic splotches of black, brown, and white.

She guided the book higher into the air as the reached the center of the room, her elvish form giving way to a much larger transformation to her natural body.

The nails of her hands and bare feet extended in length and mass to become pearlescent claws, while the blood red lightweight dress she wore seemed to melt into her skin and cover the entirety of her body, solidifying and hardening into individual diamond-hard scales.

Her tailbone extended a full fifty feet in length, growing six inch spines all along and ending in a single blade-shaped spike the length of a greatsword. Massive batlike wings sprouted from her shoulder blades before tucking up against the scales of her main body, which filled a space the size of a two-story longhouse. Her neck extended about half the length of the tail, becoming serpentine in shape with scales covering the top half and bony plates covering the underside.

As her snout finally formed, hot sulfur blew from her nostrils and she recoiled for fear of damaging the precious book in any way. Pyrwineth the Eternal, the Ravager, the Ruiner, Fear Incarnate, the ancient red dragon, rolled over to her side and turned a page with a mental flick as her attendant scurried from the reading room with a whimper.

Kel'rak and the others stared with blank expressions at Amelia, as if waiting for her to elaborate further, so she kept talking.

"In my travels, I have also learned to make my living doing the work that others might shy from," the witch began. "The first of one such assignments I found when arriving to South Peak indicated that multiple fur trappers have gone missing while on hunts in Hell's Peaks. This ordinarily would be of no concern to the city, but they are starting to feel the beginning pains of a lack of leathers in the market. This speaks to me of a larger threat than simple bears, so I have yet to venture out into the wild."

As Zekven finished translating to sign, Kel replied, "So your first thought was to find an assassin to help you hunt...a big animal?"

If Amelia was annoyed at Kel'rak's flippant reply, she was very good at hiding it.

"More likely, a band of brigands," she answered, waving a hand dismissively. "The problem is that I don't know exactly how big of a threat this is. I haven't even been out into the wilderness to check."

It was Shawna's turn for sass. "You mean to tell me you're trying to hire people for an unknown amount of money, to do an unknown amount of dirty work, for a complete and total stranger? Did I miss something?"

"No... I dare say you have the complete picture," the witch said, still maintaining her calm facade.

"You drive a hard bargain sister. I'm in!" the monk exclaimed. "I followed these dummies here with no real plan, so what's to say this isn't our plan?"

"I will admit, it is a sense of purpose we are sorely lacking," Zekven cut in.

Samarra side-eyed Kel'rak, but followed up with, "I owe Shawna my life, so where she goes, I will follow."

Zek finished signing everyone's responses and all heads at the table turned back to Kel'rak, who still just sat there leaned back in the chair with crossed arms. Though he knew what the weapon's response would be, he tossed a mental raised eyebrow to Voidtooth to ask its opinion.

It just answered with a deep, passionate feeling of pure hunger.

Yeah, that's what I thought. He sighed.

"I'll have to toss the owner a few extra gold to make sure our rooms aren't touched."

A cheer erupted around the table, with cries of "Drinks!" from Zekven. The entire mood of the room turned lighter, but two people still maintained their composure. Kel'rak and Amelia stared across the table at one another, both adopting a smile to appease their comrades. Amelia's leveled gaze was sweet, almost angelic in its sincerity.

But her smile was knowing, and Kel'rak couldn't quite place it.

I'll just have to cross that bridge when I get to it, he thought. *I seem to keep attracting these situations where I don't know what I'm getting myself into. First a god, then a demon, and now a snipe hunt affecting an entire city I don't belong to.*

Scars

Amelia rose from her chair, turning towards the door and her... pet? Glancing back over her shoulder, she said, "I'll meet you all outside the North gate tomorrow after dawn. Most places inside the city aren't as accommodating to Colson" – she gestured to the giant wolf dog, then waved in thanks to the barkeep – "as this one is."

With that, she left - the dog loping along after her, standing just above waist-height. The ragtag group of friends spent the rest of the day drinking, eating, and discussing the supplies they might need for such an adventure. Kel'rak paid double the normal rate for their rooms to ensure the highest security was placed on what was essentially their new home base.

This left him with roughly thirty gold to his name, his purse already feeling light compared to an hour ago.

They couldn't play this game with a careless attitude though. There was a very real possibility this was not their common small group of highwaymen. It could be an entire band of mercenaries, or an army of evil creatures, or something bigger. Until they knew what, no expense would be spared to ensure the safety of his companions - especially if the kind of cash flow earned from this morning's easy job was anything to say about their future prospects.

Kel already had everything he needed for adventuring stowed in his pack upstairs, which he kept ready by his bedside that night so that they might leave as soon as the first light of day crested the horizon. The rest of the group gathered the necessary things as they readied their bags for the next day. Packs with bed rolls, rations, a few lengths of rope, and some wound dressings were among the most popular topics of conversation; although, Samarra was insistent the last item wouldn't be necessary.

Everyone present packed a roll of clean linens just in case.

The barkeep sent them off with a few bundles of smoked jerky for the generous overpayment of their rooms and wished them luck on their endeavor. They exited the Cedarstout at first light, to the West towards the magister's office, in search of a few key items – chief among them: a spyglass for scouting, some sort of melee self-defense weapon for Samarra, a bow and quiver for Zek, and some form of trapping equipment.

The first shop they happened upon had several bear traps for trade, as well as a quiver and a sturdy shortbow with enough draw power to fell an elder buck in a single shot.

This westerly route past the magister's office invariably led them back towards the wharf they had landed at. The others all threw a glance Kel'rak's way when they saw him stopped, staring out over the water at the mast of the ship that had brought them, which had departed towards Hell's Ferry around breakfast time after receiving some repairs to the main mast over the last thirty-six hours.

Shaking the cobwebs from his head and dropping the horse figurine he'd been gripping back into his belt pouch, the assassin realized he had fallen behind and jogged to catch up.

The group turned North, heading towards the gate that would lead them to the mountains, after stopping inside a waterfront shop that provided a plain spyglass and the opportunity to purchase a simple cutlass and sheath for Samarra. The innocent looking woman belted it with what seemed to be great hesitation, and only then at the behest of Shawna who insisted that she have a way to defend herself should they get separated.

Zek and Kel passed a knowing, silent look towards each other at the behavior of their youngest member and chuckled.

They spent the last of Kel's four remaining gold on the rental of a few horses - if not to ride, then to at least carry many of the supplies that would weigh them down in their travels northward. This was not to say that they were completely poor – Zekven was nothing, if not an expert kleptomaniac while on the move.

He picked the pockets of any well-to-do member of the city they passed, changing shape any time it seemed like someone noticed his transgression and blending into the crowds like nothing had happened.

Amelia stood outside the cross-hatched iron gates of South Peak, as promised, conversing with one of the standard-bearing gate guards as though they were good friends. As they approached, she passed what looked like a cheesecloth satchel of leafy greens to the man, telling him to steep it in boiling water for three minutes before serving the tea to his wife for her pain.

He thanked her with a vigorous double-fisted handshake and a strong embrace, nearly strangling the poor woman and crushing her against the hard steel of his plate armor. Her wolf-dog, Colson, growled when the witch let slip a slight squeak of pain and the soldier fired off a string of apologies.

Everyone but Kel'rak had a good laugh, and Zekven decided to spare the guard further embarrassment by exclaiming, "Miss Amelia! Our apologies for not being here earlier, some of us get a tad grumpy when we don't get our full night's sleep."

He finished the last thought by jabbing his thumb over his shoulder towards Kel'rak, who just gave him a look that would wilt even the most ancient willow.

"Nothing to apologize for, Master Teluil," the witch replied sweetly. "I was just giving Master Finnegan here some muscle relaxer for his wife, who just graced his home with a newborn child."

Everyone, even Kel'rak, shook the proud new father's hand at the news. The soldier's face would split in twain were he able to grin any harder. His chest puffed up a little bit with the vigorous confidence of a man whose life just hit a major positive turning point.

"You are all obviously welcome to come and go as you please, and I will ensure to pass the same information along to my fellows," Finnegan offered. "I am in Miss Amelia's debt, and if you are her accompanying protectors, then I extend the same to you. Please, help us to figure out what is happening to our trappers."

In an uncharacteristic display of professionalism, Shawna chimed in, "By the oaths and teachings of the Temple of the Jade Dahlia, I promise you we will not return empty handed."

Finnegan raised an eyebrow towards Shawna, as if seeing her truly for the first time in the small group of people, though he had just shaken her hand.

Setting his jaw, he nodded firmly in response. "I have heard many tales of your people, young monk. I should very much like to spar with you, if time allows, when you return."

He finished the last statement by grabbing his shortsword from its scabbard in a reverse grip and raising the pommel to his brow in a respectful salute, both hands firmly grasping the hilt by either side. Shawna responded in kind, similarly grasping her bo staff in a salute and bending slightly at the waist.

He'd heard vague tales, of warrior-priests who moved with impossible speed, who could shatter stone with their bare hands. Superstition, he'd always thought. Yet, the girl's quiet intensity, her disciplined posture, spoke of a power that was undeniably real, even if it wasn't the magic he feared. His offer to spar was born of a soldier's respect, but also a burgeoning curiosity about the limits of human (or non-human) capability in a world that was clearly becoming stranger.

"Come friends, we have a couple days of travel ahead of us before we reach the lower foothills," Amelia said. "A day and a half if our horses are up for the task."

Kel'rak threw a nervous glance at the wolf dog as Zekven finished translating, but if the dog was hungry, it at least didn't see the horses as a source of food and really didn't even seem to pay them any mind. In fact, as he turned towards it, it was just… staring at him, head cocked to one side. Like it was examining him.

The assassin shuddered, shaking the thought from his head as he decided – like with everything else – not to pay it much mind. If it became a problem, he would figure it out later. High up in the saddle of a horse he wasn't familiar with, he set off at an easy trot, wishing for the fortieth time that day that he could hug Sugar around her warm thick neck.

***

Colson watched metal-tooth-shadow-human depart, thinking it quite curious how he radiated energy just like him and mother. Unlike Colson and mother's energy, which was like cold green fire, the man's energy just leaked from his skin like dusty black smoke. The boy who was a wolf dog also noted that the man's energy leaked from his entire body, while his own emanated from openings in his body like the ears, nose, mouth, and eyes.

Mother's energy only leaked from her belly – Colson's favorite spot for scratches – in a horizontal line. It looked very much like mother wore a belt of cold green fire. But she never seemed to notice it, and though Colson was a good boy and tried to tell her by putting his paw over the energy several times a day, she did not seem to understand. It was very frustrating.

As mother's strong-legs-no-fur took off in pursuit of the rest of the group, he ran comfortably by its side. The beast took good care of mother, so he didn't see a reason to make it afraid of him. In fact, he had worked together with it while they traveled, ensuring that no danger came to mother before they got to the big smelly city.

Colson did not understand the concept of sleep, other than knowing that mother needed it. Sometimes, he would pretend to do the sleep next to her, but he was always alert. When strong-legs-no-fur obliged to let mother ride it and joined their travels, Colson let it be the thing she did the sleep next to while he patrolled the night. Mother had protected him with her own life energy, so he would always be her protector.

***

The group reached the outskirts of the forest under the southernmost portion of the mountain range that night, their steeds proving surprisingly hardy compared to most. Well worth the four gold Kel'rak had paid. Though they had made it this far without incident, he felt uneasy.

Unlike the forested area to the West of the mountains that had led them to Hell's Ferry, where the green foliage provided a comforting warmth and cover to the night, the trees here felt malevolent. Like clawing arms reaching down from on high to hold them in place while some kind of terror approached in the dark.

Why any man other than him would choose to hunt here, much less by themselves, he didn't understand. Kel on the other hand… while he didn't much like the feel of the forest, he wasn't afraid of it. The most at home in the shadows of night, he elected to take the first watch while the others bedded down.

Shawna offered up her help as well, if for nothing other than company, or so she claimed. Kel'rak wasn't so naive as to think that was the truth, so when she approached his chosen watch spot after the others had fallen asleep, touching him gently on the left shoulder as she sat down, he wasn't the least bit surprised.

Though he didn't flinch away from the touch, he also chose not to be the one to initiate conversation. He was curious to see what the girl wanted.

"Good evening friend!" she greeted in a poor attempt at sign supported speech. At his surprised glance, she sheepishly signed, "Zekven taught me some while we rode today."

He sat up from his hunched-over position, stretching out his lower back. Offering his left hand as if to shake hers, he waited until their palms met before activating the serpentine bracelet. Confirming his suspicions about a few things, she didn't flinch when it activated. *So they do speak to each other.*

Evening, yes. Good?… eh, that's yet to be seen, he answered back through their link.

How can you still be so gloomy? she asked. *We are now five, and working with purpose! That is something to celebrate!*

Kel'rak cocked an eyebrow at her, saying only, *I told your… friend… I wasn't interested already.*

Oh my! No, no, no, I don't mean it like that! she backpedaled. *Besides, I don't swing that way… even if you weren't older.*

Kel'rak feigned a dagger to the heart at the dig, chuckling to himself as he scratched at his graying stubble. Alizarra's husky voice cut into the mental link.

Just because we share the same body, does not mean we share the same interests, darling, she purred inside his mind.

Hello again, "THE Demon" he replied, his mental tone indicating he was not intending insult, but only to share in their inside joke. Samarra's eyes glowed the fierce red of Alizarra's for a second, as she offered up a wicked smile.

Colson, circling the camp on the edge of the firelight, came into the view and cocked his head to one side as those eyes flashed. Parking in that spot, he ruminated on the energy. Like his and his mother's energy, it was like raging fire, but red. It did not feel good. But then it went away, and girl-who-gives-good-chin-scratches was back to normal. Curious.

Both Kel and Samarra watched the weird dog stop and stare at them. That was, until they heard a deep, throaty growl coming from the darkness behind Colson. They both jumped to their feet, Voidtooth appearing in Kel'rak's hand and Shawna showing a card of her own as she fired bright magical white light into the open forest.

The peace of the night was pierced by bone-chilling howls, as two giant wolves dressed in shredded clothing were revealed.

Chapter 15
The Pack

Clamping down on his fear and forcing his own anger at his failure to maintain watch into the magic, Kel'rak amplified his voice, shouting, "WAKE UP!" before rushing to meet the threat without confirming he had any backup.

The strength in his legs similarly amplified, he rushed past Colson like lightning made of shadow, focused on ensuring that his friends had enough time to shake off their sleep before they were in any true danger.

The first of the creatures was no more than twenty feet from Colson, having crept cautiously into the space around the camp when it took notice of the wolf dog and assigned it as the first threat. It pounced from its low crouch, loping towards the dog with savage abandon as its monstrous seven foot height was revealed.

With its front set of claws strangely more hand-shaped than paw, it prepared a powerful swipe but realized too-late that it had assessed the wrong monster as the primary threat.

Kel'rak rushed in on the left side of what he quickly assumed to be a werewolf from his childhood stories, dodging under the upraised arm and claw as he jabbed Voidtooth into its armpit once, twice, three times in rapid succession.

How the beast yowled! Though it was bleeding heavily, no major tissue tore free from the joint and the werewolf pivoted instead into the assassin's space, swiping its left arm at him with speed he had not expected. He went flying through the night with a barely audible "Oof!" as the air was blasted from his lungs.

His flight thankfully ended with a tumble through the grass and leaves, and not at an immovable tree trunk, some thirty feet from the first werewolf's location.

Bad luck for Kel'rak, the second was now in reach.

***

Samarra watched in horror as Kel'rak took a blow she thought for sure would kill him instantly. The monster whipped its head back around, loosing a snarl in her direction and dropping to all fours as it charged at her.

She froze.

As the werewolf entered the space within arms reach, Samarra's body seemed to conflict with itself. She first seemed to be pulling up her arms in a futile block, before Alizarra took control. As the arm came up, a whip of fire sprouted from the hand and wrapped around the snout of the beast, while the demon redirected its momentum around her in a semi-circle – face-first into a huge oak tree.

Alizarra willed the whip to change shape into a two-handed axe as the werewolf shook off the hit and turned back towards her.

The fiery bit swung from her right side into the side ligaments of its left knee, which buckled under its own weight. Reversing her momentum from there, the demon whipped around in another semi-circle and dug the edge of the fiery axe into the werewolf's neck, nearly severing it with the one hit.

Scars

Four more howls sounded in the night, as the beast's pack seemed to sense its demise.

Shawna was the first to arrive from the previously slumbering group. Her singing bo staff whistled through the air, cracking against the werewolf's upturned snout and ripping its head from the remaining neck skin to land at the feet of the next incoming monster. She passed her staff through a series of maneuvers to create a shrill song in the hopes that the werewolves' ears were as sensitive as any other dog.

When it tripped over its own claws after wincing in pain, she smiled evilly as she continued her horrendous song.

Zekven joined the fray then, leaping in with abandon to strike at the fallen werewolf. As it stood back up, he stabbed both shortswords into the shoulders on either side of its head, pinning down the trapezius muscle that would allow it to reach its arms above its head to retaliate. As he did so, he acted on a hunch and spoke the Elvish words "Naur" and "Khelek" in succession.

The first made the sword in his left hand erupt in white-hot flames, searing the flesh it was already in contact with and driving the blade in several inches further. The second caused the beast's left shoulder to explode in an eruption of red ice shards, as the sword in his right hand instantly froze the blood surrounding the blade that was freely pouring from the wound.

The werewolf shrieked in a pitch higher even than Shawna's staff, before Zek retracted Naur from its right shoulder and plunged it through the monster's throat and out the back side of its spinal cord, instantly cauterizing the deadly wounds and frying all connections from its brain to the rest of its body.

Three more of the creatures emerged from the woods, enraged at the sight of their pack members dying. No longer affected by the shrill song of the staff, they charged unhindered, so Shawna changed her tactic.

Halting her staff mid-swing, she planted the butt-end into the dirt beneath her feet and flipped up over it – and the werewolf – before dropping back down and executing one strike to its temple and two to where she hoped its kidneys would be.

It staggered from the series of blows, and then fell under the two-hundred pound bulk of claws, teeth, and fury that was Colson. The boy-who-was-a-wolfdog pinned the stunned beast to the ground by clamping his jaws over its throat and raked at its chest with his forepaws. It would soon be dead, which was a mercy, given how angry mother looked at the other two-leg-dog-men.

Amelia's body verily vibrated with power as her fear and hatred coalesced into green bolts of death magic, greedily crawling over the skin of her hands like living hunger as it awaited release. She threw both hands forward, launching the energy at the oncoming werewolves.

As it connected, it seemed to drain the very life force of the beasts, showing them withering away into decaying husks. She fired off two more bolts, screaming into the night with feral intent at the monsters that dared put her baby boy in mortal danger. One of them only just recovered from the first attack and dodged the second bolt, realizing the danger it was in and immediately turning tail, escaping – only barely – with its life.

The other was not so lucky. It took the second bolt in the face, still not recovered from the first hit, and the witch watched in satisfaction as the creature's entire visage aged into dust.

Zekven watched Amelia, the supposed healer, drain the life from a werewolf with a chilling efficiency. The magic of his weapons was about brute force, about elemental power. Hers was... consumption. A terrifying, elegant form of death. He felt a shiver, a faint echo of the creature's dying terror, and a new respect for the quiet woman who walked among them.

Shawna, whose power came from within, from years of physical perfection, watched Zek unleash fire and ice, and Amelia consume life. She saw the girl she was sweet on suddenly become a pillar of rage and fire.

It was magic, raw and undeniable, and a part of her, the disciplined monk, felt a deep unease. It was a power that bypassed the years of grueling training, a shortcut to devastation. She felt a strange mix of admiration for their power, and a subtle, almost imperceptible, fear of its untamed nature.

* * *

Kel'rak was not having as great of a time.

Having spent all of his time in combat since gaining his magic against foes of the human persuasion, he was used to a certain degree of ease when it came to battling enemies. It showed.

He backpedaled into the forest as the werewolf he had landed near took swipe after ruthless swipe at his head and chest. Thinking to end the fight quickly, he threw Voidtooth at its eyeball, hoping it would sink into the hilt and penetrate the brain. He had no such luck.

The werewolf he now faced had seen the speed with which he attacked, and was prepared for the desperate move, having not really committed to any of its own wild attacks. It dodged the half-effort move with ease, which sent Voidtooth careening into the darkness. Thinking Kel to be easy prey now, it moved to grapple him to the ground, where it could bite at his face and neck.

In a move born of pure desperation and fear, the assassin slid feet-first under the werewolf's legs and grabbed its ankle with the same arm that had been dislocated just the other day, howling in pain as his movement was jerked in the opposite direction by the beast's momentum and it began to drag him along the ground for several feet.

Knowing he would not live to see another thirty seconds if he didn't come up with a new plan, Kel did the one thing he had an inordinate amount of talent doing - improvising. Funneling all of the energy from his fear, desperation, and will to protect his friends into an aggressive prickling sensation in his hand, he allowed the magic to build until it felt like his hand was covered in a swarm of wasps before releasing it.

Black streaks like lightning shot up from the creature's ankle to its calf, before expanding in branches all the way up its thigh. Like a viper's venom, the blood inside the leg coagulated into a thick jelly, preventing proper blood flow throughout the werewolf's body near-instantaneous. Kel'rak let go of the ankle and let the beast go tumbling ahead of him.

Nursing his sore shoulder, he rose and started walking towards the prone creature as it made an unnatural screeching noise whilst gripping its leg and thrashing around on the ground. Many pairs of eyes glowed in the darkness around him as he stalked forward, pure hatred in his eyes.

Making a public show of recalling Voidtooth, he held his good arm parallel to the ground with the palm facing up. It appeared in an explosion of harmless black smoke, sparkling in the moonlight as if to tell its audience how excited it was for the coming feast; however, rather than allowing the dagger to release its corrosive shadow to devour the werewolf, he pumped yet more magic through his hand to coalesce around the knife's edge making it impossibly sharp.

The assassin clamped a muscular hand around the beast's whimpering muzzle from behind, drawing the snout skyward and exposing the flesh of its throat while flipping Voidtooth around to a reverse grip. Planting the edge of the blade on the left side of its neck – instead of just opening the jugular – he yanked the blade through the entirety of the werewolf's neck in a single stroke.

The corpse collapsed limp to the ground as he sent the head sailing into the darkness behind him with a mighty roar, screaming until his throat felt raw in an effort to display his dominance. A single howl, emanating from a pair of eyes that seemed maybe fifty feet directly in front of him as he turned around, sounded through the night.

It was joined by a chorus of yips, growls, and other howls that seemed to fade into the night without any indication that anything had left, such as the snap of a broken branch or twig.

The werewolves, creatures of instinct and primal rage, were utterly unprepared for the onslaught. They understood claws and teeth, the rending of flesh. But the invisible force that stole their breath, the sudden, searing heat and freezing cold that erupted from thin air, the silent coagulation of blood within their veins—these were horrors beyond their comprehension.

Their howls, usually filled with predatory fury, now contained notes of bewildered terror, a primal scream against a world that had suddenly turned against them with powers they couldn't fight or flee. They were facing not just opponents, but forces that defied their very nature.

Kel'rak's companions hurried to the sound of his conflict, thinking to help him in whatever way necessary, but dropped the tension from their shoulders as they saw him standing at ease and staring down at the headless corpse at his feet. The body was no longer covered in gray fur, instead appearing completely human – minus the lack of a head – and more appropriately filling out the shredded trapper's clothing that it wore.

The shredded trapper's clothing, the familiar lines of a man's body, were a stark, brutal reminder of what they were fighting. Not just monsters, but men twisted into something unnatural. It was a chilling realization, adding another layer of grim purpose to their bloody task.

The war against magic, he realized, was not just against mythical beasts; it was against the very humanity they sought to protect.

"I think we figured out what is happening to the city's trappers," he said.

***

Rather than opting for a shallow grave for the decapitated hunter, the group decided upon a warrior's burial for the man and his other fallen companions. They had died fighting, afterall.

It also just seemed more respectful – more *human*.

Given the number of werewolves that had surrounded their camp, it was doubtful many of them had chosen to become one of the pack, but had rather been forced into the life.

Beyond the humanity of it though, it was a warning to those that would think to come against them. The pyre blazed into the surrounding nightscape, giving off so much heat and light that the members of the adventuring party had to stand a minimum of fifty feet away not to feel it drying their eyes.

All of them, including Colson, stood mesmerized by the fire as it swayed, crackled, popped, and flared greedily at any pockets of sap within the wood used to fuel it. Zek – as usual – was the first one to break the silence.

"So are we just not going to address the wolf in the room?" he asked in sign supported speech.

"Read the room, if you will, Master Teluil," said Amelia, waving a hand toward Colson. Zek winced and grinned in sheepish apology.

"He has a point," Kel'rak chimed in. "In nearly thirty-five winters of life, I have never seen these monsters. My mother would tell me stories, to be sure, but we thought they were gone."

"Them and every other magical creature," said Shawna. Another, less noticeable, wince from Zekven.

"Exactly," said Kel'rak. "And yet, none of us look surprised. Indeed, most of us have some sort of magic of our own."

Amelia nodded with her arms crossed in contemplation, Samarra scrunched her shoulders with a tight lipped smile, and Zek patted the shortswords at his belt with a satisfied grin. Shawna was the only one to look a little irritated at the comment.

The assassin realized for the first time that everything she did, came solely from the power of her own body without any magical enhancement whatsoever. It was unfortunate and unfair for her to not have access to magic in a group such as this, as she would have to overcompensate in every action she would take from there on out.

Not that it seemed to be a struggle for her, she was incredibly powerful in her own way, and cocky about it… in fact, he might be able to work with that.

"What do you think they want?" Samarra asked, interrupting Kel's train of thought.

"Does it matter?" Zekven replied. "We were hired to figure out what is happening to the trappers, and we did. We did not sign on to invade an entire pack of were-beasts!"

Shawna was already shaking her head with her arms crossed, lips pressed tight, before the rogue ever finished talking.

"I bound myself to see this through. I promised Finnegan I would not return empty handed, so I will not."

The changeling rolled his eyes and swept a hand through his shiny black hair before scratching at the back of his head. Shawna just stared at him with a steel resolve, not providing any room for discussion as the firelight flickered in her gaze.

"Shawna is right," said Amelia. "We must see this through, as I do not think this is where it will end. You said so yourself Master Zaulyl, we are an oddity, in that we have magical means. Can we honestly state that any group the city sends to skirmish these creatures would have the same luck we did? With our magic, we had the element of surprise on the ambush predator. Men like Finnegan would be torn apart, or worse, transformed into one of them."

The assassin couldn't deny her logic. His shoulder still hurt from every minor movement after almost being ripped from the socket in the battle, and being dislocated only a few days prior.

Their magic made them faster and harder to hit, and they still won only by a large measure of luck. As if sensing his discomfort, Samarra came over to him and hesitated, clearly deep in thought.

She made a forward rotating motion with her closed fists, not unlike the act of gripping horse reins, and then pointed to herself to say "May I?" in sign language as her hands glowed with a gentle white light.

He responded only with a grim nod before turning away and closing his eyes, intent on focusing on his breathing or some other distraction, as he expected any kind of healing to come first with a sharp wave of pain as the damage undid itself.

But the expected pain never came.

Instead, he felt only warmth; though, there was a bit of an uncomfortable squirming feeling as his muscles unknotted and returned to their normal place in his shoulder. From the second her hand gently closed on his shoulder though, the pain began to disappear as if it were being washed away by a flowing river.

In place of the pain, he recognized the feelings of contentment, peace, and even joy. Her magic fixed not only physical pain, but emotional pain as well. It replaced negative feelings with positive ones she instilled in her patient.

He breathed a heavy sigh of relief, stretching both arms skyward to the full extent of their original capability.

He had seen the red glow before, but this... this was something entirely new. Samarra, vessel for something terrifyingly powerful, was also the one who could take away the pain inflicted by that power. He felt a growing sense of awe, the duality not lost on him. They were not just a group of individuals; they were a convergence of forces, a storm waiting to happen.

Kel'rak stood, raising the palm side of his fingertips to his chin and extending the hand forward and down in an arc, signing "Thank you" with every bit of appreciation he could muster on his face.

She smiled back and insisted it was nothing, her eyes darting to the tip of a burn scar she could just barely see poking out from under his shirt as he looked away.

"Speaking of magic, what was with all that fire?" Shawna asked Samarra, who blushed in embarrassment. "If you're a healer, what are you doing with all that destructive magic?"

"Whatever it is about," Kel'rak cut in after seeing where the conversation was going as Zek translated, "I am just glad it is on our side!"

"The man has a point," Zekven echoed.

Shawna could only concede the issue, shrugging away her curiosity in agreement with the men.

"So we are agreed, then?" Amelia asked.

The lot of them nodded in resolution. Tomorrow they would hunt. But first, Kel'rak wanted to try something.

***

Though it was well into the evening at this point, the assassin could not sleep yet. He was too excited at the new opportunity to expand his abilities. Shawna offered to take the next watch shift since she didn't need to sleep much – something about cycling the energy she needed from the environment around her as long as she sat still.

Waiting until everyone was asleep, he came to sit on the log just outside camp, next to the monk.

"If I stay here next to you while I do it, would you mind if I tried to give your weapon an enchantment that will assist you in battle?" Kel'rak asked. "I will need to hold onto it, and I would not dare walk away with it."

Knowing he wouldn't hear her one way or the other, Shawna thought about it for a few seconds before shrugging her shoulders and turning away once more to maintain her watch. As she did, she flicked her foot upward with a sharp motion, sending the bo staff sailing into Kel'rak's hands. He hadn't even realized it was on the ground, but it was clear she was not at any kind of disadvantage because of it.

The girl moved like lightning.

He gripped the simple-looking weapon with both hands, holding it vertical in front of him as he inspected every detail. He noted the holes in both ends of the staff for the first time, and realized they were what caused the cacophony of disorienting noise against an enemy. Paired with what he hoped to do, they would be a dangerous combination.

Scooting just a few feet away from Shawna so he could lay the staff horizontally across his lap, he lay his palms across it over top of his thighs to hold it in place as he closed his eyes and focused his inner thoughts.

This weapon needed to be an extension of its wielder, and he believed he understood that wielder better after tonight. Her natural teen cockiness was reinforced not by the belief that she was superior to others, but by the understanding of the *fact* that she was.

It was not a matter of opinion, but simple fact.

Shawna was technically still only a child, but she had grown up in the monastery, and had spent her entire life pursuing physical perfection. She had better control of every individual muscle fiber in her body than most lumberjacks did in the swing of their axe. So Kel'rak decided to focus on that concept. Her every move was based in superiority. An utter dominance of the battlefield.

A smile crept onto Kel's face as he felt the staff devour the living magic of his enchantment. Taking some of his own physical energy and jamming it in between every splinter, the energy was knit into the very fibers of the wood to reinforce every centimeter of its length.

He opened his eyes, slightly exhausted from the leeched power, but satisfied with what he knew to be a successful attempt. He handed the staff back to the monk, who accepted the weapon with silent grace as he dropped a hand to her shoulder.

"Unlike you, I am still dependent on my sleep," he said. "But I would like to spar with you tomorrow to test out my work, and see if I am improving."

Shawna just gave a quick appraisal at the apparently unchanged wood and offered a thumbs up, before turning away to stare into the darkness once more.

This should be fun, was his last thought before he gave in to the void of his dreamscape.

Chapter 16
The Sparring Match

The hunched form of Yeltnar dragged the fourth limp body to the pile he and his brethren had started. The wind howled as it nipped at his body, but he felt no cold, even this high up. The thick overcoat of his coarse grey fur bent and swayed like reeds in a storm, rebuffing the frigid wind and collecting thin sheets of constantly accumulating-then-dropping snow, while the undercoat kept him perfectly regulated.

Far from the features of a standard humanoid creature, the werewolf nevertheless was visually emaciated.

His jaw dripped with drool that froze midair as it fell to the milky white powder below. This kill – a large, well-muscled mountain goat – would have filled the bellies of him and his pack members for several days. But when Relanor the Black made his deal with her, the terms had been decisive and unwavering.

Once per week, for three years, a tithe would be paid in the form of seven kills.

If this meant the pack went without food for the week, it was not her problem – this was the payment for her part in bringing Relanor and his three sons back to the Material Plane. As magical beasts native to a plane where they were the hunted, rather than the hunter, the deal was as good as the four werewolves were ever going to get.

The deal went fine, for a time. But like all good things, the ease of the hunt dwindled over time.

The more they hunted, the less prey there was in a given area. This eventually gave way to the pack leading a nomadic lifestyle, rotating through hunting grounds along the mountain range but always staying close enough to make their promised delivery by the end of each week. The new strategy worked for the first few months, before the supply of animals large enough to satisfy her faded from the local area entirely.

Their operation had to expand.

Content to leave the hunting to his sons, Relanor the Black set out to create more pack members. It started with an unfortunate family of farmers. Their home lay on the edge of civilization at the foot of the mountains, where the snow runoff fed the soil with a constant flow of nutrients for the crops. An apex primal hunter, Relanor studied his prey, laying in wait for the time they would be at their most vulnerable.

In the early pre-dawn hours, the father of werewolves on Litharia turned his first were-spawn. Fully subservient to him, the former patriarch of the family sat in silence as he watched his creator methodically pick off the three remaining members of his house.

Eager to test his dominance and to get on with the expansion of his race, the hellish beast rutted the farmer's transformed wife until he could provide no more seed. He stalked by the cuckolded man with a snarling sneer, daring him to challenge his authority.

The family patriarch sat cowed, his head hanging low and his tail between his legs.

The process repeated in much the same way as the weeks went by, with the monster named Relanor laying claim to a young woman only barely entering adulthood. With each group he turned, he chose a female, until he maintained a harem.

After a couple of months, he changed tactics, knowing his growing group of pregnant mates would soon approach a number unsupportable by the hunting endeavors of those he captured and turned. So began the hunting trip that would take him to the fringe edge of South Peak, where the trappers existed in abundance – trappers like Yeltnar.

Yeltnar's once free-spirited existence as a trapper turned into a nightmarish servitude. His keen senses, once attuned to the subtle rhythms of the wilderness, were now shackled by the relentless demands of Relanor the Black. Forced into the pack's unholy alliance, Yeltnar and his fellow trappers were now were-thralls, compelled to carry out the bidding of their monstrous master.

The trappers, once the guardians of the fringes, now found themselves at the mercy of Relanor's pact with *Her*.

As the influence of the pack expanded, the once plentiful prey dwindled to a scarce few. The nomadic lifestyle that sustained them in the early days turned into a desperate quest for survival. Yeltnar, his body now twisted into the lupine form of his monstrous master, also dragged the corpses of his once-friends who had had the willpower to defy Relanor's influence up to the pile of animal carcasses. In the end, it was all meat, and she didn't care what type of meat it was.

The wind no longer carried the melody of freedom but whispered the mournful dirge of the enslaved.

Yeltnar, his eyes reflecting a mix of sorrow and rage, occasionally caught glimpses of the human faces within the werewolves. Those were once his kin, now lost to the curse imposed by Relanor's insatiable lust for power. The trapper, still holding onto shreds of his former self, plotted in the shadows, seeking a way to break free from the cursed servitude.

As the werewolf pack continued its relentless march, the land around South Peak transformed into a desolate wasteland, scarred by the predatory hunger of those who were once protectors. The moon, a silent witness to the tragedy, cast an eerie glow upon Yeltnar's fur as he yearned for the day when the balance of nature would be restored, and the howls of the free would drown out the cries of the enslaved.

***

Morning came to Kel'rak in the form of the butt end of a bo staff being jabbed into his ribs. He awoke with a start, doubled over and cursing both the heavens and the monk alike.

You couldn't have warned me? he said to Voidtooth.

"Aye, I could – but this was funnier."

In sign supported speech, Zekven said, "You weren't waking up to gentler methods mate."

He scoffed, sure that "gentler methods" meant trying to coax him up with words they both knew he would never hear. With one hand cradling the still-throbbing spot on his ribcage, Kel'rak raised the other hand up, which Zek grabbed as he hoisted him up from the ground. Kel raised his palm and fingertips to his chin, and dropped the hand forward in the sign for thanks, before rolling his neck and shoulders to stretch out the stiffness of the early morning.

"You said you wished to spar with me, so here I am," Shawna said, with Zekven translating.

"Indeed, but give a man twice your age some time to wake up, won't you?" he replied.

"Those beasts we fought last night will not give you time to wake up, and neither will I!"

She finished her thought with a lunge and a wild swipe left-to-right just to see whether the assassin would react. With the sun only barely cresting over the horizon, there were still enough shadows around for him to use, so Kel'rak did the only thing that made sense.

Rather than trying to dodge the blow he utilized the fear and desperation to avoid the hit as he simply disappeared, replaced by a smoky outline of his body, which the bo staff passed through without resistance. The surprise tactic combined with such a wild swing would have sent any other fighter off balance and tumbling to the side, but Shawna was not any other fighter.

Her body reacted on instinct, with her muscles going rigid to stop the momentum of the swing and to redirect the butt of the staff towards the ground. She planted it firm against the ground before vaulting up and over, spinning three hundred and sixty degrees to regain visual contact before landing behind and to the right of her previous position. She bolted forward, as fast as if the laws of physics did not apply, catching Kel by surprise.

Nonetheless, he brought the sharp edge of Voidtooth up to block as she jabbed the staff forward, grinning as he did so. The monk changed the direction of her blow in a desperate attempt to avoid any damage being done to the wood of her staff, but Kel'rak wanted to test something.

Stepping through shadow once more, he appeared in the expected path of the arcing staff, Voidtooth's edge waiting to bite into the wood just underneath the section that created its characteristic whistling music. As they connected, the two weapons met almost with a clang, like metal on metal. The monk had expected the weapon to bite into the wood, or even make a clean cut through, and therefore was taken aback at the vibration in her hands.

She dropped her weapon in shock, her eyes locking onto Kel's with evident fury that he would dare to possibly destroy her wondrous weapon.

"I assure you, your weapon was never in any danger," he stated with a calm tone.

Seething, she shook the remaining tingles from her hands as she bent to retrieve the weapon. Shawna inspected the area of impact like a mother inspecting a fallen child for injuries, turning it every which direction to ensure no permanent harm had befallen it. Once she had confirmed there was not so much as a scratch, she whipped a questioning glance towards the assassin, all anger in her eyes replaced with curiosity.

Kel'rak chuckled a bit, as Zek walked up to the monk and similarly inspected the staff with a discerning eye. He, too, looked up at his friend with a raised eyebrow.

"Our…altercation, with the werewolves last night, made me realize Shawna is the only member of our party that has no magic to rely upon," Kel'rak began.

Samarra and Amelia were now both awake from the noise that had been generated from their brief skirmish. Both young women were rubbing the sleep from their eyes as they trudged up. Amelia nodded her agreement with the observation.

"And so," he continued, "I asked her last night if I might inspect her weapon and give it an enchantment. What I did not tell her, was that I was enchanting it with its' own strength, among a few other capabilities. I thought, where I might not be able to teach her to wield magic, I might lend her my own."

"You should have!" she exclaimed. "Could have saved me a heart attack if I knew you were confident your dagger wouldn't cut through!"

Kel laughed again, a little cruelty coloring the tone red. "I wasn't."

The monk looked as if she might charge him then and there, for all of the rage that flared in her eyes. Zekven held her back, shushing reassuringly, but giving Kel'rak a look that said *What the hell?*

"Would it not have been more cruel to raise your hopes, only to have them dashed when we tried the same routine, but which met with failure?"

At his words, she calmed – just a bit.

"I may have gone about it the wrong way, but I assure you my intentions were pure. Beyond just the enhanced strength of your staff, I made a guess as to your personal nature, and imbued the weapon with that same intent."

Zek and Shawna both looked at the assassin like he had just spoken nine different kinds of foreign languages, but Amelia and Samarra both nodded in understanding, as the true magic users.

Amelia cut in next, "Magic is about intent, and emotion – at least, it is for me, and based on this conversation I'm assuming the same holds true for our friends."

"Indeed!" Samarra answered. "For me, my magic flows through my intent to spread joy, and bring peace to those around me."

"...you spread joy with a fire whip?" Zek asked with more sarcasm than he intended.

Samarra closed her eyes for a second and pinched the bridge of her nose as if nursing a headache, but Kel'rak quickly discerned it was to hide the red glow of Alizarra's presence.

"At times, wanton rage-fueled destruction is required. And fun."

"Remind me not to piss you off, healer," Zek said under his breath.

"All of this being said," Kel interrupted, "I came to the realization last night that your nature lies in your combat superiority. You are cocky, Shawna, and not for a lack of reason."

The monk bowed her head in resignation, the words clearly stinging more than the assassin had intended.

"Master Halani has told me much of the same. It is one of the many reasons I was sent out for enlightenment. Your words are but an echo of his teachings."

Kel just shook his head as Zek finished translating in real time. "You misunderstand me Shawna – you are a fantastic fighter. Your mastery of your body in combat instills fear in your enemies and is the very first weapon you have against them. Whether you understand it or not – based on the most rudimentary understanding of magic – your emotional manipulation of them is like a form of magic all on its own."

"So you are saying I should be cocky and overconfident?" she asked, taking a step back in disbelief.

"Hardly – I mean that you should strike with intent. You already treat your weapon like the extension of yourself it should be. All you need to do now is to understand that you *are* the superior fighter, and act like it. Be confident that when you strike, you strike true, and you strike like the viper with its maw full of venom. The staff will do the rest."

He finished his last statement with a surprise rush at the monk, who had been standing at ease, distracted by their conversation. Though he had intended to catch her unawares, the move had not had the intended effect. Shawna's reflexes were honed to a knife's edge, and her body reacted accordingly. She dodged to the side, unable to riposte with the staff in the position it had been in, but avoiding contact nonetheless.

As Kel'rak charged back in, he realized mid-sprint that the sun had risen too high in the sky to utilize the shadows any longer, as he tried to shadowstep in a zig-zag pattern towards the monk but only managed to give himself a severe migraine.

Undeterred, he concentrated on the adrenaline rush that came from sheer desperation and boosted the muscles in his legs to gain a burst of speed. The assassin's blade met the monk's staff with a resounding CLANG! as he passed by, but Shawna was not done.

She allowed the momentum of the over-committed assassin to spin the staff out wide, before redirecting the force into a three hundred sixty degree arc. The staff connected with only a single point of touch as Kel'rak continued his rush by, but that was all that was necessary as it flashed a brief dim green light.

Kel felt the magic hit him before he even realized he was tumbling forward, the blow having hit him in the crook of the knee and sending him off balance. He rolled and came back up in a ready position, grinning, but feeling slightly drained. Shawna on the other hand had felt the energy surge from Kel'rak and into the staff.

Even now, she felt it vibrating with a gentle buzz.

The magic did not sap much, but she felt it could hold so much more.

The two fighters collided once more, neither landing a hit on the other as they shoved off in a brilliant display of dexterity and strength. Their sparring match became a dance of singing steel and birch, the blade whipping through the air with a slight whistle as the staff was spun through a series of maneuvers that created a reverberating screech in the immediate area.

It had no real effect on the deaf man, but the combat form allowed Shawna to pass through a series of rapid strikes that – while not hard-hitting – all managed to connect. Each hit sapped just a little bit more energy from Kel'rak. She was adapting to the magic quicker than he had anticipated, and he was already feeling the exhaustion set in.

"Hold!" he cried out.

The staff itself gave no outward sign that it held any form of energy, magic or otherwise. But Shawna could feel it. Buzzing like the stone floors of the monastery during an earthquake, her staff would be begging for release were it alive.

"Please trust me for just a moment, if you will," Kel'rak said while holding Voidtooth's blade down towards her forearm.

Shawna recoiled at first, as her danger sense flared, but forced herself to calm when the man raised his other hand palm forward to show he wasn't meaning true harm. Deciding he had earned the trust, she extended her arm forward, exposing the underside of her forearm. Kel'rak made a precise, gentle one-inch cut with the blade only to begin to draw blood before retreating a few steps and sheathing the weapon entirely.

"The enchantment should work in one of two ways, and you should have enough energy stored to try out both now," he began. "The first, is to clamp down on the joy you should feel from your prowess and/or subsequent victory in combat. Direct the energy you feel inside the staff to flow up your hand and through your body to heal your ailments – in this case, a small cut. Or in sustained situations with a stronger opponent, to slowly even the playing field by zapping their stamina and giving it to yourself, so that you never get tired while they huff and puff."

Shawna did as she was told, closing her eyes to orient her mind's eye with the now-familiar buzzing of the weapon. Congratulating herself on severely whooping the arrogant shadow man's ass, she felt the energy collect near her right palm where it made contact with the staff, then directed a tiny amount of it to flow up through her arm and past her chest towards the left arm.

There it paused, as the energy found something to do. Knitting the cut back together in less than a second, it left a mild itching sensation. When she moved the other hand to scratch at the itch, she wiped away the blood to reveal flawless skin underneath. The monk's smile grew ear-to-ear, her characteristic youthful sense of wonder returning to fill Kel'rak with happiness.

"What is the other way?" she asked with tears forming in her eyes.

"This one, your Master Halani will hate me for, I think," the assassin chuckled. "You need to embrace the arrogance of your superiority and release the energy into your opponent instead of yourself."

He looked around, not willing to be the target this time. His eyes landed on one of the fallen logs they had used the night prior as benches near the fire.

"Imagine this log is your enemy. Imagine that it is threatening you or someone you care about, then push forward the energy in the weapon to the striking zone, and hit it."

So she did.

Closing her eyes once more, Shawna called forth the memory of Samarra, her screams of terror in the woods when they met ringing out into the forest. She thought of the way her shocking green eyes seemed to have a laugh of their own after that rescue, and how her chocolate brown hair cascaded down her shoulders and over her ample chest…

Shaking the cobwebs from her head to get back on track, she backtracked to the memory of Samarra under attack and growled at the thought, remembering how she had trounced the group of idiot men.

In an overhead swipe, she brought the staff down like a hammer. As it impacted, thunder sounded out like lightning had just struck the ground nearby. The entire pool of energy still within the weapon was released in that one strike, shattering the one-foot-thick log like a twig and sending splinters flying out in a fifty foot cone to either side of the monk.

She blinked away the shock of the moment, before rushing over to Kel'rak and wrapping him in a hug. Not knowing what to do, he patted her on the head with the one hand he still had free while she continued her bear hug.

"Thank you," she weeped, "for believing in me."

Chapter 17
The Discoveries

I am not that person. I am not a father. I am not her father. I am not responsible for her – I am hardly responsible for myself. I already failed at being a husband.

This litany of denial repeated through Kel's head all day as the group journeyed deeper into the forest. He hardly knew the kid. She was explicitly not his problem.

And yet… *nope, not my problem.*

The deeper the five people and a dog moved into the woods, the colder it got. Winter was officially in full swing. Though the thick canopy of pine kept away most of the snow and freezing rain, it did nothing to stop the wind.

If anything, the space they walked amongst the bare trunks became like a wind tunnel. The gusts seemed to flow down the mountain side like white water rapids over a cliff, the dense cold air replacing any warmth that might appear. The group moved trunk to trunk, taking shelter from the wind in the eight foot wide bases between each movement.

"Samarra," Zekven shouted, "Might some of your fire magic be willing to come out and play?"

The healer, caught unawares, shifted her eyes nervously from one person to the next, finally landing on Kelrak. He nodded with chittering teeth, fighting back his own desire to beg for warmth. Colson's mop-like body, soaked in freezing cold water, nudged against her hand – he didn't need it, couldn't feel it, but Mother could use it.

She passed a quick glance towards Amelia, who smiled sweetly, motioning with her hands to get on with it. Samarra sighed.

"Okay, but I promise you, I have no clue what will happen – i-in all this wind, I mean."

The healer closed her eyes, looking inwards and taking a deep breath to center her energies. When she opened them once more, they glowed with a red smoke, and her lip curled into a sneer as she spoke in a huskier tone.

"Let's give this a go, darlings."

A bubble of heat exploded outwards in all directions from Samarra's body. Flames licked at her clothes, areas of exposed skin, and hair – but did not burn. Instead, she was like a living torch, radiating life-giving heat. Kel'rak swore he could see a tail, a pair of wings, and a crown all made from that fire. But it had to be an illusion.

Mind trick or not, the heat was real, and everyone breathed a deep sigh of relief. Even Shawna, whose training taught her to withstand the subzero temperatures of the winter seemed to relax a little bit under the magical warmth.

Feeling the blood rush back into the capillaries of his hands like little needle-pricks of discomfort, Kel shook his arms violently to distract himself from the pain. As he looked towards Samarra's blazing form, Alizarra met his gaze with a leveled smile.

He let one of the serpentine bracelets drop to the ground and slither its way to her ankle, where it wrapped in place snug enough not to jingle. The assassin walked away with a casual gait, appearing to inspect the full scope of the spell's effects –

which he really did. Within about a thirty foot sphere, everything was now warmed.

Guess it's time for sweet Sam's nap. It's ok, mama's here to… take care of you, she said through the mental link with a suggestive tone.

He snorted, the sound of which was drowned out by the surprising continued howl of the wind. It seemed the magic couldn't get rid of sound at least, but *damn* was it feeling good. Alizarra's hand came into view as she reached for his shoulder, and he couldn't suppress a flinch.

She just chuckled and patted him three times instead.

I just thought the fire surrounding you might burn me, he said.

At least make it convincing if you're going to lie to me darling, she replied.

She stepped away and moved to the direct center of the group to ensure everyone stayed within the bubble as they walked.

I told you already, I'm not interested, Kel'rak said, fiddling with a metal band in his neck purse. *Even if I was, that's not your body to offer up.*

You're no fun, she said, passing the mental equivalent of a pout. *You're the only person other than prissy pants here that I get to talk to.*

Am I not talking to you now? he asked.

Yes, but it's so much more fun when both parties are horizontal, she purred.

Still good, he said. *But thank you for saving all of us like this. I will not forget your kindness today.*

Don't thank me yet, it only lasts so long, she said. *Besides, I already told you I don't do it for everyone else. The girl goes, so do I.*

He smirked. *Tell yourself whatever you need to, to feel better about it.*

Aloud, he asked, "So, will this last all day and night, and forever more? Or do we need to find shelter while it lasts?"

"We have about one hour until the magic fades," she said, swaying Samarra's hips just slightly more than the girl herself as she walked.

"Shelter time it is, ladies and gentlemen!," Zekven announced. "Thank you for the heat Lady Samarra, however long it may stick around."

Alizarra stared him dead in the eyes and bowed, never breaking eye contact.

"You are most welcome, darling," she said.

"Can any of you magical people turn a pile of sticks into a house?" Zek said in sign supported speech, either not noticing the awkward social interaction or ignoring it entirely.

Amelia was the first to shake her head in contradiction to the idea, saying her magic tended to be reactionary towards danger. Kel was going to say no at first, but thought about it for a few seconds before answering.

"I might have an idea," he said. "Let me think."

While they continued their march towards the foothills, he asked Voidtooth for advice; however, the weapon was silent at first. When he pressed it for anything at all, it snapped back a response.

"Oh, ye need me now, do ye?"

By the gods' ancient grey beards, what are you on about?

"E'er since the Baron came to ye, ye've not had to rely on ol' Voidtooth have ye? Treatin' me like a common dagger."

It mentally wretched inside his head. A feeling he really hated.

"Not even feedin' me!"

You went a hundred years without anything to eat, you can go several days while we find our prey.

"The demon lass be speakin' true then. Ye *are* no fun."

I'm aware, Kel answered. *Please just answer my damn question.*

The weapon scoffed. "Fine. Ye wanna make a shelter? Think about isolation, loneliness, and fear. Use that."

Just how in the hell am I supposed to tap into loneliness when I'm surrounded by people who have already shown several times over that they will die with me?

"I already told ye, magic isn't one and done. The rules are flexible, Lambie."

I am not picking up what you're putting down.

"Adjust it," he weapon snapped. "Ye're so protective of these twats, use that."

Pleased with himself for setting off the weapon that was the manipulator in most any other situation, he cut off the mental conversation at the same time it did out of annoyance. He thought long and hard on the problem.

Fear is the basis of my affinity. Not hard. Protecting these people, that's a new one, but I can work with Isolation. We're needing to be isolated and protected for fear of the night's predators. Okay. Let's try.

He signaled for the group to halt some thirty minutes into his contemplation. Knowing Alizarra's magic wouldn't hold much longer, he got to work. Feeling a massive drain begin on his physical energy, he moved near the demon in the center of the whole group, so as to encompass the heat with what he planned.

Widening his stance and thrusting both hands like knives to either side, he spun a slow circle. A grinding noise emanated from the ground on either side of him as he did so. The magic circle "drawn", he touched the centerpoint of the circle with both hands held together and seemed to pull on an imaginary string.

As he did so, a cylinder of mixed stone and clay materials rose from the ground, reaching a height of about eight feet before stopping. He reached out once more, this time at shoulder height, and seemed to grip onto thin air in either direction. After doing so, he spun a circle once more, the top–most portions of the cylinder spinning and stretching with him until it formed a dome with a slight hole in the top for fresh air.

Kel'rak slumped to the ground, every muscle in his body shaking with the exertion. If the heat from Alizarra's sphere was no longer active, any onlooker would think him to be shivering from hypothermia without any control of his body. The man shook as if his very bones were icing over.

"Let's not... do that... again..." he said through chittering teeth and ragged gasps.

The heat from Alizarra's spell dissipated as Samarra took control once more. She rushed to Kel'rak's side and knelt nearby, closing her eyes with outstretched hands. A soft white light emanated from both hands, as Samarra seemed to slouch with the passing seconds.

She held the magic until the assassin's weakness visibly eased, passing her own energy directly to him as she did so. The amount of energy she had to feed into him just to stabilize was astronomical – his vast pool of energy far exceeding hers. After the longest minute of her life, she too, collapsed sideways only just catching herself with her right hand.

The new dome shelter held onto the existing heat it had already entrapped. Amelia, Shawna, and Zekven all stretched and clenched their hands as the increase in temperature also opened the veins of their hands. The sudden rush of blood flow left their digits feeling a mix of burning with pins and needles creating a wholly unpleasant experience.

With Kel's breathing normalized at last – though he was still exhausted – he said, "I probably should not have done that."

Samarra smacked him across the face.

"No, you shouldn't have!"

Not used to the outburst of emotion from the otherwise timid girl, he just blinked away the sting in his cheeks and stared her straight in the eye, dumbfounded.

"How are you the strongest one here and you do not know that your magic cannot just be used without restraint?" she exclaimed.

The first part of her statement she said without hesitation, as a matter of simple fact. Just another thing to add onto the pile of items keeping his mouth moving without sound escaping.

"It is most likely just natural talent, Sam…" Amelia began, but was cut off.

"Natural talent or no, he has protected all of us countless times in the last weeks with more ease than should be possible! He should know that his energy is not infinite!" Samarra said with tears beginning to roll down her cheeks, Zek translating in real time.

"The lass speaks the truth," Voidtooth said in Kel's head.

Not helping.

"Ye only yet live because the girl gave you her own energy. Not healing, but direct energy transfer. Yer body was on the verge of total failure, Lambie."

Why? It was magic, like anything else I've done to this point.

"Eh… my knickers being in a twist is mostly tae blame," the weapon confessed. "I encouraged ye to experiment with magic ye were not prepared to create."

Elaborate, now.

"Ye had the base knowledge and the creativity, but ye lacked the understanding and connection to the moment. Therefore, the magic fed less efficiently on yer energy. Even the simplest spell can kill a man if he does not understand it," Voidtooth finished.

"This is why when ye fell in my hole, I spared ye instead of consuming. Natural affinities play a large role in the use of magic – yours happens to perfectly match mine, so I had confidence ye would live through accelerated teachings."

Kel'rak sighed and patted Samarra's shoulder.

"You are right, I should know my limits. I have admittedly never had to push out that much energy into magic, and I misjudged my ability. I am sorry."

Samarra hugged her legs to her chest for stability, ignoring Kel's apology entirely as she seemed to withdraw inside her own mind. Shawna dropped her own pack on the outer edge of the hut and approached. Dropping to one knee next to Samarra, she pried the young woman's fingers apart with a gentle hand and lifted the heavy pack from her shoulders.

Setting herself to the process of preparing Samarra's bedroll, she gave the assassin the full silent treatment.

Zek was the next to speak up. "You are just lucky that we were somewhere of relative peace, and not under attack, mate."

"And that Sam has the abilities that she does," Amelia said. She now sat cross-legged at the outer edge of the shelter, Colson sitting at attention and panting happily with the knowledge that Mother was in no current danger.

Kel'rak just sat and leaned against his pack, trying to take in the fact that he had almost died. He stayed that way for over an hour, as his companions succumbed to sleep one-by-one in the comfort and security of the shelter they were all furious with him for creating.

***

The next morning the group of adventurers found, much to Kel'rak's chagrin, that the walls of the shelter were not as thick as they all believed. Since his crude formation of the shelter had left no door, Shawna decided to test the thickness of the wall with the end of her staff.

She impaled a clay section of the wall large enough for each of them to pass through should the wall be broken. In doing so, she learned that the dome surrounding them was about the thickness of a human hand. It was a miracle the shelter had survived the wind storm from the night prior.

She kicked through the wall, walking through the small hole and letting it crumble around her.

As they all shambled out of the earthen shelter and stretched under the morning sunlight, Kel'rak's embarrassment only deepened. The last to make it out of the shelter was Colson, who nudged the wall just a little too hard, and sent the whole thing tumbling down in a pile of dust and the sharp crack of rock on rock.

Kel'rak and Zekven took up the rear, with all three ladies taking the lead. None of them were happy with Kel'rak right now, and he could not blame them. Zekven, though, would not abandon his friend regardless of his personal feelings on the matter.

He knew what it was like to be shunned.

"So… the red eyes. That's not Samarra is it?" Zek signed without speech.

Kel'rak just glanced sideways and gave a noncommittal shrug. "What makes you think that?" he responded in kind, taking the hint that Zek intended to keep the conversation private.

"I may play the part of a bumbling idiot, but I am not so good at it as for you to believe that," Zek replied. His facial expression was one of dry amusement.

"Let's assume I know a few things," Kel'rak said. "What clued you in?"

"Her voice is different when it happens, for one thing," signed the rogue. "Though I guess you probably didn't know that."

"It actually matches up with her mental voice."

At Zek's raised eyebrow, Kel sighed and pointed at his friend's left wrist. Touching his own right wrist to Zek's, the serpent bracelet came to life for a moment and slithered across, anchoring itself once more before the green light in its eyes flared out.

The snakes let us talk in our heads, said the assassin.

Zekven reeled as though he couldn't figure out where the voice was coming from, but thought back, *Can you hear me?*

Kel sighed through the mental link. *You could at least make it look less obvious.*

Sorry, this is new!

It was for me as well. Alizarra was the one who knew what they did, outside of the whole strangling thing.

Ali-who?

Alizarra. Good ol' red eyes, the demon riding Sam's body.

Zekven snickered. *That sounds wrong.*

Yeah, well, it's right. Demon lady tried to possess her and failed. Something about trying to possess a repentant soul. Now they're stuck together in the same body.

That's really gotta suck.

It's better than the alternative. And Alizarra's been pretty helpful so far. We would've been in far worse shape with those werewolves without her, and who knows if we would have survived the cold last night.

Wild… so the fire, that's all the demon?

Yup.

Glad she's on our side, said Zek. The ladies turned back to glare at them as a collective, before turning around once more.

Kel'rak just sighed, the silent treatment reminding him of the time Cecilia had been furious with him for being gone for training with Laird Delmar's army for too long. He had had no control over it, and desperately wanted to be close to her as soon as he got home, but gave her the space she needed to cool off. She came around soon after, and their reunion was as sweet as blackberry wine.

Though the memory pained him, he held onto it in his mind's eye just a little bit longer. How he missed her. How he missed her advice, which never steered him wrong. Just then, Shawna called out over her shoulder. A lone mountain of a man wandered their way dressed in shredded clothing.

The entire party fanned out, preparing arms and magical energies as the man seemed to stagger forth in pure exhaustion. He looked just like the others they had killed, shredded all to hell, with no wounds to show for it – save for the ones inflicted by the group themselves.

He raised his head, jumping in alarm at the sight of a growling behemoth of a dog and five total men and women brandishing threatening modes of murder his way. He extended both hands in surrender, making it clear he meant no harm as he knelt to the ground as a form of submission.

"I see you're already acquainted with my kind!" he said in a raised voice from his position about fifty feet away.

"Intimately," said Zek.

"Please, let me tell my tale, then judge my fate for yourselves," he begged.

"Give me a reason," said Shawna.

"Because I can help you stop them."

Chapter 18
The Hunt

Yeltnar sat in terror, not sure whether this group of strangers would end his life then and there, or let him say his peace. At this point, he didn't care. He wanted to help them end the blight of the mountains, but would also be content to welcome the cold embrace of death. He had seen too many of his friends die already – he didn't deserve to live.

A man with a shaved head stepped forward, his intense gaze boring into the depths of Yeltnar's soul. This man's aura was danger incarnate. He would tell the man anything he asked for. Before he could, the man also knelt down and held the tip of a wavy bladed kris to the underside of his chin.

"Show me," the man demanded.

The trapper-turned-werewolf looked at him in confusion for a second, before the other man with shoulder length black hair gave an amused smirk and made a mocking claw motion while baring his teeth.

Yeltnar sighed. The transformation wasn't fun. Nor was it exactly pleasing to watch. Still on his knees, he turned away from the group, trying to spare the young women some horror. A werewolf could still be a gentleman.

Kel'rak felt the vibrations of the transformation as everyone else heard it. This close to the trapper, he could feel the reverberations through the air as bones cracked and grew, the trapper crying out in pain with each passing moment. The bones of his hands and feet grinded against each other as they shifted to accommodate the paw structure of the bestial form.

Worse than that was the sharp snap of Yeltnar's skull, which shattered in the face and grew forward to form the lupine snout. Coarse grey fur sprouted from every square inch of his body. Even kneeling on the ground, he grew to five feet. But when the transformation was complete and he stood to his full height, turning to face the group, he towered over them all at a hunched seven and a half feet.

The werewolf flexed the pain out of his joints, paws, and claws, looking for all the world as if he were going to pounce. Kel'rak took two involuntary steps back from the imposing figure, stopping only once the sharp-toothed maw was in full view as he looked up.

Yeltnar's wolven features seemed to mimic an expression of sorrow and regret as he reverted back to human form, with yet more cracks and groans while his bones broke once more and shrank.

"What do you know so far?" he asked through huffed breaths, while glancing around nervously and adding, "We should walk and talk."

***

"Contrary to the stories my nan used to tell me," Yeltnar announced off-hand as he led the group while walking backwards, "We lycanthropes are not under some sort of weird blood craze and change because the full moon cycle hangs above the world. I am just as much in control as the lot of you."

Scars

The lycan put this on display by choosing to only grow the claws from his human bare hands and feet – something he had told them he didn't care to fix, as the transformation did not take clothing into account, and he had long since destroyed his best pairs of boots. Even this part of the transformation was clearly agony though, as his fingers bled like a tap while the nails extended and retracted. Interestingly, the bleeding stopped within seconds of the transformation ending.

Kel took note of this rapid healing effect and seared it into his brain to always go for the kill when facing one as an enemy, lest he tire himself out before victory is assured. He watched the mountain man's face closely as they walked, also taking note of his apparent heightened senses.

Several times he stopped mid-sentence to listen to something only he heard or smelled, then decided to turn in another direction. He had yet to lead the party into any confrontations, so there was no reason to believe he was taking them anywhere other than safety - or into a trap.

They would be prepared either way. Kel'rak mentally commanded his snake bracelet to make contact with each member of his group as they traveled, steadily ensuring that everyone was prepared to fight at a moments' notice. To their credit, neither Shawna nor Amelia made any verbal reaction to the metal snake's actions, as Kel'rak made his intent clear during periods where Yeltnar's back was turned. They would touch wrists briefly, and the snake would change hands, all done while seemingly randomly shifting marching positions to appear alert.

Shawna, who had seen the snake strangle a man during Samarra's rescue in the woods, was understandably nervous but let the snake travel and establish the link. Kel got a brief moment of her thoughts focusing on Sam's rear-end in an effort to stay calm, before letting her know through the link that they could speak this way. He spared her the embarrassment of letting her know what he saw.

Amelia, having watched the interaction with Shawna the first time Yeltnar's back was turned, made her way to the assassin's side and touched wrists to acquire the item in one smooth movement as she took a front position in the marching order just behind the lycan. Unlike Shawna, she felt the magic probing her mind and actively poked at it in her mind's eye.

She felt it tether to Kel's mind and simply said, *Fascinating*.

Zek'ven spoke up with sign supported speech, jumping back to the prior statement, intending to further distract their guide while the others interacted.

"If your kind are not in some sort of blood craze, why did your… brothers?… attack us," he asked, raising one black eyebrow. "We did not hunt them down or attack them first. The kind of ambush tactics they sprung on us while we camped weren't unlike your standard pack of wolves looking for their next meal. There did not seem to be any reason left in them."

Yeltnar winced. "While I would like to say we are still civilized folk, I'd be lying if I did. We don't get that luxury."

"How do you mean?" Amelia asked.

"Not many of us were willing converts," the trapper answered. "Most of us are victims of a deal between *her* and Relanor the Black."

Kel'rak almost didn't notice the near subconscious hunch of Yeltnar's shoulders and the way his eyes darted back and forth as he said that, because he was busy watching Zek translate the conversation to sign.

Shawna jogged up behind the man and rapped him upside the head with her staff. "We're going to need more information than that, guy. We're not from around here. Who are 'her' and this Relanor?"

Yeltnar stuttered mid-stride and stopped, gesturing with a hand to quiet down. "One can never know when he's listening - you really must be careful when throwing around names out in the wild."

Every bit the over-confident teen, Shawna struck a power pose with her staff in-hand leaned out to the side, and - in a louder voice, daring the woods to come at her - asked, "Who are 'her' and this Re–"

The trapper cut her off with a hand over her mouth, as the others drew their weapons towards him.

"Are you trying to get us all slaughtered?!" he hissed. "I don't know about you, but I am not keen on dying slowly over the course of a week as my skin is flayed from my muscles! He once made an example of a man who dared to flout his authority by opening his body from head to toe, taking care not to nick a single major artery and keeping that man bound and alive in a cage for a full moon cycle."

Zekven and Samarra gagged a little, Kel'rak raised an eyebrow, Amelia took an involuntary step back, and Shawna just blinked. She peeled Yeltnar's hand off her face, keeping it in an iron grip.

"People like to think that our monastery teaches only passivity and self defense, but we're also quite well educated in human biology," she began. "For example, do you know that it only takes twenty-five pounds of pressure to fracture a small finger bone?"

This, she asked, as she shifted her grip to his pinky and dragged it backwards, wrenching a cry from his lips and sending him to the ground with no more effort than a babe playing with their toy choo-choo train.

"If you ever touch me like that again, I just might have to conduct an experiment to see if the masters' teachings were true," she finished. "Now, be a good dog and take us to the bad dog that shall not be named."

Zek didn't translate the wounded whimper that escaped from Yeltnar's lips as Shawna walked away, so Kel'rak thought his companions were judging the monk for being too harsh when he saw them make various pitying looks.

Yeltnar led the party through several loopbacks in an attempt to mask their true trail from anyone that might be tracking them, while continuing to elaborate on the truth of his pack. He explained as much when Kel noted he had seen the same tree no less than three times.

"As you pointed out, we are not so far from wild wolves ourselves," the former trapper began. "We retain many of the same abilities one might associate with the average hunting dog - heightened hearing and smell. If we loopback on the same points enough times, it should serve as enough confusion to give us extra time in the event that we are discovered and can break line of sight."

"Regarding the alpha, what can you tell us?" Samarra prodded.

"He is terror incarnate," Yeltnar whispered. "If you think my lycan form is imposing, you may consider me a runt. He is the father of every one of my kind in these mountains."

"Yes yes, we get it, he is horrible. Big bad wolf," Shawna chimed in. "But what do we need to know to fix this problem?"

The werewolf just chuckled. "That you think you can fix the problem, is cute."

Shawna just leveled a flat stare at him until his smug smile faded. He looked around at the rest of the party seeming to beg for some support, but found none.

"Bunch of killjoys," he muttered.

Zek's sensitive ears caught the words, and he translated to sign.

"We can have fun when we're not all in immediate danger," said Kel'rak, whose eyes leaked a little shadowstuff to add to the seriousness of the moment. "So far, you have led us through the woods in circles under the guise of covering our trail, but have done nothing else to gain our trust outside of giving us a little bit of information as to how your curse works. How should we expect that you are doing anything other than distracting us into a trap, if you don't give us something to work with?"

Yeltnar sighed. "I suppose if you want to stand a chance, I cannot expect to lead you into a fight blind. As I mentioned before, our Father is larger than any of the rest of us - if you were to compare him to the size of a cottage, his head would just crest over the roof."

He lowered his head, shoulders rising and falling with visible hesitation. "As his name would imply," he said, "he is covered in fur the color of a clear night sky—minus the stars. And he is vicious, to a fault. In most cases, he would rather attack than speak."

Samarra cracked her knuckles. "Good. Talking's overrated anyway."

The trapper rolled his eyes before continuing, "As you might have guessed from prior encounters with my kind, he is incredibly strong. But as with everything else, he is stronger even than the rest of us."

Yeltnar gestured for silence and pointed forward through the thinning tree line. The air shifted—colder here, more sterile. No animal sounds. No wind. Just the sharp scent of sulfur and scorched pine.

They crept forward until the trees broke into a clearing. The moon hung high overhead, full and swollen, casting pale light onto the circular basin below. Blackened stone lined its edges like teeth, with patches of melted snow hissing steam in the corners. The trees here had burned, some still standing like charred skeletons.

At the center stood a crude throne of jagged stone, cracked and steaming. Perched atop it was the Alpha, Relanor the Black.

He was massive—twice Yeltnar's size—with fur so dark it devoured the moonlight, absorbing the color around him like ink on paper. Horns curled from the sides of his head hinted at a demonic lineage, bone twisted into antlered spirals that seemed wrong in every way, like they grew in defiance of nature. He sat like a king surveying his court, one clawed hand resting atop a pillar of bones that might have once been a person.

The Alpha slowly lifted his muzzle, sniffing the air. His eyes snapped open—blazing crimson—and he let out a slow, deliberate growl.

Yeltnar whispered, "He knows we're here."

"Then let's stop wasting time," Shawna said, twirling her staff through a few passes that seemed to make it whistle in anticipation. "Light him up."

Scars

The Alpha's howl cracked the silence. In an instant, shadows exploded from the far tree line—half a dozen werewolves tearing through the dark like the worst kind of nightmare fuel. Alizarra surged forward with a roar that shook the trees, her blade alight with infernal flame. Shawna met the first beast head-on, parrying claws with her newly enhanced staff and dancing in a whirlwind of footwork. Zekven slipped behind a boulder and loosed a flurry of arrows with clinical precision.

Together, the trio halted the first wave of lycanthropes, with Shawna acting as the distraction. Dancing and twirling from foe to foe, her staff whistled a shrieking song that set the canine monstrosities on edge, disrupting their naturally enhanced reflexes. Each of Zek's arrows found their mark, embedding in a neck, eye, or lung. Alizarra leapt into the fray, fully beheading her first enemy with a single overpowering strike.

The stump of its neck instantly cauterized, not even leaking a single drop of blood.

Amelia took down yet another spawn, her sickly green magic seeming to flow into the beast's maw and flood its' lungs, stealing the very air from it. Colson took the opportunity to lunge at the werewolf, tackling and pinning it to the ground as it suffocated. The magic reversed course, now tinged with a pale blue as it flew back toward's Amelia's awaiting outstretched hand.

Yeltnar moved with reckless abandon as his body made the rapid transition into his lycan form, rage lending him strength. In a loping bound, he charged shoulder-first towards the throne, claws flexing, leaping for the Alpha in an attempt to rip his throat out.

"I am not afraid of you anymore!" he shouted.

Relanor caught him mid-air by the neck, slamming him to the stone.

"You were never meant to be," the beast rasped, voice and breath thick with heat and the scent of rotting meat.

Kel'rak closed the distance at breakneck speed, enhancing the strength of his legs to hit the Alpha from the side, Voidtooth's edge flashing in the firelight. The blade bit deep, deeper than it should have, seeming to swim into Relanor's flesh like this was the best meal it had ever had and it couldn't get enough. Shadow bled from the wound like ink in water.

Still in control of Samarra's body, Alizarra followed with a scream and a burst of fire straight to the Alpha's back, searing flesh from bone. The Alpha howled—once. The sound died in his throat as his body burst from within, fire tearing through his chest and up his throat in a pillar of light. They all stepped back, breathing hard, blood and sweat painting their skin. Yeltnar rolled aside, coughing and heaving, as the corpse smoldered.

But Alizarra's fire didn't stop, her eyes widening at the loss of control.

The stone throne beneath the Alpha began to glow—lines of red light carved into the rock like veins, symbols pulsing outward in a ring. The heat intensified, and the air grew thick with power. From the fire, smoke twisted upward—not lazily, but with purpose. It spiraled, then narrowed into a vertical slit of gold and red.

An eye opened in the air above the throne. A massive, reptilian, intelligent eye.

The eye seemed to swell, dilating with pleasure as it viewed the scene.

All parties involved, even the remaining werewolves, froze.

Then came the voice—deep, melodic, and cruelly patient. It did not echo; it invaded the mind.

"Pyrwineth sees you now."

Zekven stepped back instinctively, his fingers losing their grip on the bow, which fell with a clatter to the stone. "That's… that's a name I've heard before. From the stories. The Vault of the Eternal."

Alizarra brandished her flaming weapon again, though her hand shook. "That's no myth."

"The debt is paid. The contract fulfilled," the voice continued. "And so I collect."

Relanor's body burst into embers and vanished—no bone, no ash, no trace. The surrounding lycans tentatively shuffled back into the forest, no longer under the compulsion of the Alpha.

Only a single scrap of parchment fluttered down, blackened at the edges. It landed at Kel'rak's feet.

He bent down and picked it up slowly, fingers trembling.

The script on it was delicate, refined, and horrifyingly mundane in its cataloguing:

Inventory #CXLIV: Obedient Beast, Prime Condition, Delivered.

Kel'rak read it aloud, voice hollow.

Nobody spoke for a long moment.

Then Shawna muttered, "Knew it was too easy…"

Yeltnar swallowed hard. "It would appear we just opened the door to *her*."

Samarra didn't move, the glow of Alizarra's presence notably absent. Her eyes remained locked on where the eye had been, her voice nearly a whisper. "We were never hunting the source of the infestation. We were hunting the distraction."

Chapter 19
The Weight of The Task

The forest was too quiet.

Not the hush of peace, but the vacuum of aftermath. Every sound felt wrong. Colson's low growl as he paced the perimeter. Zekven's boots grinding softly over broken pine needles. Shawna tearing cloth into bandages with her teeth.

Even the wind seemed to hesitate.

A vague outline of a body lay upon the scorched ground, where the flame had seared into the dirt surrounding the vanished corpse of the Alpha. The air stank of burned fur, soulfire, and the faintest tang of ozone; Alizarra's last spell had cracked something in the weave of the world, like lightning that overcharged the ground it struck.

Relanor had died with confusion in his eyes. Not fear. Not rage.

Confusion.

He hadn't expected it to end here. And neither had they.

Kel'rak hadn't moved since the moment it ended. He stood statue-still over the bloodstained circle, one hand slack at his side, the other locked tightly around Voidtooth's hilt. The dagger had gone silent. Eerily so. No whispering. No demands. No hiss of satisfaction.

It had fed.

And now it waited.

Samarra sat nearby with her back against a half-burned log, knees drawn to her chest. The glow of Alizarra's presence was absent from her eyes, and for once, there was no sly smirk or teasing lilt to her voice. Just quiet. Stillness. Her hands trembled once, and she gripped her elbows to stop the shake.

Zekven and Shawna were triaging quietly. A long tear in Shawna's trousers revealed an angry welt from where one of the werewolves had grazed her with a claw before falling. Zekven dabbed it clean with a cloth and offered her the last of their alchemical balm.

"Ow," she muttered.

"That's what you get for showing off," he replied, signing one-handed while pressing the ointment in.

Amelia had wandered toward the tree line, her expression unreadable. She wasn't pacing, exactly, but she was drifting. Floating in thought. As if she needed motion to keep the panic from coiling too tight.

"We were played," she said, barely louder than the rustle of pine needles.

Zekven looked up. "That wasn't a fight. That was a staging."

"For us," Shawna added, chewing the inside of her cheek. "He stalled us."

Samarra glanced toward the ashes. "I counted nine werewolves. That's too few for a real pack. There should've been dozens, maybe hundreds."

Amelia nodded. "And Relanor didn't rally them. Didn't retreat. He didn't even try to survive."

"He was a diversion," Kel'rak said.

His voice rasped like bark being peeled from a tree.

The others turned to him, watching as he finally straightened, his movements deliberate.

"He wasn't meant to win," Kel'rak continued. "He was meant to die. On display."

"Like a warning," Zek said.

"No," Kel'rak corrected. "Like a receipt."

They all fell silent.

Then Samarra stood, brushing off ash from her trousers. "Let's not stay here."

"Agreed," Amelia said. "The energy's all wrong. It feels... sticky. Like it wants to hold us."

As they moved to break camp, no one needed orders. They worked in practiced rhythm—rolling up packs, checking weapons, cataloging wounds. Even Colson stayed close to Amelia's side, no longer scouting ahead or sniffing around.

The dog was afraid.

They traveled downhill, half a mile or so, until they found a bend in the forest where the trees were thicker, huddled together like gossiping elders trying to keep a secret. There, beneath the leaning stone face of a collapsed cliff, they set a minimal camp.

No fire.

Just huddled cloaks, shared canteens, and the weight of what they had witnessed.

Samarra tended to Shawna's leg first, her healing magic dulled but functional. Golden light drifted over the torn skin, knitting it together in slow pulses. Shawna winced but didn't flinch.

"You could at least hum a lullaby," she muttered.

Samarra's eyes narrowed. "You want me to sing, I'll pick something with fire and brimstone."

"Romantic."

Zekven chuckled under his breath but said nothing.

Colson nestled beside Amelia, who sat with her knees drawn to her chest, staring up at the clouds that now hung unnaturally low over the ridgeline to the north.

She spoke quietly, but her voice carried.

"We're being watched."

Kel'rak nodded as Zekven signed. "We were from the start."

The changeling finally stood and stretched his legs. "I'll say what we're all thinking, then."

He turned slowly, eyes sweeping the circle of his companions.

"That wasn't the real threat. That wasn't even close."

Nobody interrupted.

"Relanor... he was a gatekeeper," Zek continued. "A loose end. She used him to slow us down, maybe to study us. But he was never the goal."

Amelia looked up. "Pyrwineth."

Samarra grimaced. "She saw everything. The fight, the fire, the deaths."

"Let us win," Kel'rak added.

Zek pointed at him, tapping his nose in confirmation before continuing to sign. "Exactly. Because she didn't need to stop us. She wanted to see how far we'd go."

The clouds had coiled tighter around the ridge line now, forming a dip in the sky that throbbed slightly—like a heartbeat pressed against a thin curtain.

"We need to leave," Zek said. "We go back, find allies, bring more firepower."

"And risk giving her time to prepare?" Shawna asked. "She's already five steps ahead."

"Yeah, but we're five people and a dog," Zek snapped. "And she's a goddamn draconic archivist of death and memory!"

Kel'rak's voice cut through the argument like a blade.

"We finish this."

Everyone turned.

He rose from his seat and walked to the edge of the rock face, staring toward the clouds.

"Relanor's death wasn't a victory," Kel'rak said. "It was an invitation."

Samarra stood beside him. "You're saying this was the opening act."

"It was a test," Amelia said, rising slowly. "A way to see what we were capable of. She needed to know which of us might be... collectible."

Shawna shuddered. "Don't say that."

"It's true," Kel said. "You felt it. The parchment. The inventory note. He was catalogued."

Amelia's fingers twitched. "And now, so are we."

No one spoke for a long while.

Finally, Shawna broke the silence. "So... what now? We can't exactly punch a dream dragon into submission."

Amelia reached into her satchel and withdrew a length of black ribbon. Arcane sigils shimmered faintly in threads of silver.

"I'm going to ask the dead."

Samarra looked up sharply. "That's not safe."

"It's necessary," Amelia said. "Relanor's thralls weren't just foot soldiers. They were bound. The magic—twisted, corrupted—it wasn't just lycanthropy. There was something deeper. Older."

Zek muttered, "Every time someone says 'older' in a forest, something awful happens."

Amelia approached the nearest intact corpse; a smaller werewolf, now reverted to human form. Male. Maybe nineteen, if that. Dirt still clung to his hands like he'd been digging. His face was frozen in quiet shock, not rage.

Kel crouched beside her. "What are you hoping to find?"

"Location. Hierarchy. A clue." She hesitated, then added, "Maybe a warning."

He nodded and stepped back.

The others gathered in a loose circle, watching.

Amelia laid the ribbon across the body's chest. The symbols pulsed once, then again, brighter. She placed her hand over his heart and whispered a word none of them recognized.

The shadows shifted.

Not just the light, but the actual shape of space around them warped. Cold air spiraled inward, and frost crept from the corpse's fingers.

Then it gasped.

Shawna recoiled. Colson barked. Zek swore under his breath.

The young man's eyes flew open—milky, unfocused. His lips moved without sound until Amelia leaned closer and whispered, "You are safe. Only memory."

The corpse stilled, then spoke.

"She dreams."

The voice was thin. Ragged. As if memory itself had splintered into sound.

"We obey."

Amelia nodded, eyes flicking to Kel. "Did Relanor serve her directly?"

The corpse blinked.

"Bound. Name etched in blood."

Kel whispered, "What was the purpose?"

"To guard the path," it rasped.

"Where is she?" Amelia asked.

"Beneath," said the corpse.

"Beneath what?"

"Between," it said.

Then it pointed, slowly, toward the northern ridge—toward the place where the clouds coiled and pulsed like a living heart.

"Below."

The hand dropped. The ribbon faded. And the body stilled.

Amelia sat back with a shudder. "That was more than just death magic. It… reached across something."

Kel helped her to her feet. "What does it mean?"

"She's not just under the mountain," Amelia said. "I think she's under reality."

Zek groaned. "Why does everything always come back to 'beneath the veil of the world'? Why can't we just have a nice wizard in a tower?"

"Because you're not that lucky," Samarra said.

They didn't make another fire.

No one slept deeply.

And when dawn came, Kel'rak was already standing at the edge of the camp, Voidtooth in hand, staring toward the dip in the clouds.

Toward the Vault.

Toward the breathless dark.

Dawn came slow and heavy, like it had second thoughts.

Scars

The sun breached the edge of the horizon but failed to cut through the low, sagging clouds that clung to the mountainside. Light seeped in, pale and indifferent, doing little to warm the frost-cloaked undergrowth or the tension thick in the air.

Kel's silhouette faced north, toward the ridge line and the place where the clouds had grown darker, lower—dense like wool soaked through with wet and rot.

Amelia was the next to rise, wrapping her fingers in Colson's fur before pushing herself upright. Her face was drawn, eyes smudged from lack of sleep. She rubbed the side of her neck and exhaled hard through her nose before stepping up beside Kel.

"No dreams," she murmured.

Behind them, Zekven cursed softly as he emerged from his bedroll, brushing frost from his shoulders. "I think I dreamed about numbers."

"Numbers?" Shawna asked, stretching. Her voice was tight.

"Just columns of them. Endless pages. Something was adding and subtracting."

"Were you winning?"

"I don't think I was playing."

He ran his hand through his uncombed hair and took a long sip from his canteen. "I've decided I hate magic forests."

Samarra packed quickly and without comment, her face calm but her movements a little too precise. She hadn't said a word all morning.

By the time they'd shouldered their gear and checked their weapons, the light had shifted again. It didn't brighten. It flattened, color draining subtly from everything. The leaves were still green, but the wrong green. The trees stood, but their bark seemed less textured, as if drawn with too few lines.

"I don't think this is the forest anymore," Amelia said, eyes narrowed.

Zekven adjusted his quiver. "Then what the hell is it?"

Kel'rak stepped forward. "A memory of one?"

At first, the path appeared normal—narrow, rocky, bracketed by frost-nipped ferns. But within minutes, the terrain changed. The trees began to lean subtly inward, like they were watching. Not all of them; just one here, another there. Their trunks tilted a few degrees too far. Their shadows lingered even when clouds passed overhead.

Samarra muttered something under her breath in another language.

"What?" Shawna asked.

"It's… nothing. Just a prayer."

"That didn't sound like any prayer I know."

"Good," Samarra said. "It wasn't for you."

They pressed on.

The wind was gone entirely now, but leaves occasionally drifted down from the branches overhead, spiraling in perfect, symmetrical arcs. They didn't seem to touch the ground.

Kel noticed the first time a rock shifted behind them.

He stopped, watched, and waited. Then kept walking.

He didn't mention it.

The path narrowed as it wound along the shoulder of the ridge. The drop to their right grew steep, jagged with scree and half-exposed roots, while the slope to the left rose into a wall of crooked trees.

Something cracked deep in the woods behind them.

Zek turned sharply, drawing a dagger in one hand and reaching for his shortbow with the other.

Nothing emerged.

Just that too-perfect stillness.

Then Shawna spotted it.

"Wait," she said, pointing ahead. "There."

A boulder—large and angular—sat squarely in the center of the trail.

"It wasn't there when we came through yesterday," she said.

Zek approached it cautiously, circling once. "Fresh scrape on the left side. This slid."

"By itself?" Amelia asked.

"Or by something bigger than us."

Kel knelt and placed his palm on the stone's surface. It was warm.

He stood. "We're close."

Samarra gave him a sharp look. "How do you know?"

"Because everything around it is cold, but this rock is warm. Even hot, depending on your body temperature."

They pressed on, slower now. Tension coiled in their limbs like drawn bowstrings. Each footstep felt heavier. The light continued to dull. Shadows lingering longer than they should, sounds muffled and strange.

Then came the whisper.

Soft. Dry. Faint.

Not from ahead. Not behind. Not even beside. From inside their minds.

Kel turned toward the trees, slowly. The others followed his gaze.

There, nestled between two leaning trunks, was a structure.

Or the suggestion of one.

A stone wall, partially collapsed, half-swallowed by moss and roots. No door. No roof. No markings.

But there was something about the stones themselves. Too smooth. Too symmetrical. As if carved by magic, not hand.

Samarra tilted her head. "That wasn't there ten seconds ago."

"It didn't appear," Amelia said. "We just noticed it."

They stared in silence.

Then Kel walked toward it.

Amelia reached out. "Wait—"

He brushed his fingers against the stone.

It pulsed, once. A single ripple of something that wasn't magic, wasn't heat. A presence. Like the wall had exhaled recognition.

"Her hoard," Kel whispered.

Amelia's voice dropped to a whisper. "You think this is part of it?"

"No," he said. "This is something she forgot. Or tried to."

He stepped back.

The wall faded.

Not like it dissolved; like an illusion was wiped from their minds, the way a dream slips the moment you try to recall it.

Only the memory of stone remained.

Only the sense that something should have been there.

Colson growled, low and uncertain.

"Let's keep moving," Zek said.

They did.

The trees began to change.

Bark peeling in curls like paper. Branches twisted into unnatural patterns, some resembling glyphs, others just jagged wounds. At one point, they passed a fallen trunk whose core had been hollowed into hexagonal chambers.

Amelia slowed, touching it with two fingers. "This is... patterned. Someone shaped this."

"No," Samarra said. "Something did."

And then, finally, the ridge.

The trail ended in a shelf of cracked stone overlooking the basin below. Snow clung to the rocks in uneven patches, and the clouds above sagged like the ceiling of a cavern, too low and too dense to belong to the sky.

There, nestled in the cliffside just ahead, was a break in the stone.

Not a cave.

A slit.

Thin. Tall. As if something enormous had once forced its way through and left only a scar.

They had reached the Vault.

It breathed.

Softly. Inward and outward. Like the sigh of a dying world.

No door barred it. No guards. No traps. Just that sense of presence, of attention.

Samarra backed away a few steps. "It's not just a structure. It's awake."

"I feel it," Amelia whispered.

Colson flattened himself to the ground and refused to move.

Zek looked around. "We're too exposed here."

"Then we stay one night," Kel said. "Enter at dawn."

No one argued.

Not because they agreed, but because they couldn't speak. The words would not come.

Something in the presence of that fissure stole them.

As they set their meager camp against a stone overhang just above the Vault, Shawna sat beside Samarra and whispered, "You ever wonder if we were supposed to get this far?"

Samarra's eyes were locked on the dark slit in the rock. "I think we were always supposed to."

She turned to Shawna.

"I just don't know if we are meant to make it back out."

The fire was shallow, fueled with dry moss and twigs, not to give heat or light, but to satisfy the old instinct of warmth. It barely smoked, but the smell of it—faint, woodsy—grounded them just enough to keep from unraveling completely.

They sat in a rough circle. No one ate much. Rations were passed from hand to hand more out of obligation than hunger.

Shawna was the first to speak.

"Do you remember when Kel sang the sun into the sky? That day on the ship?"

Amelia blinked at her. "What?"

"I'm just trying to think of something nice," she said, shrugging. "It was before you were with us. Kel'rak saw me struggling to keep my lunch down and broke into a song about being new at sea."

"I remember," Samarra said. Her lips tugged into the barest smile. "We danced about the deck without a care in the world."

"I was dying of embarrassment," Shawna said. "I thought he was making fun of me."

Zekven snorted, interpreting the exchange for Kel'rak. "I remember that all too well. Kel here pounded out a beat and just started a'singing, and the crew took it over."

"It was so warm and bright. So unlike him," Shawna snickered.

Kel'rak stared into the fire. "And then I ruined it."

Shawna turned toward him. "No, we are remembering the happy part. Do not go there."

He shifted his eyes towards her in a glare. "Why wouldn't I go there? That's the day Sugar died. The day I failed her, the same way I failed my wife. Through my own sheer incompetence and fear."

Shawna, Samarra, and Zekven shut their mouths. Amelia bowed her head, rubbing her belly and scratching Colson's head. "I can relate."

The whole group sat in silence.

They didn't elaborate. Neither needed to.

Samarra sat with her cloak wrapped tightly around her, arms crossed. "I used to think I would die falling from a trapeze - now I just wish my mama was alive to do it with."

"You were in the circus?" Zek asked, incredulous.

"I miss it..." she trailed off, a single tear welling in her eye and trailing down her delicate cheek. "But I cannot go back. I am why they're dead."

Silence settled again. Not oppressive. Just heavy. Familiar.

Amelia took a deep breath. "We should talk about what happens inside."

Zek stiffened. "You mean if it's a trap?"

"No," she said. "I mean if we're separated."

Samarra rubbed the tears from her eyes and grinded her temples. "Great. Just what I needed. A discussion about worst-case scenarios."

"She's not just going to fight us," Amelia said. "She's going to test us. Study us. Pick at whatever thread we least want her to pull."

Shawna stared at the crack in the rock ahead of them. "Like what?"

Amelia didn't answer.

Kel shifted. "She's going to try to rewrite us."

The others looked at him.

"Think about it," he said. "She's a vault, right? She stores. Archives. Curates. That means she decides what's worth remembering. And what gets erased."

Zekven let out a slow exhale. "So we don't just need to win. We need to remain ourselves."

"Exactly," Kel said.

Samarra frowned. "That's not always easy."

"No," Amelia said. "But it's necessary."

A long pause.

Then Shawna pulled out a small carved token from her satchel. It was shaped like a tree leaf, no bigger than her palm. "My father gave me this when I left the monastery," she said, turning it in her fingers. "Said it would keep me grounded."

She held it out. "Pass it around. One word each. Say what you're holding onto."

Zek raised a brow. "You serious?"

"Yes," she said.

He took the token. "Fine. 'Clarity.'"

He passed it to Samarra.

She held it a little too long. "Absolution."

To Amelia.

She didn't hesitate. "Loyalty."

To Kel.

He stared at it. Ran his thumb along the edge.

"Remorse."

They didn't ask him to explain.

He passed it back to Shawna.

She nodded. "Balance."

The fire crackled gently. Colson shifted and let out a quiet, half-conscious huff. The Vault loomed, silent now, the slow inhale and exhale barely perceptible.

"I hate this part," Zek said.

"What part?" Amelia asked.

"The waiting. The knowing what's next. Pretending we're not scared."

"I'm not pretending," Shawna said. "I'm terrified."

They all were. But no one mocked her for saying it aloud.

Kel rose first.

He walked to the edge of the camp and stared down toward the vault entrance, shoulders squared.

"I've been hunted my whole life," he said. "By my past. By my name. By the things I've done."

The others turned toward him, quiet.

"But tomorrow, I hunt back."

No one clapped. No one cheered.

They just nodded.

Because that was all there was left to do.

One by one, they found places to rest. Samarra leaned back against a tree, her head dipping forward with sleep - until Alizarra awoke to keep watch. Shawna leaned against the stone wall with her arms folded and eyes half-lidded. Zek sat with his legs crossed, trying to meditate, failing, then trying again.

Amelia lay on her side, fingers twined in Colson's fur, whispering something to herself.

Kel sat last, alone by the edge, staring into the dark.

And the Vault watched them back.

Notes From the Garden

The Monster's Account

Amelia, the healer. Amelia, the gentle soul who believed in the inherent goodness of people. What a pathetic, naive fool you were. You thought a poultice and a kind word could mend the world.

You recoiled from blood, from violence, from the harsh realities of existence. You saw yourself as a beacon of light, a protector of the fragile.

That Amelia, with her soft hands and softer heart, was a sickness. A delicate bloom destined to wither in the first harsh wind. She preached compassion, while the world sharpened its teeth. She believed in remedies, while true wounds festered beyond the reach of her tinctures.

How I despise that fragile, trembling girl, so utterly unprepared for the true nature of existence.

I remember the metallic tang of blood, the faint scent of decay from a simple wound, and the nausea that would churn in my stomach. A healer, made ill by the very essence of life's fragility. What a mockery.

My hands, now stained with the true cost of survival, once trembled at the sight of a scraped knee. The irony is a bitter laugh in my throat.

You thought you were a protector? You were a lamb, leading other lambs to slaughter with your blind faith in goodness. Your 'light' merely illuminated your own vulnerability, making you a brighter target for the wolves that always, always come.

When did the scales truly fall from your eyes? Was it the first time you saw true malice, unadorned by circumstance? Or the first time you realized your 'gentle touch' was a weakness, a liability in a world that demanded teeth?

That innocence, that gentle nature—it was a scar, wasn't it? A gaping wound of vulnerability that the world, in its brutal wisdom, had to cauterize. And it did so with fire and blood, leaving behind the ugly, hardened tissue of what I am now. A scar I wear with grim pride, for it marks the death of the fool I once was.

That 'healer' persona? It was a shield, wasn't it? A way to avoid confronting the ugliness, the necessary cruelties. A way to avoid becoming what you needed to be.

You were so busy tending to superficial wounds, you ignored the rot festering at the core of everything. Your compassion was a luxury you couldn't afford. Your aversion to darkness, a handicap. How many times did your soft heart hesitate when a hard hand was needed? How many times did your 'innocence' leave you vulnerable, or worse, make others vulnerable because of you?

But then, the world kept coming.

It didn't care for your delicate sensibilities. It demanded a different kind of strength. It demanded adaptability. And I, the new Amelia, found it.

Found it with an ease that would have horrified the old me. The world didn't ask politely. It tore my life apart. It ripped my child from my womb. It left me for dead in the ashes of everything I held dear. It didn't whisper for change; it screamed for it, with the voices of the dying and the cackles of the victorious.

And in that cacophony, a new voice rose within me—a voice of cold, clear purpose.

They say darkness creeps in, insidious and slow. For me, it was a welcome guest, a forgotten part of myself finally allowed to breathe. It wasn't a struggle; it was a revelation. A shedding of restrictive garments.

The darkness wasn't a creeping chill; it was a profound, satisfying warmth. A liberation. It filled the hollow spaces left by grief, not with comfort, but with a terrible, beautiful strength.

It was the shedding of a skin too thin, too porous, for the harsh realities of this existence. Every shadow that coiled around me, every whisper of forbidden knowledge, felt like a truth unveiled, a secret weapon finally unsheathed. The shadows offered clarity, efficiency. They offered power. Moreover, they offered the promise of our child's continued life.

And all of it, every single step into this beautiful, terrifying abyss, was for Colson. For his continued breath, for his laughter, for the promise of a future where he would never know the vulnerability I once suffered. He is the anchor, the justification, the living proof that this transformation, however monstrous, was not only necessary but righteous.

This power, this willingness to step into the shadows, it has left its own mark. A scar, perhaps, on my very soul. A blackened, twisted thing that would make the old Amelia weep. But this scar, unlike the others, is a source of strength.

It is the proof of my ultimate adaptation, a testament to my unyielding will to survive, no matter the cost to my former self.

When that werewolf lunged, its maw gaping, the old Amelia would have sought a way to incapacitate, to bind. This Amelia? I simply took its breath. I watched its lungs collapse, its eyes bulge. And felt... nothing but cold satisfaction. Efficiency. The air, tinged with its last, desperate gasp, flowed back into me, a subtle surge of energy. A fair exchange, wouldn't you say?

To touch the dead, to pull secrets from their dissolving minds —the old Amelia would have recoiled from such a violation. But the corpse of that young werewolf, his face frozen in quiet shock, held answers. And answers are power.

The chill of that magic, the way it warped space around us, it felt... right. Necessary. A tool, nothing more. A means to an end. It was the quickest path to understanding Pyrwineth's game.

It's not cruelty; it's pragmatism. It's not evil; it's necessary. I adapt, because the alternative is to break. And I refuse to break. Not when there's still so much to learn, so much to control.

Cruelty? Evil? These are words for children, for those who haven't truly seen the world's teeth. There is only efficacy. Only outcome. The werewolf was a threat. It ceased to be a threat. Its essence served a purpose.

The dead hold information. Information serves a purpose. Every action, every decision, is now weighed on the scales of utility. Sentiment is a weakness I can no longer afford.

This cold satisfaction, this efficient detachment—it is another scar. A chilling absence where warmth once resided. The old Amelia would have wept for the werewolf, for the violation of the dead. This Amelia feels only the hum of power, the clarity of purpose. It is an ugly scar, perhaps, this erosion of empathy. But it is a necessary one, forged in the fires of survival.

It is the mark of a predator, not a healer.

Scars

They still flinch at the sight of true power, at the necessary ugliness. They don't understand that the true terror isn't the magic itself, but the will behind it. The will to survive, at any cost. Their ignorance is their shield, but it is also their ultimate vulnerability. And mine is the hand that will eventually shatter it.

They still cling to their quaint notions of 'good' and 'evil.'

Zek's 'clarity' , Samarra's 'absolution' , Shawna's 'balance'. Even Kel'rak's 'remorse'. They are useful, yes. Their strengths complement mine. But they are pieces on a board, and I am learning to move them with increasing precision.

I chose 'Loyalty'. And I am loyal. Loyal to the truth of this world, to the necessity of power, to the understanding that only strength can truly protect our baby. Their loyalty is to each other, to a fading ideal. Mine is to the inevitable.

They are pieces. Each with their own unique function. Kel'rak, the shadow, the blunt instrument of fear. Zek, the nimble hand, the gatherer of secrets. Shawna, the unyielding will, the physical force. Samarra, the wellspring of raw emotion, the conduit to power. And Colson, my heart, my justification, the ultimate beneficiary.

They believe we are a team, a fellowship. I believe I am learning to conduct an orchestra.

My loyalty is not to their fleeting ideals, to their 'goodness' and 'balance.' My loyalty is to Colson's future. To a world where he is safe, protected, and perhaps, eventually, in control. If that means sacrificing their innocence, their comfort, their very lives, then it is a price I will pay.

A necessary, ugly scar on my conscience, for the greater good of my child.

The old Amelia was a victim of circumstance, tossed about by the whims of fate. This Amelia? I shape circumstance. I bend it to my will. The whispers of power, the subtle currents of influence—they are intoxicating. A far more potent balm than any salve I once applied.

The whispers of power, the subtle currents of influence—they are more intoxicating than any wine, more invigorating than any herb. They are the true balm, the only remedy for the wounds of the soul.

To feel the world shift beneath my will, to see events bend to my intent—it is a sensation I will never relinquish.

Pyrwineth collects memories. Perhaps I will collect something else. Perhaps I will be the one who decides what new memories are forged. What new realities are cataloged. The world needs a firm hand. A guiding force. And if that force must be cloaked in shadow, then so be it. The old world is dying.

And I, the new Amelia, am ready to build what comes next. On my terms.

The 'healer' is dead, a soft, pathetic memory. Long live... something else. Something forged in fire and grief. Something far more resilient. Something far more real. Something utterly, beautifully, terribly scarred. A monster, perhaps.

But a monster who will ensure her child's survival, no matter the cost.

Chapter 20
The Vault of The Eternal

The stone throat swallowed them one by one.

Kel'rak led, stepping first into the narrow gap, followed closely by Amelia, her hand resting on Colson's collar. The tunnel was too tight for comfort, just wide enough for a person, and not quite high enough to stand upright. Samarra cursed softly as her shoulder scraped a wall of uneven stone. Zekven brought up the rear, his bow slung and twin shortswords drawn.

They didn't speak.

Even Shawna, normally the first to break a silence with sarcasm, kept her mouth shut. Words felt like they might echo too far, touch things they didn't want to wake.

The passage twisted downward in slow, deliberate spirals. The walls changed, stone gave way to something else. Not carved. Not molded. Formed. The texture became smooth in some places, rippling in others, like water frozen mid-motion. The air grew heavy with pressure that pushed into their ears, their temples, their memories.

Then came the darkness.

Not a lack of light; true dark. Sensory starvation. The kind that made you forget what colors were. What breath was. Kel pressed a hand to the wall and felt nothing. No cold. No texture. Just absence.

Then the floor shifted.

One by one, they stumbled through an unseen veil.

The darkness ended not with light, but with awareness.

Suddenly, they were standing on a wide stone platform overlooking a vast interior chamber that defied geometry. Pillars bent at unnatural angles. The floor rippled like sand disturbed by wind. Ceiling? There wasn't one. Just an expanse of night sky that didn't belong underground. Stars flickered in strange constellations, patterns none of them recognized.

They had entered the Vault, but it wasn't filled with gold or treasure.

It was filled with… art.

Thousands of objects stretched across the stone plains. Musical instruments suspended mid-air, each strumming or vibrating on their own. Abstract paintings, some of them pulsing softly as if alive, others flickering between shapes when viewed from different angles. Murals wrapped around invisible walls, painted in pigments that seemed to shift as the viewer moved. Thousands upon thousands of books lined shelves.

Samarra stepped forward slowly, eyes wide. "What… is all this?"

Amelia turned in place, awe overtaking her fear. "It's a gallery."

Zekven approached a statue—half-marble, half-crystal— depicting a tall, hooded figure with three faces, all turned away from the viewer. "I thought dragons hoarded treasure."

"Treasure isn't always coins," Kel breathed out with amazement.

They moved deeper into the Vault, weaving through aisles of history.

One sculpture was carved from a single piece of darkwood, polished to a shine. It showed a family of four—halfway through embracing, halfway through turning to ash. The detail was exquisite. Even the cracks in their smiles had been captured. Amelia paused before it, reaching out but stopping short of touching.

"What kind of mind makes this?" she whispered.

"Not makes," Kel said. "Finds. Collects."

Farther in, they came across a series of musical stands holding impossibly intricate instruments. Lutes with strings of glass, flutes made of bone and humming with tones the ear couldn't follow. One violin played itself in the corner, the bow suspended mid-air. The melody was haunting, like a lullaby sung by someone who had never heard a child.

Shawna stood before it, transfixed. "I think I've heard this before…"

"No," Zek said quietly. "You've almost remembered it before."

He pointed to an oil painting beside the violin. It showed a battlefield that none of them recognized, soldiers wearing armor with blank heraldry, no faces. Only one figure was painted in detail: a little girl hiding behind a tree, eyes wide and watching. The brushstrokes were delicate, emotional. The expression on her face mirrored the Amelia's.

The woman blinked in shock, and stepped back.

"That's not possible," she said.

Kel turned slowly. "She's been watching longer than we thought."

Then the lights shifted.

From above—if "above" could be called anything here—a slow golden glow unfurled like dawn, though no sun could be seen.

And with that light came a voice, speaking directly into their minds. Low. Smooth. Cold.

"You walk barefoot through eternity's bones. I wonder if you understand the privilege."

They turned as one.

Pyrwineth.

She stood—or floated—at the far end of the chamber, her body half-shrouded in an opalescent mist that gleamed with too many colors. Her form was that of a ruby-red dragon, but it was wreathed in a shimmering glamour that made her appear as the art she lived among. Her wings were like thin sheets of shimmering vellum, and her eyes were hollow lanterns filled with pages instead of flame. Where her claws touched the ground, glyphs burned briefly and vanished.

The fire in Samarra's eyes lit up as Alizarra took over. "Back."

Pyrwineth tilted her head.

"Oh no. Not yet. You've barely begun to appreciate the collection."

Amelia stepped forward, her voice steady. "You've taken from people. Lives. Histories. Souls."

"I preserved them," Pyrwineth said simply. "The world forgets so easily. I do not."

Kel's hand hovered over Voidtooth. "You kill to catalog."

"I catalog to prevent extinction," the dragon replied. "Do you mourn a seed placed in a vault for future generations?"

Zekven muttered, "You're not saving us. You're taxiderming us."

Pyrwineth smiled.

"Only those who earn the honor."

Pyrwineth circled slowly, the glamour leaving a trail of gently drifting paper in her wake. It dissolved in the air like falling ash.

"You see corruption," she said, "but I see continuity."

Alizarra stepped closer to Shawna, a blazing blade like magma drawn. "We're not here to be stored."

"No," the dragon said, "you're here because you're rare. Unique. Threads in a pattern I thought broken."

Her wings unfurled slightly, pages fluttering and catching on invisible winds. She didn't breathe like a beast—she exhaled knowledge, thick with certainty and arrogance.

"You made it farther than I anticipated. Few ever do. Even fewer without leaving a piece of themselves behind."

Zekven glared at her. "We've left plenty behind."

Pyrwineth cocked her head. "You misunderstand. I speak of shedding burdens, yes, but also names. Histories. Futures. These things become… fragile under pressure."

She turned to Amelia.

"You, in particular, have already rewritten more than most."

Amelia's stomach clenched. "You don't know me."

"I knew your mother."

The words struck like thunder.

Everyone froze. Even Kel took a step closer.

Amelia's throat went dry. "That's not possible."

Pyrwineth's smile did not change, but the light around her eyes pulsed.

"She once brought me a song," the dragon said. "Not for safekeeping—but to forget. It was too painful to carry. So I archived it."

A ripple passed through the room—faint, invisible, but palpable.

Amelia turned in a slow circle. One of the violins stopped playing.

The mural of the battlefield now had a figure leaning beside the girl. A woman, her face obscured by strands of hair, holding a lute.

Amelia stumbled backward.

"No. That isn't…"

Samarra caught her by the arm. "Don't look at it. She's baiting you."

Pyrwineth's tone turned amused. "I don't lie. I display."

Kel stepped forward. "Enough of this."

The dragon turned toward him.

"Ah. The one who carries the void. Your blade has an older name, doesn't it?"

Voidtooth pulsed in its sheath, like a heartbeat skipping.

"You dream of undoing," Pyrwineth whispered. "But you still fear what you might become."

Kel drew the dagger slowly, letting its curve reflect the unnatural light.

"I fear nothing that bleeds," he said.

Pyrwineth chuckled.

"Bravado. How quaint."

Then she turned, gliding several paces away and gesturing to the art that surrounded them.

"You misunderstand my purpose. This is not a trap—it is a sanctuary. A timeless capsule. I take what might otherwise be lost."

"Then take a memory," Amelia said. "Not the person."

"Ah, but the person is the memory. Stripped of context, all things wither. A melody without the hand that played it becomes hollow. A painting without the artist becomes a mystery. I preserve wholeness."

Kel raised Voidtooth.

"Then you'll preserve our defiance."

The air shifted. A low hum began, distant at first, then building; like the pressure that accompanies being deep under water.

"I could offer you each a place," Pyrwineth said softly. "Not in chains. In stasis. A room of your own. The moment you most cherish. Or most fear. A loop. A comfort."

"No," Shawna said. "We've already lived our lives. And they belong to us."

The dragon's gaze swept over her. "Even the broken parts?"

"Especially the broken parts."

Then the Vault moved.

Not physically, but in essence. The floor didn't shift. The walls didn't tremble. And yet suddenly, each of them was alone.

Separated.

Divided by their memories.

***

Kel

He stood in the dank dark of Voidtooth's well.

The smell of mildew, the cold of the fetid water, the sound of things crawling—it all came rushing back.

Except it wasn't real.

He turned and saw himself—ten years younger, leaner, hunched over a body, his calloused hands covered in Cecilia's blood. Somewhere, a child cried.

Voidtooth's shadow pulsed in his hand now, but younger Kel had nothing to exact vengeance.

"You were made here," a voice said beside him.

Pyrwineth again. Watching.

Kel said nothing.

"You became a weapon for revenge. And yet… you are still caged by fear and grief."

He closed his eyes. "I escaped."

"You did," she said. "But only by upward growth. Not away."

***

Amelia

The battlefield from the painting stretched out before her.

Only now, she stood among the fallen.

Men and women she knew her mother had entertained with her music, faces familiar and half-forgotten, lay at her feet. Some with eyes open. Some missing limbs.

In the distance, the melody from the violin played again.

She turned and saw her mother, fully formed now, sitting beneath the same tree, strumming a half-broken lute.

Amelia stepped toward her.

"Why didn't you tell me?"

Her mother looked up. "Because I wanted you to survive me."

Tears welled in Amelia's eyes. "I needed you."

"A minstrel could never provide enough for her child by herself."

"A tragedy," the dragon cut in, "but one that put you on your path."

Then the light shifted again—and her mother was gone.

***

Zekven

He stood in a vault—not Pyrwineth's, but one of ledgers, charts, and numbered scrolls.

He recognized it. The compound inside the Kingdom of the Nine. Before he left. Before he betrayed them.

Papers fluttered in the air, each labeled with a version of himself: soldier, thief, son, exile, friend.

He tried to catch one.

It turned to dust in his hand.

"You spend your life rejecting definition," said Pyrwineth, appearing behind a column. "But do you not wish to know which version was most true?"

He snarled. "I'm all of them."

"Then you are none."

***

Samarra

She stood in a courtroom.

But there was no judge. No jury. Only shadows behind a bench, watching her. Accusing. Waiting.

She recognized none of them, but somehow felt the verdict press against her skin.

"You took a life once," said Pyrwineth, seated in the jury box now. "And you told yourself it was for justice."

"It was," Samarra cried, choking back tears..

"But what if it wasn't?"

A mirror appeared before her.

In it, she saw not herself—but the face of the one she killed. Still. Cold. Asking for answers.

Samarra clenched her fists.

"I am so sorry mama," she whispered.

***

Shawna

She walked through the monastery.

The hallways stretched too long. The walls curved inward.

She passed her old teachers, frozen mid-lesson. Students with faces blurred. Her footsteps echoed like memory struggling to form.

At the center of the hall was a gong.

Unstruck.

She approached it.

"You always feared you were the wrong student," Pyrwineth said from behind her.

Shawna looked down. "I was the loud one."

"You were the real one," Pyrwineth said. "And that scared them."

Shawna turned, striking the gong. The noise shattered the illusion.

***

The group snapped back to the real Vault. They stood together once more. Pyrwineth hovered above, watching.

"You endure," she said. "Curious."

Kel gritted his teeth. "We fight."

"Yes," the dragon said softly. "I suppose you must."

Voidtooth pulsed once in Kel's grip.

A warning.

He advanced slowly, blade drawn, but already he felt his footing falter. Not from any tripping hazard, but a change in terrain.

The floor wasn't stone anymore.

It was pages.

Thousands of them, layered and bound by nothing, shifting underfoot like sand caught in the tide.

And Pyrwineth was rising.

Her body no longer a shape, but a concept. Her head towered above them, her wings spread wide with inevitability. As if she'd already seen this moment unfold and found it unremarkable.

Zekven fired first.

A glinting arrow hissed through the Vault's stale air.

It never landed.

It slowed mid-flight, as though entering syrup, then stopped entirely and crumbled into ink.

"Expected," Pyrwineth said.

Shawna leapt next, closing the distance with a burst of momentum. Her staff struck the stone beneath Pyrwineth's massive claw—but met nothing. The surface shimmered, her blow passed through the illusion, and she stumbled forward into air that pushed her back with crushing weight.

"Derivative," the dragon muttered.

Alizarra, eyes blazing red on Samarra's normally kind face flanked left, her blade of fire flashing. It first twisted down mid-swing, cutting her own leg. On the reverse cut it passed through Pyrwineth's neck as if striking fog.

"No comprehension of the text."

Amelia tried to cast—tried—but her magic stuttered. Illusions of her past harried her, disrupting the focus on the emotions necessary to bring forth her terrible might. The spell shorted out with a puff of ash.

"You do not belong here," Pyrwineth boomed. "You are footnotes scrawled in a sacred tome."

The Vault darkened.

The art around them retracted. Murals peeled into flat palettes. Sculptures crumbled into powdered marble. The music slowed until notes stretched seconds long, then minutes.

Reality was erasing itself to make room for her.

Colson bayed; a desperate, warbling sound, while backing away, hackles raised. Even he could feel it: this wasn't a battle. This was a lesson.

And they were failing.

Kel ran forward.

Voidtooth screamed in his head. It vibrated with fury, but also... futility.

He shadow-stepped upward into the air, stabbing down and aiming for the dragon's eye.

The blade struck, and stopped. Inches from contact. Held in place by nothing visible.

Pyrwineth blinked, amused.

"You seek to correct a story you have not read," she said. "Your anger is illegible. Your defiance, expected. Your fear... stale."

Then she breathed.

Not fire. Not frost.

Words.

They filled the air like wind-chimes and thunder, layered and harmonic, impossible to isolate. Each one was a name, a phrase, a citation of the party's lives.

Shawna dropped to her knees, clutching her head. "Stop—"

Zekven screamed something no one heard.

Alizarra staggered into a pillar and fell, blade tumbling from her hands.

Amelia clutched her pendant, lips moving silently.

And Kel—

He stood, barely, Voidtooth clutched to his chest. Knees shaking, his mind filled with memories not his own.

He saw himself as a child again—but not just his own childhood. Someone else's. Hundreds of them. A thousand different versions of who he might've been. All lost. All catalogued.

Pyrwineth pressed closer.

"I could preserve you," she whispered. "But you are unfinished. Incoherent. A first draft."

She opened her wings.

And the Vault answered.

The ground dropped.

Literally dropped, like a stage giving way. The platform beneath them unraveled into floating ribbons of narrative, symbols, phrases. The group tumbled through them, falling but not falling, each of them colliding with fragments of memory too sharp to hold.

Alizarra's presence faded, and Samarra saw the sister she'd orphaned.

Zekven saw his own gravestone, labeled with an incorrect date.

Shawna saw the monastery's bell tower collapse, crushing everyone.

Amelia saw her mother—again—only this time, her eyes were empty.

And Kel saw himself, surrounded by books with blank covers, and his own face staring out of each one, identical and wrong.

Then—

Stillness.

They were back on the Vault's stone platform. Bruised and broken, but alive.

And Pyrwineth... was just watching.

She did not attack again.

She did not need to.

"You are unfinished," she repeated. "But not without merit."

Amelia coughed, blood on her lips from some unseen injury.

Zekven helped her up, barely standing himself.

Kel staggered to his feet.

"We're not done," he rasped.

Pyrwineth nodded slowly.

"No. But you will be."

The great dragon turned away, warping reality once more. The Vault sealed ahead of her, seeming to forget their very existence. The passageway out blurred, like a page turned too fast. Light returned in fractured pieces. The platform beneath Kel's feet shattered into fractals, the endless void extending in all directions around him.

And the dragon was gone.

Only the echo of her voice remained.

"I will remember this failure. Will you?"

Smoke—not real, but a memory of fire—spiraled across the broken Vault floor. Every breath tasted of ash and parchment.

Kel'rak could barely stand.

The fight, if it could be called that, had turned one-sided from the start. Pyrwineth hadn't struck them down out of malice. She hadn't needed to. The gallery itself had folded around them, warping the laws of space, muting their spells, bending their strikes into irrelevance.

They hadn't landed a single meaningful blow.

And now, Kel was alone.

Somehow, he'd become separated again, isolated on a drifting stone slab above the Void. The others were there in shouts and silhouettes, muffled and distant.

Pyrwineth loomed above, wings spread like the open covers of an ancient tome.

Then came the wind, hot and absolute. One wingbeat sent the platform shuddering. Her gaze fixed on him. Kel raised Voidtooth in shaking hands, but the dagger no longer radiated its shadowy caress.

It knew.

This was beyond it.

He couldn't dodge. Couldn't run. So, in desperation, he reached for something else. His hand closed over the horse figurine in his pocket.

"Baron," he breathed. "If you ever meant any of it—please. Help me."

The world slowed, time seeming to crawl around him.

Just enough.

Just long enough.

Then he felt it; a pop in reality. A presence, galloping through the world like thunder rolling across stars. A glowing white shape barreled toward him. Light given form, warmth given speed. The spirit of Sugar—his old friend, his companion against loneliness— reborn as something eternal, crashed into him and somehow lifted him up.

He was on her back before he could speak her name.

Her hooves beat against the air, and the vault beneath them warped as they ran. Through every single illusion. The roar of Pyrwineth's breath missed him by inches, curving like water around a rock.

Sugar galloped across the impossible space, and no one else saw her.

Not Amelia. Not Shawna. Not even the dragon.

Only Kel'rak.

She carried him all the way out of the Vault. Away from the dream-turned-nightmare. To the cold, real edge of the mountain once more, stopping gently on a slope of cracked stone.

He slid from her back, legs wobbling. "You're here," he whispered. "You're really—"

She nuzzled his cheek, her eyes shimmering with something more than starlight.

Then, slowly, she began to fade. Mane to mist, hooves to smoke, until all that remained was the figurine, warm and still, resting in his hand.

A joy blossomed in Kel's heart that he hadn't felt since that day on the lake.

***

The others found him minutes later – bloodied, scraped, but alive.

Shawna pulled him into a hug so hard he nearly dropped the figurine. "Don't ever do that again! We thought you didn't make it."

He didn't answer. Not because he didn't want to, but because there was no way to explain what had happened. Not yet.

Samarra looked around. "Is she gone?"

No one answered.

Because they didn't know.

The Vault behind them collapsed without a sound. Not an explosion, not a spell, just a shuttering of space. As if the book had been closed, and their chapter removed.

The wind returned.

The snow. The smell of pine. The rhythm of the real. It all felt dull after the Vault's impossible clarity. But it was something they could hold onto.

They made camp in the shadow of the next hill. There were no jokes. No debates. Only small kindnesses. Zekven tossing a stick to Colson, Samarra healing Amelia's bruised ribs, Shawna brewing everyone a muscle relaxing tea from some herbs she found nearby.

Kel sat alone for a time, the figurine in his palm.

Alive. She was still in there.

And maybe… maybe so was he.

***

The silence wasn't grief. It wasn't defeat.

It was focus. A gathering storm beneath still water.

Tomorrow, they would plan.

Tomorrow, they would prepare.

Pyrwineth had shown them her strength. Now they would find her weakness. They didn't speak it aloud, but the fire had not gone out. It had only been banked.

When the time came, they would strike again.

Together. Stronger. Ready.

As the sun set behind the ridgeline, they stood, packed up their camp, and began walking toward the next hill.

Chapter 21
The Icons Burn

They camped in silence again. Not for stealth, or for mourning.

But because there was nothing left to say.

They had seen the Vault. Had felt its weight. Had been bent beneath the spine of memory. Pyrwineth had not simply beaten them, she had shown them what they were. Flawed. Incomplete. Unworthy.

And yet, they had lived.

That meant something.

Samarra stoked the fire low, casting only enough light to warm hands and reflect off steel. Zekven paced quietly near the edge of the clearing, watching the ridge beyond for any sign of movement; physical, or imagined. Shawna sat with her legs crossed, eyes half-lidded, occasionally tightening her fists and releasing them. Kel held the figurine of Sugar in one palm and stared at it like it might disappear. Amelia hadn't stopped whispering to herself since dusk.

At some point in the night, Zekven dropped beside the fire and said, "We need a plan."

Everyone looked up.

He tapped the hilt of his dagger against a charred log. "We can't face her on her terms. No matter what we throw at her, the Vault will warp it."

Amelia nodded slowly. "Unless we break the terms."

Samarra tilted her head. "How?"

Amelia's eyes gleamed. "By breaking her things."

Zek raised a brow, signing and emoting his shock to Kel. "We're robbing the dragon?"

"We're dismantling her collection," Amelia said. "She didn't just show it to us. She fought us with it."

Kel looked up. "The gallery... it was her weapon."

"And it's all connected," Amelia continued. "The icons. The art. The illusions. They aren't just trophies. They're anchors. The more she archives, the more power she has to shape the Vault."

"If we start removing pages from the book..." Samarra began.

"We might break the binding," Amelia finished.

Silence settled again.

Then Shawna said, "Good. Let's start smashing."

Zek gave a lopsided grin. "Reckless and righteous. My favorite combination."

Amelia stood.

"We go at dawn."

***

The second entry into the Vault felt different.

Not quieter, or louder. Wrong.

The air as they descended twisted in spirals. The walls of the passage were still stone, but they pulsed slightly, like breathing pages. The descent was faster this time. Not measured physically, but felt—as if the Vault remembered them and was done playing with subtlety.

When they crossed the threshold, the light inside was colder.

The gallery remained, but it had changed.

Where once the collection stretched in pristine symmetry, now it was fractured. Paintings hung crooked. Sculptures slumped and cracked. Musical instruments hummed discordantly.

The Vault was decaying.

"Our presence last time wasn't meaningless," Amelia said. "Did we force her to use too much power by fighting off the illusions?"

"She'll remember us now," Samarra said.

Kel stepped forward, one hand near Voidtooth's hilt.

"She already does."

They spread out.

Shawna moved directly toward the center of the gallery, where a mural depicting an impossible sky turned slowly on invisible rails. She struck it with her staff.

The frame cracked.

Immediately, a ripple passed through the air. One of the floating violins nearby dropped to the ground, strings snapping.

"She's watching," Zek said.

"Good," the monk muttered, and broke the mural again.

Kel stood beside a marble statue of a woman holding a bleeding book. He stared at it for a moment, then sliced the spine of the book with Voidtooth, releasing its corrosive shadow.

The statue split in half. The Vault trembled.

The floor under their feet vibrated with a pulse of fear. A shiver through the nervous system of a living archive.

One by one, they moved through the chamber, striking what seemed central. There was rhythm to it. Intent.

Zekven fired a bolt into a canvas depicting a tower of timepieces.

Samarra severed the strings of a harp suspended mid-air.

Shawna smashed a gold-masked bust with one clean sweep of her staff.

Each act chipped away at the integrity of the space.

The sky above them, once infinite, flickered then dimmed.

"This is working," Amelia said. "We can collapse her domain."

"Then she'll come," Kel warned. "And she won't let us leave twice."

As if summoned by the breath between words—

Pyrwineth appeared.

No wingbeat. No trumpet of power.

Just presence.

She stepped forward from the folds of space itself, her body now less mist, more flesh. Solid, scaled, but cracked—small rents between her plates where shadow leaked like ink.

Her wings were shredded.

Her voice was not.

"You defile my curation."

The dragon opened her mouth, but no breath came.

Instead, glyphs spilled forth. Jagged, searing letters of pain and judgment. They writhed toward the group.

Zek slashed the air with Naur, the flame blade's magic disrupting the spell's focus. "She's bound to the collection. She is the collection!"

Kel turned his attention to Voidtooth. But something was wrong. The dagger was silent.

No hum.

No pressure.

No snarky voice.

It felt... inert.

He looked down and saw that its once-shifting blackness had dimmed to a dull gray. The blade was cold.

Voidtooth had left him.

"No," he whispered.

Samarra shouted something he didn't catch. Pyrwineth had lunged, her claws distorting the air.

Amelia raised her hands and shouted in defiant terror, blasting the dragon back with a sickly-green shockwave.

Kel's hands shook. "It's gone…she took it from me…"

"No," Amelia said. She turned to him, eyes burning with clarity.

"She didn't take it."

Kel hesitated, then tossed the dagger to her. Voidtooth caught the light mid-air and flared.

Not black.

Not red.

Not gold.

Its normal shadowy hue was running through with rivers of green.

Alive.

Amelia caught it, and charged.

Her feet struck the Vault's fractured floor with thunder.

Voidtooth gleamed in her grip; not a just dagger anymore, but a spearpoint of hunger, lengthening and warping in her hands with black and green eruptions of raw power. It responded to her, neither with words nor sass, but understanding.

It had been forged to unmake.

And now it would do just that.

Pyrwineth reared back, shadow bleeding from her scales, wings twitching erratically. One of her legs smashed through a row of glass-encased sonatas, the noise a scream of dying music.

"You wield something beyond your right," the dragon spat.

Amelia didn't stop.

She leapt, feet finding a crumbling stone bridge that hadn't been there a moment before. The Vault twisted to stop her, but too late—she had already learned the rhythm. The beat of unmaking.

She drove Voidtooth down, striking Pyrwineth's chest. Not enough to bite deep, but enough to draw blood.

A ripple of shadowstuff erupted from the point of contact. Ink and memory and hunger all spilling outward. Pyrwineth screamed. She twisted violently, wings hammering the air, trying to shake the connection loose.

But Voidtooth clung, and poor Amelia was no longer touching the ground. She was being thrashed through the air, keeping a tight grip on the weapon that fed on her wrath.

Kel watched in awe, shielding his eyes as another icon burst —this time a sculpture of a thousand eyes, each one closing in synchronized death.

"She's unraveling!" Shawna shouted. "We have to help her!"

Zekven sprinted toward one of the central murals, still intact —a vision of Pyrwineth herself in regal pose, the gallery pristine around her. He slashed it once, twice, then lit it with Naur's fire.

It didn't just burn.

It screamed.

Samarra knocked over a row of ink-capsuled soul jars, each one labeled in a language no one had spoken in centuries. They shattered with a chorus of fading voices.

Scars

The Vault groaned. The illusion of sky in the ceiling above flickered.

And for a moment, the party could see it: The bones beneath.

This was no temple.

It was a carcass.

The remains of every body belonging to every moment Pyrwineth had stolen, shaped into a prison masquerading as a sanctuary.

Amelia twisted Voidtooth deeper.

The blade hissed in delight.

Pyrwineth collapsed to one foreleg, snarling, her form buckling inward.

"You dare destroy my legacy?" she rasped.

"No," Amelia said, hovering just beyond her reach. "I liberate it."

Pyrwineth lunged toward the remaining icons. Her claws reached for a fractured statue, desperate to reclaim even a sliver of what remained.

Amelia retracted her arm and struck again. Voidtooth entered between Pyrwineth's ribs, deeper this time.

The eruption was immediate.

Shadowstuff poured from the wound, liquid void, spilling upward against gravity, surrounding the dragon's torso and winding up her neck like strangling vines of ink.

Pyrwineth reared back, roared once and began to collapse.

Amelia remained.

Floating at the eye of the storm, suspended by the blade and whatever final reserves of power she had called on.

The void thickened around her.

It tore pages from the air.

Cracked illusions.

Broke light itself.

And then Colson leapt.

The wolf-dog-boy—loyal and frantic—broke from Shawna's grip with a ragged snarl. He darted across the fractured gallery floor, paws scrabbling on blood-slick stone to reach Mother.

"Colson, stay back!" Amelia cried, her last words before the void swallowed her whole.

He reached her too late, the shadowstuff surging upward like a wave. A burst of kinetic force exploded outward, launching Colson sideways, his body crashing into a collapsed column of petrified songbooks with a gut-sickening thud.

"Colson!" Shawna screamed.

But he did not move.

The wave collapsed in on itself.

Voidtooth disappeared into the spiral.

And Amelia was gone.

***

Silence, the kind that follows the crescendo of an orchestra.

The party stood in stunned quiet.

Shawna dropped to her knees beside Colson's still form, pressing her hand against his fur, searching desperately for breath, for warmth.

Nothing.

Zekven looked to the center of the ruin, but no shape emerged. No ripple. No sign of life.

Kel walked to the edge of the blast crater, searching through the black-stained stone.

But there was no sign of Amelia.

Only the scorched outline of where she had last stood.

No body.

No blade.

No trace.

"She's gone," Samarra said.

Kel didn't answer, because he didn't know how to.

Shawna buried her face in Colson's fur.

Zek turned away.

The Vault finally, fully, fell still.

***

The mountain did not weep for them.

Its wind cut clean and cold, unsoftened by loss, unconcerned by sacrifice. Snow drifted down in dry, quiet flakes, hissing faintly as it landed on warm shoulders and cooling skin.

No one spoke as they left the Vault behind.

Its mouth had collapsed in on itself. Folded, silent. Not sealed by spell or curse, but by emptiness. There was nothing left to guard. Nothing left to hoard.

They walked single-file down the broken slope, too tired to speak, too wounded to mourn out loud.

Shawna shambled her way down the path, hugging her arms around her body as if trying to hold onto a memory. Sniffles accompanied her silent march, the monk only able to make her way through the blinding tears by following the shape of Zekven in front of her..

Kel walked behind her.

His hands hung at his sides, empty. Voidtooth's absence was more than a weight, it was complete silence. A hollow in his thoughts where another will had once waited, coiled and dark, but loyal in its own way.

Now there was only his own voice.

And it wasn't strong enough yet to fill the silence.

The lake waited below, still and wide, its surface smooth as obsidian.

Samarra and Zekven built the pyre.

It wasn't made of fresh logs or dry firewood from the forest. It was shaped from driftwood lashed with wax-treated cloth, bound with ceremonial herbs Amelia had kept in her pack. Even in death, she had provided the tools for goodbye.

Shawna lay a small tuft of Colson's fur down first, tucking it under the stick she had thrown for him the night before. She pressed her fingers to her lips, touching the kiss to the memorial and whispering something no one else could hear.

Zekven added a folded scrap of parchment, a sketch she'd once made of all of them, clumsily drawn but full of laughter.

Kel added nothing.

He had nothing left to give.

Not now.

They floated the pyre out with a gentle push from Samarra.

It drifted, farther than expected. As if the water itself understood.

Alizarra made herself known, floating a lazy spark out to the craft, and watching it alight. Kel stared with no emotion as the flames caught with languor, curling first in orange, then blue, then white-hot at the center. There was no wind, and the smoke rose like a column.

He imagined he could see Amelia there—standing just beyond the heat.

Watching them.

Watching him.

***

They returned to camp that night in silence.

The fire crackled.

The world didn't end, it just... moved on.

Kel sat apart from the others, legs drawn up, arms around his knees. The figurine of Sugar lay in his palm. Cold now. Dormant.

No voices spoke to him.

No void offered strength.

He'd called on the Baron. He'd seen Sugar return. He'd believed that would change everything; and maybe it had.

But now, with Voidtooth gone, he felt... untethered.

For so long, he had walked with the dagger like a crutch. A voice in the dark to lean on when his own failed. But now, the weight was his alone.

He didn't know how to carry it.

He looked at his hands.

Calloused. Dirty.

Human.

"I wasn't supposed to outlive them," he whispered to the flames.

He didn't know if he meant Amelia, or Colson.

Or something older.

They did not stay long.

The lake still shimmered with the afterglow of firelight, but the pyre was gone. Burnt down to a smear of charcoal, drifting embers long since swallowed by the deep.

Samarra was the first to rise. She checked her pack, tightened her boots, and nodded once at Shawna, who returned it without speaking.

Zekven pulled on his cloak and adjusted the strap of his pack. His mouth was drawn, not with grief, but determination. Something behind his eyes had settled into place. A plan, perhaps. A shape to the pain.

Shawna lingered beside the blackened stones of the fire pit, arms wrapped around herself, watching the sky.

No one asked where they would go next.

They simply began walking.

Southward.

Down the slope where the mountains flattened and the trees grew tall again.

No more dragons.

No more Vault.

Just dirt and air and the long road.

Kel'rak walked a little behind the others.

Not from shame, or guilt. But because everything felt slower now.

He had always heard that grief made the world feel unreal, like walking through fog. But this wasn't fog.

This was clarity. Too much of it.

Every crunch of gravel beneath his boots. Every flicker of wind against his neck. Every ache in his legs. It all felt sharper, more vivid. There was no great force to mute it anymore. No dagger humming with hunger, no distant voice stirring in the edge of thought.

Voidtooth was gone.

Amelia and Colson were gone.

Cecilia was gone.

And Kel was still here.

That felt like a gods-damned mistake.

They reached the base of the slope by late afternoon, a crooked tree leaning over the path like an old sentinel. Shawna stopped there, staring at the horizon.

Samarra walked a few paces ahead, then paused and looked back. "Are we stopping?"

Shawna shook her head. "No."

Zekven gestured toward a low hill. "That's a good place to rest. Set camp."

"Then we'll move from there," Samarra said.

Kel stood at the edge of the tree's shadow and didn't move.

The others began ascending the hill, one by one. No fanfare. No speeches.

Just the motion of people too tired to stop.

Kel looked down at his empty hands.

For a moment, he wondered what he would become without the weapon that had defined him. If he could still use magic. Still fight. Still lead.

Then he took a breath.

And stepped forward.

From the top of the hill, the land stretched out in every direction. Forests. Glens. Roads that curved beyond sight.

It was not the end of anything.

Only the end of one chapter.

They stopped just long enough to adjust their gear. No one unpacked.

They didn't need rest yet, just a few moments to breathe.

Kel turned back once, scanning the tree line. As if—maybe—something would appear. A sign. A voice. The shimmer of light on metal.

Nothing did.

So he exhaled, and began walking toward the next hill.

Epilogue

Within the collapsed Vault, in a hollow of stone and silence, something stirred. An illusion fell, revealing a charred skeleton amidst a pile of rubble and ruined memories.

Amelia gasped, bursting up from a fever dream, as she consumed another soul to bring herself vitality once more.

Air, so thick it felt like smoke, rushed into her lungs. Her chest convulsed, wracked with pain. Her skin was scorched. Her tunic shredded. Blood crusted her lips.

She was alive.

She lay within the shattered ribcage of Pyrwineth the Eternal, surrounded by bones older than empires, the last heat of the dragon's body fading into ash.

Voidtooth lay beside her, humming softly.

"Well hello, dearie," it whispered into her mind, calm and warm. As if nothing had happened.

Amelia didn't smile.

She audibly wept—but only once, choking on the sound. One sob. One tear. One long breath. Then she sat up.

Colson's body lay just outside the arc of the ribcage, halfway buried in debris. The wolf-boy's fur was burned away in places, his form still. The green fire that animated his body smoldering under the rips in his skin.

Amelia crawled to him, trembling, every limb screaming in protest.

She placed one hand on his back, and he whimpered.

Dragging herself closer, she placed both hands on his chest.

Colson tried and failed to lean into her touch.

"No," she said, voice shaking. "Not like this."

Voidtooth pulsed at her side.

She understood.

It wasn't words now. It didn't need them.

It was invitation.

She drew a ritual circle in the dust with the tip of the blade. Symbols she didn't know she knew poured from her mind into the stone. Old, broken magic fed by the dagger, now gorged with power after drinking the essence of a titan. The kind carried only by weapons that fed on grief and darkness.

She carved the symbols in silence, tracing each with her fingertip. They bled shadowstuff behind her.

One hand on Colson's heart.

The other on Pyrwineth's skull.

A rumble emanated from her throat.

Low. Old. Terrible.

The Vault pulsed. Even dead, its magic stirred. Voidtooth drank it in, and glowed a shade darker. Smoke curled from Colson's chest. Emerald green light flickered in the space between his ribs.

The ground trembled.

Pyrwineth's skeleton shifted, slow and ponderous, like something waking for the first time in centuries.

The draconic skull rose.

Two hollow sockets caught fire—green fire.

Not flames of hunger or wrath.

Flames of the soul.

Amelia's voice rose, louder, as the ritual reached its end.

Colson howled in recognition of his mother as a soft light burst from the wolf-dog body and vanished into bone.

Scars

The transformation was slow, reverent.

The dragon's frame twisted, bones that had fallen apart from each other reshaping. The bones darkened. The wing membranes, half consumed and rotted by shadowstuff, stretched as the wings themselves stretched experimentally. A third eye opened between the skull's sockets and burned with emerald fury.

The creature that rose was no longer Pyrwineth.

Colson was alive.

He was something new.

Something Amelia's.

A sentinel.

A guardian.

A monster made from loyalty and grief.

She stood before the dracolich she had created.

Voidtooth purred with satisfaction in her grasp.

"We never have to worry again sweet boy," she cooed. "No one will ever hurt you, ever again."

The creature bowed its head.

Amelia placed her hand against its snout.

The green fire in its eyes flared.

Then dimmed, and steadied.

She climbed the bone-laddered ridge of his neck and sat between his shoulders.

Voidtooth purred in her palm.

"Let's show them what comes after," she said.

Colson's massive soot-stained bone jaws opened wide in a triumphant roar.

End

Scars

About The Author

J.A. McCoy is a debut novelist who dreams of being published by the likes of Tor or HarperVoyager. A graduate of Southern New Hampshire University and an Air Force Veteran, his home is wherever his wife, daughter, and two Cavalier King Charles Spaniels decide to call their next adventure. He grew up on R.A. Salvatore's Legend of Drizzt, stories from the Dragonlance  setting, Lord of the Rings, Eragon, and the like with his head in the clouds. He began writing his first attempt at a novel in middle school, after learning that Christopher Paolini had been published doing the same. Now in his mid-thirties, he finds himself with a stronger drive than ever to tell his story, while stuck in the corporate world where he is the "editor in chief" for his team's monthly and quarterly newsletters.

www.ingramcontent.com/pod-product-compliance
Lightning Source LLC
Chambersburg PA
CBHW031138160726
47991CB00004B/1473